ALL THAT REMAINS

JEREMY DORFMAN

ISBN: 978-0-578-09271-3

This is a work of fiction. Names, characters, places, and incidents are the products of the author's imagination or are used fictitiously. Any resemblance to persons, living or dead, is purely coincidental.

Published in the United States, 2011.

Book design by Jenelle Rittenhouse.

Cover design and artwork by Jeremy Dorfman.

TABLE OF CONTENTS

PROLOGUE

i.

Later, the events of Michael's birth would be investigated and analyzed, and over analyzed and reinvestigated, until its principal players started creating fantastic untruths, not out of any intentional desire to beef up the story, but out of a subconscious exhaustion that inevitably grew from repeating the same unassuming, unhelpful facts over and over again. It got to the point where the nurse even believed that the umbilical cord briefly illuminated in a shade of gold. Where the doctor actually remembered Michael's cry reaching a pitch that recreated the musical notes scale. Where Michael's own mother was certain that she felt the burning of the sun in her uterus as she went into labor. It couldn't be helped. The events that followed lent themselves to this illusional past far better than the actual truth. That the birth of Michael Bailey on September 1, 1987, at Montgomery Hospital, was nothing other than typical, undramatic, and unparalleled in its utter normalcy.

Michael would come to know this and when asked about his birth would say honestly that the facts were hardly worth discussing. The importance of the story of his birth lied only in its unimportance of in any way explaining what was to come. Further, Michael eventually concluded after years of research that no events from his life could provide an answer. For it was not that he was finding the wrong answers, but asking the wrong questions. And the correct questions, wherever they were, were so foreign to any standard conception of human understanding that he had no hope whatsoever of locating them. As his life went on, all of those around him kept analyzing the events of his existence, striving to uncover some central significance buried within it all. Michael would witness their attempts and smile kindly. "There's nothing to find," he would say. They always found his words comforting. But they went on searching anyway. He did not expect anything else.

Later, the events of Michael's life would capture the attention of every man, woman, and child walking this earth. But anyone who may have witnessed Michael's birth would have merely seen the arrival of a newborn boy, indistinguishable from the process that brings millions of other miniature people into the world each year. A living being of joy to family and friends, one of countless adorable, but unremarkable new children to everyone else. A boy to live a life similar in structure and progess to the rest of the population, and yet dramatically unique. A man who would be faced with questions of purpose and meaning similar to those faced by every man and woman each day. A man who would be forced to answer these grueling questions in his own way, just as every person who comes face to face with them eventually must. For in the end, the question of "Why?" is one we all have to answer alone.

ii.

He hit her. He immediately forgot why.

Jake watched, completely still. He was already numb to his father's drunkenesss at the age of six. Night after night he would return home, stinking of alcohol, and would launch into a verbal tirade on Jake's mother, about seemingly absolutely any subject that popped into his head. There would be the alcoholic classics such as:

"Where the fuck is my dinner?! I bust my ass all day and I expect to return home to a fucking hot wad of meat on my fucking plate! And some fucking potatoes!"

Howard Porter may have been a traditional man but it could never be said he wasn't original. His alcohol fueled rants included nights where he would blame Jake's poor mother for a bad day on the stock market, yell that she would single handedly ruin the education of every child she came across, insult her for there being nothing but re-runs on the prime time television lineup or tell her she was responsible for the inability of humanity to realize world peace. And all the while Jake would watch. Silent, knowing no other way of life, but with the vague, unacted on notion somewhere in his mind that something was wrong with such a way of living. A notion quickly beaten down by the unchanging reality of the situation.

Melanie Porter had bought the wrong kind of chips. That was the reason Howard could not recall. The reason he had seen fit to break her nose, leaving her a bleeding, crying mess. She had bought Ruffles, which were on special, rather than Howard's preferred smooth chips. She argued that they tasted the same, so he hit her. Less so because they did taste any different to him than because he did not wish to be proven wrong.

Howard would never apologize for his fits, but he would feel the need to justify them. He would never make any comments indicating there was anything wrong with fueling himself daily on whisky and rum and gin and ale and beer. But he would call himself Jekyll while on the bottle, mistaking which of the famous novel's characters was the evil incarnation, and imply that he was in no way responsible for any of his actions while drunk, for they were in fact the doings of a completely foreign individual. And Melanie would always accept these inane explanations and the abuse they were explaining away for the simple stupid reason that she was in love with him. And even though his actions had killed her spirit, they annoyingly failed to kill her love.

Jake, not yet old enough to be fully conscious of his decisions, paid as little attention to his parents as possible. He would observe their interactions but was never fully present, filling his mind mostly with thoughts of nothing.

It was clear, however, that the argument over the Ruffles and the strike that followed had crossed a threshold. Melanie could not bring herself to wipe away the blood and apologize for the chips' purchase even though her love was telling her to. Jake could not continue to be an inanimate object. So as Howard mulled over why it was he had attacked his wife, and Melanie quickly tried to reorganize her life plan, Jake calmly walked over to his father and kicked him, with all the force he could muster, on his left shin.

Howard let out a piercing cry of pain and forgot about forgetting. He also forgot that the menace who kicked him was his own son, and that he was only six years old. His instincts were primal. Something had hurt him and he would obtain immediate retribution. With very little aim he rapidly swung his arms, every moment of contact he made with his child's head a satisfying brick in the house of revenge.

To Melanie, it was horror. Not simply because she was witnessing her husband pummel the person that they together had created, although the circumstances were enough to kill her remaining drive to live for the remainder of her days. But the true sharp terror, so strong that it froze her in place when every aspect of her being told her to jump up and do anything possible to throw Howard from her son, was the look on Jake's face. A look of complete indifference. Even boredom.

Melanie left Howard. She would have liked to say that she had finally gained the strength to walk away from the abuse she was receiving, but that would have been a lie. Others might have seen a woman with the tragic will to leave the volatile man she loved in order to protect her son, the person she had brought into this world, from pain. This was also not the case. Rather, it was the worst kind of fear that drove Melanie. An incapacitating fear of witnessing the blank painless stare on Jake's face ever again. A look of pain she could have stomached. The emotional breakdown of her little boy she could have gotten over. But the complete lack of humanity she saw scared her. It scared her in a way she could not fully explain, to her deepest core. She was determined never to see such a look on her child again.

She took Jake to the doctor. The pretext for the visit was that her son had sustained a beating from her bastard of a husband and although he appeared to be okay after the initial cuts, she was concerned about internal injuries she might not see. The subtext was that she suspected a much deeper non-physical wound. A flaw scarred into Jake's essence that she had no real hope a local doctor trained only in medicine and the human body would be able to find. Melanie was feeling desperate and any course of action was worth a try.

Dr. Neilson was a sixty-four year old, established professional, who rushed to reach a diagnosis as if he was in competition with two other doctors on an all medical edition of Jeopardy. Many patients found themselves with prescriptions in their hands before they even finished describing their symptoms, impressively always bottles of pills that effectively eased whatever malady inflicted the office's visitor. Neilson's whole identity was based on the concept that he had a sixth sense in prying out his patients' conditions rapidly and spending as little time with them as possible.

It became obvious to Melanie within the first moments of the examination that Jake's presence was a frustrating anomaly to the doctor. Every ten seconds he would pause, glance at Melanie, open up his mouth to speak, and shut it again as quickly as possible, somehow believing his observers would not notice his intention if he transitioned quickly enough out of it. Each time he resumed his analysis of the continually expressionless Jake, a look of greater confusion and anger spread across his face. He was trying to ease the pain of his failure in living up to his usual world record time work by outwardly expressing his bafflement so extremely that some idea would have to invade his brain, simply because it could not get past the rather cartoonish representation of annoyance visible in his oversized eye balls.

It didn't take long for him to send Melanie out of the room. The pressure of coming to a conclusion for an expectant audience member was too much under the already quite stressful conditions.

And so she waited. For minutes. And hours. She was not a religious woman but she prayed. She prayed to any spiritual source that would possibly listen. It wasn't a concern to her if her frantic prayers brought Zeus himself down from Mount Olympus, heaving lightning bolts every which way, causing immense destruction in his path, if he could eradicate whatever demon inhabited her son. Whatever force that made him so unexplainably and frighteningly different from the rest of humanity.

She listened. A cascade of unexpected noises escaped from the closed door of the examination room. Dr. Neilson was constructing and breaking down his methods of investigation, leaving back no tiny parcel of knowledge hidden in the recesses of his brain which might provide the answer to the enigma facing him.

Finally, after two and a half hours and a last bit of unusual and downright terrifying sound, the door was opened. The doctor himself must have been proud of the speed at which Melanie relocated herself into the examination room upon hearing the click of the handle.

There sat her son. A bandage on his arm. A bruise on his knee. Boredom on his face.

"Can we go home now, Mom?"

It was not the question of a child who had been through major trauma. It was the question of a child who had spent too long in the backseat of a car, was exhausted with sitting still, and was anxious to reach his next location simply for a change of scenery.

She broke down in tears. Dr. Neilson, so close to retirement, was consumed with thoughts of medical malpractice for the rather physical experiments the exasperatingly unexplainable condition had led him to perform. He comforted Melanie with his hands while spouting out sentences of made up legal jargon with his mouth, trying to keep her off guard and confused about her son's particular rights.

A lawsuit, however, was the last thing on her mind.

"What's wrong with my son?" she cried.

The doctor's nonsensical contract words immediately ceased.

In his selfish state he had not been expecting such overflowing motherly concern. It touched him. And for the first time since his days in medical school, he paused for a long moment before delivering the diagnosis.

"We'll have to take him to a doctor more trained in the area of rare conditions to be sure, but there is a rare condition that I believe your son has."

"What is it?"

"He can't feel pain."

iii.

Adam loved the smell of blood. He even enjoyed its taste. That gruff bitter mixture stored with such easy accessibility in every human body was the only drug that ever appealed to him. Partly for the thrill of what actions it took to gain access to it, but more for the purest of sensual pleasure he felt at engraining himself in that paste of life. If Adam's predominant nasal ecstasy had been flowers or brownies or even something more consistent with the stereotypes of his gender, such as a slow roasting steak on a coal grill, his life decisions may have been very different. It was a schoolyard fight in grade school over a disputed call in an impromptu kickball match which had first revealed to him the power that red wonder held over his body. His instinct towards violence had always been present. But perhaps he could have outgrown his instincts, had the will to overcome his often painful circumstances, if not for his consuming addiction to blood.

Adam never mentioned his morbid fixation to anyone, despite his usual goal of maximum possible intimidation. Though the vampire comparisons, inevitable with a revelation of his vice, would no doubt increase the fright of everyone he came across, Adam felt the need to hold the detail secret. He understood his fellow human beings just enough to know that his literal thirst for blood would make him an outsider. It thrilled him to be a figure of domination. His ability to lead the group of peers who could only be referred to as his friends (terrified followers would probably be more accurate) might have become suspect, were this more bizarre aspect of his personality to become known. A transition would occur from Adam being a figure they simultaneously feared and loved, to one they only feared and therefore, he kept quiet. He thrived on the love they showed to him, even if he had none to give in return.

• • •

Adam Giacorozzi grew up as the centerpiece in a house of three males and still managed to feel testosterone deprived. His mother left before he could remember for reasons that Thomas, his father, either failed to explain or did not understand. Thomas never volunteered the circumstances of his wife's departure and Adam never inquired, having no drive to search out information that did not want to find him. He heard his younger brother, Justin, once ask about the roots of his female parentage. He was met with the vague and slightly cryptic:

"One day perhaps, we'll all know."

Justin was planning to inquire more into this matter until he spotted the look on Adam's face. One of complete disapproval. Any definitive opinion of Adam's which Justin gained access to immediately became the opinion of two. He worshiped his older brother and Adam enjoyed being a figure of total influence even though he sorely lacked the necessary qualities of maturity and responsibility to properly hold such a position in another's life.

These glaring flaws were demonstrated on one occasion in which Adam, in front of his adoring peers, tested out an old cliché and witnessed Justin seconds from jumping off a bridge merely because he was asked to. Perhaps because of some unconscious brotherly instinct of which he was entirely unaware, he stopped his younger sibling before he inflicted serious injury or death upon himself. But he mainly viewed the incident as a thrilling display of his power.

Although he had been prepared to jump off a bridge at his brother's beck and call, Justin was far from moronic. He merely valued loyalty to his brother to an unhealthy extreme. He was the type of child whose inevitable failure teachers would always lament over lunch time, possessing obvious intellectual potential that was squandered beneath misguided notions of what was important and a general lack of effort. While Adam formed an image of intimidation amongst his peers through action alone, Justin, not as naturally vicious, tried to do the same amongst the kids his age by amping his attitude. He had far more charisma than his brother and also far more natural likeability, but he rarely took advantage of these gifts, finding most of those his own age worthless to associate with. He only had one close friend of his own age.

It would be unfair and inaccurate to say that the formation of the Giacorozzi children's personalities was a direct result of their dear old Dad. Thomas could not be described as a bad father. He also could not be described as a good father. In fact, to a certain extent, he could not be described as a father at all beyond in the obvious biological sense. He was more of an older roommate, who would occasionally offer adult perspective and guidance to the boys, but who rarely delved into their existences on a personal level. On a rare unexplained day he may have given Adam a hug, or offered Justin help with his homework, unaware that school studies were a practice both boys consistently ignored. Meanwhile, these attempts at reaching out struck all parties involved with a loudly ringing false cord and left all three of the Giacorozzi's, including Thomas, wearing an uncomfortable expression of confusion, only healed by an immediate dispersion to separate rooms. It was not so much that Thomas felt he should be a father figure and failed, as that he felt he should feel remorse at failing to be a father figure but failed even more miserably at that. And as his feelings of remorse, over no feelings of remorse, over a course of action which became increasingly muddled and forgotten in the shuffle became overwhelming, Thomas's outward personality vanished and he became a disconnected boarder in his own house, spending most of his time trying to figure out where his remorse began and ended and why it existed in the first place.

Thomas's mental disappearing act left a hole in the psyche of both of his children, each abandoned to a desperate search for someone or something to look up or latch on to. The hole needed to be filled as quickly as possible before either suffocated from the prospect of facing existence alone.

For Justin, the solution came quickly and without deliberation. He would invest himself fully in admiration of his brother. Adam became the holy trinity of figures necessary for survival. Brother. Father. Friend. If Adam was lacking minorly in one of these designations and majorly in others, it did not dissuade Justin. Adam's presence gave him the will to live and all faults went unnoticed.

For Adam, the hole was not filled so easily. He could not tilt his head upward along the family tree and find a living, breathing person to properly inform his every move. His difficulty was twofold. He had to face the necessity of forging himself into something concrete without any guidance and he had to sculpt something out of his brother, a responsibility he would not have fully desired even if he were ready for it. He needed an identity to rapidly cease the chasm and give him the sense of being anything more than a fleeting persona, washed away because no one ever took the time to finish his construction. He found his remedy at a fairly young age in the ever accessible quality of violence.

The way in which violence could fulfill Adam like no human ever had first became apparent to him in grade school. It was the sensation of blood experienced in that first fight which initially hooked him on physical confrontation. But even more, it was the satisfaction of defining himself through dominance which convinced him that he had found his calling. He thrived on seeing fear in the eyes of those who looked upon him.

And so Adam woke up each morning throughout his early teenage years, determined to locate a conflict where there was one, coax a conflict into the open where one was hiding, and create a conflict where none existed, all in order to satisfy his ever growing need. Those other self described tough guys who wished to preserve their image to whatever extent was realistic joined him as followers, submitting themselves to Adam as a leader rather than have their positions of supremacy pierced in a situation of opposition. Adam allowed these sheep to graze on his lawn because they further reinforced his identity as an unstoppable force.

When his altercations with schoolmates became tedious (and hard to come by, since his reputation indicated he should be avoided at all costs) he led his loyal crew into the outside world. There, the opportunity for random acts of violence appeared endless. His attacks showed no discrimination. Neither a twenty-something frat boy nor a middle aged mailman were safe. Usually nothing was taken, though Adam did, in the interest of laughs, confiscate what he imagined to be a love letter from the mailman. Unfortunately it turned out to be an electricity bill, which was not nearly as humorous. No females were ever attacked, but Adam's lackeys saw this gender selection as mere chance, a result of his spontaneous decisions that could just have easily veered in another direction. Close calls with policeman were inevitable, but Adam always managed to avoid being caught in the act and once he had escaped the initial threat there was not the slightest bit of motive which would ever cause an investigation to lead to his door step.

After two years of such activity a fatigue started to develop within his cronies. They were losing excitement over the repetition of assaulting innocent victims and some were even getting the gnawing sense that what they were doing might possibly be wrong.

"I wonder if this is how the Nazis felt?" asked one of Adam's crew on one such occasion in which they were sitting around, mulling over the somewhat disturbing trajectories of their lives.

They tried to consider the implications. But unfortunately, the question did not convince them to rebel against Adam. It merely made them feel more sympathetic to the Nazis.

Adam sensed the restlessness of his not so merry band. Normally he was not concerned with anything that originated in their minds, but mistaking the reasons for their distress and in a rare mood of generosity to those who had followed him so loyally, Adam informed his men that he would step up the excitement level. Material goods meant nothing to him but they would enact a burglary anyway and he would allow them to keep the spoils.

Even though Adam's reward in no way addressed what was actually bothering the group, it had the same effect. The notion of acquiring free goods as a result of an expedition, as they liked to refer to it, wiped away any doubts they were currently feeling. They were easily swayed by the pure thrill of materialistic gain. How could they have ever questioned their fearless leader?

The plan was as follows. On the second Friday in the month of October, in the three o'clock A.M. hour, they would set out driving in no predetermined direction, with no intended destination. They would pick a house only when every member of the team agreed that it should be their target, at which point they would hide their vehicle and converge to enter the building by whatever route was deemed easiest. They would fill their bags and boxes with any items they considered worthy for twenty minutes. When time expired, they would be required to leave. Though they felt limited by the time constraints Adam set, they also found the limitations exciting.

"It's like we're going to be on a game show," one said.

Justin often eavesdropped on Adam's conversations. Whenever he got wind of a particular action being taken, he would ask to participate. Adam never denied him from inclusion, nor did he show any anger at being listened to when permission had not been granted. Justin took this as indicative of the great brotherly bond they shared, but the truth, which was buried under only the thinnest level of surface, was that Adam didn't think much of Justin at all. He never thought twice of allowing Justin to tag along because he had no concern for his well being. He was simply another unspecific individual who surrounded him as he made his way through life.

To others, the reality was clear. Jimmy Fordham was Justin's one real friend. He had been close with Justin since first grade and remained close with him despite the very divergent paths their lives were already taking. When they had met they were just two seven year olds who liked baseball and bonded over trading cards. They talked sports for hours and were inseparable at recess. Over the years the friendship stuck, the old habit of affection now deeply rooted, but their personalities became more and more disparate. Jimmy was an excellent student who took pride in seeing A's on his report card and Justin just barely escaped being left behind with each passing year, not bothering to do any work assigned to him even though he could have grasped it all mentally if he had just bothered to listen to what the teacher said. Jimmy strived to fill his time by becoming involved with community service, driven by the satisfaction of helping others. Justin provided a great disservice to the community by not turning his brother over to the police. Jimmy branched out and made friends with other students. Justin barely spoke to anyone, always anxious to rejoin his brother's merry band.

Most of the time Justin kept his old friend completely in the dark as to what went on when he followed his brother into the night. But on the current occasion Jimmy managed to catch wind of his plans. He overheard Adam talking when he arrived at the Giacorozzi residence to ask his friend to participate in their favorite recreation, the suddenly overly innocent game of catch.

"You can't go through with this," said Jimmy.

"Why not?"

"Because if you rob a house and the police catch you, you'll go to jail."

"They're not going to catch us. Adam has it all worked out."

"And so what if they don't? It's still wrong. Would you want someone coming to your house and taking your things?"

"There's a lot of people doing lots worse than this. We're just taking some stuff. And I'm not even going to take anything. I'm just going along for fun."

The conversation continued along these lines for about another twenty minutes and was followed immediately by silence. A silence that said more than any of the many words which had just been exchanged. Their long dying friendship had finally reached it's end point. They could both sense it.

"You know your brother doesn't really care about you."

"Fuck you."

"He doesn't. He wouldn't give a shit if you got killed."

Although he had only been a bystander, Justin had witnessed enough of Adam's physical dominance to know how to deliver a beating. And that's precisely what he did. He beat Jimmy who frantically tried to defend himself to no avail. He beat his best friend until his face was unrecognizable.

Jimmy could have easily revealed the name of his aggressor to his wailing mother, or his distraught father, or the sympathetic policeman who came to question him. But he didn't. He told all of his questioners that he did not see the individual's face. He never told anyone the truth. Not for the entire remainder of his life.

• • •

The night of the robbery Adam was calm, almost distracted, apparently daydreaming of what he found to be more interesting times. Justin and the rest of his crew, however, were boiling over in excitement. It took a good hour to determine the location they would invade. One would argue that a house with a balcony would contain higher end items even if it appeared a bit smaller, another would argue that no matter the size of the house, nothing of value would be found if the mailbox was designed to look like a puppy. Finally, after a number of intricate architecture discussions, they all settled on a nice suburban residence with a normal mailbox, no balconies, a front porch, and three garages.

Breaking into the house would have been astonishingly easy if any of the troop had taken the time to be astonished. Instead, they rather naively saw the effortlessness of their entry as evidence of their expert burglary skills, impressive all the more so because it was their virgin voyage on such an undertaking. They passed through the doorway patting each other on the back, basking in their collective glory, as a treasure trove of goods awaited their taking. It was Christmas morning.

Perhaps they should have been tipped off by the living room

walls, plastered with posters of Charlton Heston classics like Ben-Hur and The Ten Commandments, but that may have required a more extensive knowledge of both film history and political minutiae than anyone present possessed. And as it was prior to Mr. Heston's presidency of the National Rifle Association, the resident may simply have been a fan of sword and sandals epics.

They more likely should have become suspicious upon discovering a room that existed purely for the purpose of displaying deer heads.

"An animal enthusiast," one of the more intelligence deprived members of the crew stated, grossly misunderstanding the situation.

And they certainly should have fully grasped the nature of he who they victimized when they walked by the framed, blown up display of the Constitution's second amendment prominently displayed in the main corridor. At the very least these clues should have caused them to keep their voices down, remembering that they had put in no effort to choose a house they knew was empty, and that there might more than likely be someone home. As it happened, it wasn't the absurdly incautious volume of their voices that woke up the gun-toting master of the house. It was Justin.

While his followers were joyously looting their surroundings, scampering back and forth, acquiring one useless item or another simply because they had the power to, Adam placed himself in a leather recliner and waited for the dull proceedings to wrap up. He thought of better days when his limbs gnashed the skin of another and released that wonderful red. He had no interest in being involved with the gift he was providing his men. He neither took a second look at any material goods nor provided any much needed rules of precaution, which he knew were well needed. He had no fear of being caught and the others were too dim to recognize the possibility.

So he didn't know what it was that made him stand up and follow when he saw his brother separate from the pack and venture up the staircase. He might have recognized the strange pang as brotherly concern if he had ever felt such a sensation in the past. He may have sat back down if he had taken a moment to inspect what he would have normally considered an entirely irrational action, relocating to a more precarious area of the household purely for the sake of another. As it was, he was hit by an instinct, and acted.

"Justin!"

"What?"

"Where the fuck do you think you're going?"

"To see if there's anything good up here."

"Did it occur to you that the room you're about to enter might contain an actual person, who lives here, and may not be too happy to find out they're being robbed?"

"So what?"

"What are your plans if they wake up?"

"I don't know. I'll beat the shit out of them."

"Yeah, alright."

"I can do it. I've seen you beat the shit out of people lots of times."

"Come back downstairs."

"No."

"Justin."

"What's your problem anyway? I'm not a baby."

"Justin!"

The card carrying NRA member who had been sleeping in the bedroom occupied the left side of the bed. His wife slept on the right. She claimed that the left side caused severe insomnia while the right side was a sleep inducing miracle. Her husband questioned the validity of her statements but obliged nonetheless.

The human object blockage of his dear spouse caused the man a delay of about two seconds between springing from his sleep, awoken by Adam's voice, and reaching the drawers where he kept his rifle. If the sides of the beds had been switched, he would have retrieved his gun a moment faster, and Justin, the first entrant, would have been shot in the head. Instead, the delay allowed Adam time to enter the room and angrily throw his brother to the ground. The gun was aimed. The trigger was pulled. The target was hit. And as a last brotherly gesture, Adam managed to give Justin his favorite thing. Blood. His own. Spread all over Justin's terrified face.

BOOK I

THE BEST MAN

I.

The smell reminded him of something. It wasn't necessarily a positive something or a negative something but it was definitive something. A something that was giving him some of the strongest feeling he'd felt in years. It didn't make a damn bit of difference what memory the smell was connected with and he didn't attempt to search the depths of his thoughts for it. Instead, he just stood still, hanging on to the smell. Hanging on to the feeling.

And just like that, it was gone.

He snapped back into his dire present circumstances.

"Reed, tonight, has died. Becky killed him."

Colin Benson had never mastered the art of facetiousness and his morbid attempt at humor was met with actual silence and perceived annoyance. He had always been told that no more personal connection could occur between two individuals than direct eye contact but as he looked from guest to guest at Reed's wedding, all focused on him, polite smiles on their faces, trying to excuse the failed opening statement of the best man's speech and hope for better, Colin felt he could not be more disconnected and alone. He got the sense that despite acting as the current visual attention center of the room, he could walk off, out of sight, and not one of his observers would know the difference. Colin did not fear public speaking, although he was in fact terrible at it. In order to be afraid of speaking to those who surrounded him, he would have to feel at least some concern as to their opinion of him. He felt nothing for these people. No affection. No dislike. Simply no connection whatsoever.

Becky watched him. Or rather, her eyes did. Her body had heard his comment but her mind had not. Her shoulders were anxiously hunched, her muscles tense, prepared to destroy if the speech continued along the same path, in any way diminishing the meaning of her wedding day. At the same time, she had not heard him at all. She was entirely focused on her love for Reed.

Reed, with his inexhaustible charm, which easily won over every person he met. Reed, with his impossible to deplete source of energy and magical ability to rouse anyone to a level of excitement, even if the circumstances were uncommonly dull. Reed, with his skill of always knowing how to end a gap of silence with just the right sentence, somehow never coming off as fake. Reed, with his boyish good looks and killer smile that probably could have sold a million tubes of toothpaste should he have ever become the face of a dental hygiene campaign.

Colin was not like Reed. With his bland physical features, his rather monotone voice, and his inability to think of anything to say in ninety percent of all situations, he usually failed to make any impression whatsoever on those he met. "We've actually met before," was something he often found himself saying. It used to bother him how little adhesiveness he had in other people's memories but over the years he had gotten used to it. Besides, the truth was that most people bored him just as much as he bored them. Everyone followed their own particular personality's rules of behavior and barely anything of interest ever happened. Life was rather monotonous, Colin thought, and he found little use in not being so himself. The only two things that ever managed to excite him were rare, impossible to clarify physical sensations, like the smell which had just briefly penetrated his consciousness, and Reed. For whatever reason, Reed had always possessed some quality that could crack Colin's shell of existential tedium.

Colin watched Becky clutch her new husband. She did love his friend. He recognized that. But he didn't think that recognition would be enough to stop him from delivering the very well thought out speech he had been rehearsing in his mind for months. A passionate declaration denouncing the union of Becky and Reed as a tragic mistake. A series of perfectly planned words that provided Colin with that oh so rare feeling of enthusiasm every time he repeated them. Colin had known he would not find the courage to speak up during the ceremony's "speak now or forever hold your peace" moment. Though he has still imagined doing so. Now that had come and gone and he found himself in an instance in which, as best man, he knew he was going to have speak anyway. If he was already speaking, he figured, he could get past his apprehensions and say what needed to be said. Reed and Becky were already legally married but divorces were common these days and perhaps the right words could start them on the path to separation.

As the rest of his audience uneasily waited for the doomed speech to continue, restless, awkwardly whispering to each other, Colin's attention shifted solely to Reed. Reed returned Becky's undistracted physical affection with his own devoted clutching, his body showing his commitment to marriage better than his fairly well written vows ever could. But his eyes were fixed on Colin, their full attention given over to the speech.

Colin paused and tried to gain the composure to speak the words he had planned. He ignored the snickering, confused, bored stares of the rest of the wedding party and looked only into the steadfast eyes of his best friend Reed, the only person he had ever really loved.

• • •

It is sometimes hard to pinpoint the exact moment that a friendship begins. A bond is rarely formed on an initial meeting, although there are certainly exceptions. There are instances where a relationship takes years to grow into an entity that can be truthfully referred to as a genuine friendship, and there are instances where deep connections come so rapidly it is as if they were preplanned before the first meeting, only to dissipate with astonishing speed. There are friendships that are obvious, practical, and leave every observer nodding at the inevitability. And then there are friendships that defy logic, for which no one, including the immediate parties involved, can identify any characteristic matching justification for. Yet these often baffling human unions can become unbreakable, expanding on the confusion of their very existence with a fixed surface layer covering of temporal eternity, irremovable as long as the friendship remains unexplainable in the first place.

Colin and Reed shared one such friendship.

Colin Benson was the type of child who would have been bullied if he had only had the fortune of being more interesting. His physical frame certainly matched the bullies' considerations. He was scrawny, short, had knobby knees. But he was so unassuming, faded so much into the background of every situation, that most of the students usually forgot he was even there.

Reed was precisely the opposite. He was fun, attractive, quick witted. The type of child the bullies tried to impress when they beat up on helpless twerps, hoping he might take notice of their strength and request their services as a sidekick. But he was generally too lost in his own world of wonder to even notice they were there.

The two first met in the third grade class of Mrs. Figelfor, a woman working past retirement age who treated her students like disappointing meals at a usually reliable restaurant. The years withered her and the atmosphere of constantly surprised disappointment in the classroom could not help but affect the student's enthusiasm. Colin, at age eight, already found learning to be a burden. He was not incapable and his performance throughout his school years was always more than adequate, but his accomplishment of the tasks assigned to him was continuously more of a default afterthought than any sort of conscious decision. A youth of schoolwork was the life structure he had fallen into and he found no purpose or energy in rebelling against it anymore than he found any drive to excel at it. Colin's parents could be said to have been constantly supportive. But they provided a support that was so quietly accepting, it gave him no indication any increase of effort on his own part would provide either of them with any heightened pride for their child. Any grade he brought home was met with an automatic, "Good job," always unemotional, always ending in a period, never an exclamation point. Any discussion of knowledge he had gained during a school day was met with respectful listening, but never the sense Colin looked for actively in his earliest years that any of the facts which now inhabited his brain were of any importance whatsoever. Colin viewed his parents as living evidence that the expression, "You learn something new everyday," was actually a fallacy. Mr. and Mrs. Benson might have sometimes had new facts latch onto their memories, but rarely could this process be called learning. Never did these facts enlighten their conversation or behavior. There was no sense that any piece of knowledge had ever more than minutely affected the paths of their lives and certainly had not improved their well-being. So Colin would sit in front of the eternally let down face of Mrs. Fiegelfor, acquiring facts through the method of simply not ignoring what he was being told, all the while planted inside him the ever growing tree of boredom.

Reed was affected by the atmosphere of that third grade

classroom in quite a different manner. From his earliest infancy, he was a child who produced and fed off human joy. It would be difficult to identify the precise age at which Reed realized the full power he and all children possessed to harness this delight. It was not yet as a baby, when the mere sight of his unchanging expression induced uncontrolled smiles. It may have been as a toddler, when painting his face with now manipulated cuteness caused observing adults to find him all the more adorable. It was definitely in full force by age five, when, encouraged by his parents, he arrived at gatherings of family and friends, told often nonsensical children's jokes, sang, and even on several occasions, attempted, and failed miserably at juggling. There were a few who viewed his whole display as more of a circus act than a child and questioned his parents' judgment in rearing such a trained beast, but they always remained quiet, while the vast majority delighted in young Reed's exploits. It should not be said that Reed was a mini-philanthropist, entertaining selflessly. His actions were always reciprocal, even if he never realized it. When he witnessed the spontaneous smiles his presence provided, his sense of self worth grew. Experiencing an atmosphere of joy, particularly one he substantially provided to, became a drug to Reed. A drug that at the age of eight, in Mrs. Figelfor's class, was suddenly becoming harder to acquire.

Reed was already beginning to notice the diminishing power of his cuteness. He could still coax a smile out of most adults, but the task was requiring increased effort. Nothing he had faced prepared him for the daily smog of disappointment that consumed the classroom of Mrs. Figelfor, with no sign of anyone opening a window. Reed was not ready for the extreme loss of energy he felt just by being in the company of such a downtrodden adult. He was even less ready for the more powerful blow that came from being seated next to a misanthrope of his own age. A boy by the name of Colin Benson.

It would have been easy for this to have been the moment when Reed was unknowingly pushed down the lifelong slide of cynicism on the jungle gym of depression. But he was made of stronger stuff. He would not be like most of the other children in that classroom, or for that matter, most of the other children in the world, or for a matter that is still the same matter, most of the other people in the world. Confronted with those drained by the difficulties of life, Reed, at the age of eight, made a decision that many people cannot find the strength to make at any age. The decision to be happy. The decision to fight what would often in the future appear to be an impossible fight against the force of sadness, and always come out on top.

Ours is a social existence and Reed recognized that the only successful strategy in his war to maintain enthusiasm amongst the beaten down drones would be to share his happiness with others. Reed was, of course, a child. He made decisions on instinct alone, not able to grasp why he acted the way he did. Although, to be truthful, acting from the gut was a quality he held onto most of his life. So he was unaware of his own imperfections. Of the fact that the need to force reciprocated joy from the depths of other individuals' minds was as a validation of his own efforts. And was also a source of evidence that in some way he was superior to those other individuals. The contradiction in wanting others around him to share in the positivity that flowed through him, while at the same time relishing in the ability to see himself as a better person than those same others, was one Reed would never fully recognize, even years later.

His focus was on action, not motivation. He needed to decide where to begin his mission. So he chose the individual closest to him, proximity wise. The quiet isolated building block of a personality known as Colin Benson.

On an unspecific day in March, after a particularly unenthusiastic butchering of a classic children's story by the expressionless reader Mrs. Figelfor, Reed turned to his classmate and uttered what he had concluded was the perfectly formed sentence of friendship initiation.

"Hey, you wanna come over this weekend and play Nintendo?"

Colin really had never had any friends. He barely spoke to others. In the school yard he sat against a wall in a shadowy corner and waited for the bell to ring. He had never considered that anyone would be interested in being his friend. All of the other boys spent recess running around, playing sports, and Colin, feeling far from athletic, thought that without possessing the ability to throw or catch a ball he was better off just being ignored. For Colin, being asked by Reed to hang out was the equivalent of being asked to be the godfather to someone's child. A tremendous honor he had never expected, a gesture that personally jumped into his body and gave his lonely heart a high five, instantly raising its self-esteem countless degrees, and a real responsibility that he was excruciatingly afraid of mishandling. What he lacked in courageousness was fulfilled in great quantity by the unusual emotion of inclusion, created upon hearing Reed's invitation. He accepted.

On the day of the hangout, Colin's father dropped him off, then drove away without bothering to see whether his son had been left inside. Luckily, Reed was home, and was waiting with a snack tray of delicious goodies, both healthy and not, and a brand new copy of Duck Hunt. At first the get together was a bit awkward as the children struggled through conversation greetings, but something significant happened once the two became engaged in the video game. They seemed to come to an immediate understanding. Reed was going to talk, about his games, and his snacks, and his house, and his family, and almost anything at all that came to mind, and Colin was going to remain quiet except for the occasional sentence of necessary contextual information. All while engaged in a friendly competition to see who could kill the most ducks. Somehow Colin felt free to be himself around Reed, no pressure to be less socially awkward than he actually was. This made him smile. Reed caught the smile and felt so satisfied with his victory that he ended up having a great time himself, thoroughly enjoying the freedom to ramble energetically to someone who loved nothing more than to listen.

One Saturday Duck Hunt session quickly became two and three and then a regular weekend routine for the boys. The fact that the friendship actually worked was as much a surprise to Reed as to the bewildered other children in the class who wore their stereotypes on their sleeves and had never pictured the outgoing lively Reed associating with the silent slothful Colin. It was not precisely that Reed had gotten Colin to open up, because Colin was the person that he appeared on the surface to be. An easily bored stiff entity who found it uninteresting to communicate with most people. Opening up the door of his personality would merely have revealed another door. It was rather that the prospect and occurrence of social activity in his life gave Colin enough enthusiasm to allow Reed to form an almost brotherly affection for him. What was created was a friendship in which two divergent personalities perfectly meshed.

Thus their bond was forged.

As Colin got older, Reed became nothing less than life support. The contentment which resulted from the friendship did nothing to change his basic nature. Throughout his early teens the chore of having to trudge personally through each indistinct moment of his life between the sporadic points of interest only intensified. The exciting minutes that came and went and usually involved Reed were enough to prevent him from ever leading down the thought road to the town of life is not worth living, but his method of being was very far from a lust for life.

Reed, in a somewhat similar fashion, stayed true to the first draft of his personality. Though Colin's lack of change did broaden his awareness of the conflicting mind sets of others. His passion for excelling at life led him to perform exceptionally in his studies, which caused him to have a prominent status in school, which caused the cloak of popularity to drape itself over his shoulders quite comfortably. As they moved on to larger education institutions, Reed's list of friends grew rapidly in number. Some with whom he was quite close. Some with whom he was barely more than acquaintances. None of whom could understand his friendship with Colin.

"He's my best friend," Reed repeatedly told his confused associations.

One of his other friends quietly questioned whether Reed understood the meaning of the words he was using. He did not think Reed was an imbecile when it came to the English language. But this baffling explanation was the only conclusion he could come to that could explain the contradiction between this oft repeated sentence and every other piece of knowledge he and Reed's other friends could gain.

"If someone is told the word cat means the animal dog from a very early age, for years and years, they will think a dog is a cat and they will be right. They will just not be able to communicate properly with the rest of us. Maybe this is like that."

The others did not buy his theory. They searched for answers nonetheless. How could the naturally socially gifted Reed be best friends with an individual who would routinely stand to the side of their hallway circles of socialization, saying nothing, avoiding eye contact, when he even approached the circle at all? How could he pass by the circle without comment when his supposed best friend was involved?

"Is he shy?" they asked Reed.

"Just uninterested I think. But sometimes it's hard to say with Colin."

"Does he talk more when it's just the two of you? Does he say interesting things which he feels strange bringing up around other people?"

"Not particularly. I mean obviously he talks but our friendship is not overly conversation based."

"What is it based on then?"

"I can't say exactly. Some quality that language doesn't really have a word for."

These answers left Reed's friends incredibly unsatisfied and made the questions more a part of their daily mental routine than they had any right to be.

A couple of Reed's closer friends actually viewed his friendship with Colin as a personal insult. They were envious of Colin's etched in stone position as Reed's best friend, a title they felt they were far more entitled to hold. They tried to isolate Colin and tease him when Reed was not around, but gave up on their attempts at hazing when they determined that it was impossible to tell whether stone faced Colin was affected or could even tell what they were doing.

Colin could tell what they were doing but he told himself it didn't matter much. He never expected to connect with people.

He tried occasionally to spend time with Reed's other friends because somewhere in his mind was the desire to be more like others. To bond with multiple individuals. But his minimal efforts always failed and he realized again and again the only person he had desire to be around was Reed. Colin was not bothered by Reed's ever expanding network. He recognized his need for a larger social map. Yet he didn't have a desire to have any of these individuals enter the close quarters of his own life. Reed was enough and Reed would be steadfast.

Inevitably, Reed's good looks and the magnetic pull of likeability he had on those around him caught hold on members of the opposite gender. The first in a long line of teenage suitors, waiting their turn somewhat impatiently, was Suzanne Apler, a girl displaced in time who insisted on being pinned. Reed thought she was using a wrestling term. After, came Jamie Crudstein, who ate cereal three meals a day and Stephanie Kushlek, who had never heard the word insistence. Quite literally. The relationship ended after three dates when Stephanie insisted that insist could not be transformed into such a form.

Reed's teenage flings were of various lengths. Some lasted days, some months, and all inevitably ended before any needful personal tie was formed. Many in this steady stream of girls were sent away by Reed. He always maintained enthusiasm over being alive but found it difficult to transfer his passion from its natural all expansive nature into the image of a single individual. Some became fed up waiting for this shift of zeal and dispersed with the frustratingly unaffected Reed themselves. And a select few simply could never get over the paradox of Colin. It was inconceivable to them to be second fiddle to an individual with no engaging qualities.

As for Colin, he found himself, much to his own surprise,

longing for love. He was not especially fond of any of Reed's companions and his self esteem was constantly boosted when each of these girlfriends failed to form a connection as strong as the one he and Reed shared. He was, however, hit with a strange, unaccustomed feeling of yearning each time he saw Reed's hand clasped to another. It was not the individuals involved but the action itself he found himself longing for.

So Colin began searching for the elusive quality of love, without the slightest bit of knowledge as to what it was he was looking for.

He initially expected his search to become somewhat easier after leaving high school and ceasing to be around the already proven low grade stock of females. It did not. In his college classrooms, in bars, in stores, on the street, and in every conceivable location in which Colin might have and did meet a member of the opposite sex, he found that his yearning for love grew exponentially and every female realized in actuality provided him with nothing but forgettable tedium.

At times he told himself falling in love with another in the world was in two words, not necessary, and in five words, an utter waste of time. He also considered the sixteen words, a desire that would never live up to the abstract expectations and high hopes he had, but he forgot the sentence completely after its trial run. He increasingly preferred to imagine love rather than actually search for it. In his mind his expectations could actually be met. Real people only detracted from the imaginary and far more powerful feeling, although minor in itself, that he already felt in his mind. He saw his search as pointless if the contents of the shoddy treasure chest were worth less than the plastic shovel he used to dig it up. In truth he knew exactly what he wanted, even if the thought embarrassed him. What he was looking for was a romantic relationship that gave him the same feeling he got from his friendship with Reed.

In quiet secret moments when no one was around to observe even the slightest shift of his eyes or adjustment of his pose, Colin questioned his own sexual orientation. The only time he had ever felt anything close to what was commonly described as love was in time spent with Reed. Perhaps a deeply engrained biological tendency was the reason his love failed to expand. In some ways he wished this was the answer. It would concisely explain his failure at finding a female to love. Or, at the very least, one he felt even the faintest desire to be around. It was a concrete solution to the void. It just happened to be, annoyingly, not the case. His sexual desires were only for members of the opposing gender. Desires that terrified because of their complete lack of emotional connection. Cold biological instincts that he hoped falling in love might thaw.

But the thing that bothered him most was the fact that he could not manage to get more upset about it all. On several occasions he sat down with the intention of crying. He wanted to wail over his endless lack of satisfaction, his inability to be more like everybody else, his complete failure to experience the world of emotions the way everyone else seemed to, and the lack of love that was available to him. But he could not even manage a single tear.

His disappointment turned to dissatisfaction which turned to bitterness. Not that he knew the difference. All of these negative emotions were buried under the far more prominent lack of emotion he had hoped falling in love would erase. In the end this erasure was the true purpose of his search. The slight pangs of emotion obscured deeply in his mind were desperately trying to crawl out. But each actual woman he met only failed to live up to the sensation he desired but could not describe, and pushed those emotions he knew but could not feel further into the recesses of his mind. Falling in love appeared increasingly unlikely, and with each passing day Colin let go of hope and decided to hold on to what he had. Reed.

It likely comes as little surprise that while Reed was an academic steam train at college, chugging along, racking up one marvelous grade after another, simultaneously finding time to frequent parties and special university events, all the while avoiding any stress, Colin found himself in an ambitionless sand pit. He entered his four year term majoring in the fine art of undeclared, and left with an incredibly ironic diploma which labeled him as an expert in the field of communications. His particular major had not been any more appealing to him than any of the hundred plus choices in the course book. He picked it completely randomly when declaring became a requirement because the label on his degree didn't seem to make the slightest bit of difference. The only appeal he ever found in the concept of doing something was that he wouldn't be doing nothing. The differentiation was slight.

Upon graduation, while Reed was hard at work determining which high quality law school's colors he should be adding to his wardrobe, Colin browsed the endless online list of unappealing jobs, one of which the need for funds would soon require him to occupy.

He ended up accepting an office assistant position at Feldman Staffing. It was fitting that he perform menial tasks at a company whose purpose it was to find individuals jobs filled with menial tasks.

At Feldman Staffing he met Becky, of whom he promptly thought nothing. Reed, of course, had a very different reaction.

"Who's she?"

"Becky."

Colin had a concise way of answering questions.

In all his time across the room from her, Colin learned very little about Becky. Reed, on his visits, quickly started up friendly conversation with her, desperate to get to the essence of who she was. Becky was the type of girl who liked to wear her hair in a ponytail, then rest it through the loop in the one size fits all cap of her favorite baseball team. She could easily be one of the guys with her sports addiction and unusual amount of knowledge about car maintenance, but she also never lost her obvious female qualities, pretty even in a football jersey, gorgeous in makeup and a dress. She was incredibly affable and had what seemed to Reed an endearing obliviousness as to whether those she talked to pleasantly had any desire to converse back with her.

Reed, after much deliberation, managed to create a proper balance of enough visits to Colin at work that he could frequently steal a conversation with the new object of his affection, but not too many that Becky might think he and Colin were in a homosexual relationship.

The thought never entered Becky's mind. She was as immediately and completely taken with Reed as he was with her. The standard question of how such a charmer came to be best friends with the cartoonishly uncharismatic co-worker to her right did enter her mind, but to her credit, her reaction to the strange bond was only to become certain that anyone so close with someone as wonderful as Reed must be a terrific person himself, even if he lacked any surface level appeal.

The two were inseparable. Colin immediately knew there was a world of difference between this and any of Reed's former flings. This was real. This was Reed reaching a previously unknown height of enthusiasm. A rather difficult feat. This was Reed with a look of complete satisfaction whenever he looked at Becky and a subtle look of confusion when he looked at anything else, as if his eyes no longer understood the purpose of their use if they were not fixed upon the love his life.

Reed was being stolen from him and Colin was angry. He was angry for an instant when he realized he would soon lose his position of prominence in Reed's life. He was angry for a while when he embraced the feeling of anger as at least being a feeling. Colin did not hate Becky. He could not even bring himself to dislike her. To dislike her would be to recognize her as an individual. It would force him to learn about her specific personality traits, to disassociate her from the numerous crowd of unknowns who often inhabited his personal space but could not in any way be said to have entered the narrow confines of his life. And he was determined that she would remain a symbol. No more or less than a tangential figure who had taken the place of Colin as the dominant connection in Reed's life. What he hated was their union and the idea of his inevitable displacement. When they got engaged only seven months later, Colin felt a new powerful jolt of hate. A hate that was constantly fed with each detail of wedding plans he overheard Becky discussing at work and each mention of the big event by Reed in their dwindling but still consistent hang outs. The hate fueled the speech he planned to deliver as Reed's best man.

And there he stood, the day of the wedding having finally arrived, two hundred plus restless guests waiting to hear what he would say, Becky and Reed staring at him, trying not to show discomfort with his growing pause, hoping that his speech would swiftly continue, and he realized that he could not go through with it.

It was partly the look on Reed's face. A look that vowed he would be proud of Colin's speech regardless of how good it was. That really, the content of the speech was irrelevant. Reed was merely delighted to see his best friend addressing the crowd, speaking on his behalf, on this, the happiest day of his life. His eyes gave recognition of Colin's natural apprehensiveness at public speaking, not realizing that his apprehensiveness was of a more sinister nature, and reassured Colin that the act of continuing, in and of itself, would show the bond of their friendship, in a way Reed knew Colin could never express verbally. Reed had never actually given any indication Colin would be replaced. In fact, knowing Colin well, he made effort to insist clearly, without room for doubt, that their friendship remained strong as ever. He went out of his way to make sure his best friend never felt excluded or ignored. He wanted Colin to know that no matter what happened, they would always be best friends.

But even more than because of Reed's reassuring look, Colin suddenly knew he would not deliver the planned speech because it was built on a lie.

The truth was he had been unable to maintain the feeling of hate he had tried to immerse himself in. After some initial small pangs of sadness, thoughts of the loss of Reed had turned into nothing but lethargy. The truth was that the hate was false. It was a self created delusion that got him through the days. As always, what he really felt was nothing. For years and years all he really wanted was to be like everyone else. To communicate and connect and feel. He was unconsciously jealous of all those he felt nothing for because he could not be like them. He wanted to be swept away by emotions the way every other person in the world seemed to be. But instead he was faced with infinite boredom. Not even the loss of the only person he had ever loved could

46

shock him into an emotional upheaval. It was this thought, at this moment, that almost caused him to shed his first tear in many many years. Almost. Or at least, he liked to believe.

The remainder of Colin's speech failed just as miserably as the opening. He stumbled through thoughts of praise and nostalgia that lacked any filling. His unprepared words lacked any content and were simultaneously repetitious. The relief of some listeners at the speech's end was second only to the surprise of others that it had still been going on. At the finish, Colin wasted no time in returning to his seat. He remained there for the duration of the affair.

•••

"Colin, I'd like you to meet someone."

Becky interrupted him from his solitary contemplation. He was previously accompanied only by a morsel of shrimp wrapped in bacon, whose journey to his mouth this intrusion interrupted.

Becky glowed. The glow did not extend to the female she stood with. Colin could hardly see her face.

"This is Lisa."

"Hello," he said.

Colin did not support the use of phrases like "Nice to meet you" until the interaction was actually proven to be nice. "Unpleasant to meet you," could easily be a more accurate statement, or more often then not "Unmemorable to meet you" would fit the bill.

"Hi," said Lisa.

Lisa was either shy or felt the same way. The prospect of sharing characteristics with her did nothing to raise his excitement level.

"Well, why don't you two get to know each other a bit. I should get back to my *husband*." Lisa smiled at Becky's intentional over-enunciation of a long delayed term she was now permitted to use. Colin ate his shrimp.

As Becky departed Lisa looked kindly at Colin and waited. She expected Colin to initiate the proceedings. He fully under-stood her expectation and had no intention of obliging. If neither had anything to say, then nothing should be said. It seemed only practical.

Eventually, she broke the uncomfortable silence.

"So you work with Becky?"

"I do."

"What do you do there?"

"Nothing that you'd actually be interested in hearing about."

"You never know."

"Sometimes you do."

"My job's pretty boring too."

"Most are."

"Do you want to hear about it?"

"If it's boring, then not particularly."

"At least you're honest. I like honesty."

"You wouldn't if you knew what I was thinking right now."

She laughed. He wasn't joking.

"Becky seems to think we'd be a good match."

"Does she?"

"Yeah. I've known her for a really long time. We used to live next door to each other when we were kids."

"Ok."

"Where'd you meet Reed?"

"In our third grade class."

"And you guys have been best friends ever since?"

"Yeah."

"That's sweet."

Colin nodded. He was becoming exhausted of responding with words.

Lisa seemed to notice that the non-conversation had arrived at its tipping point with no lack of haste.

"Well it was really nice to meet you."

"Yeah."

"Maybe I'll see you a little later."

"It's entirely possible."

He was not about to deny the obvious.

Colin hoped that Becky's intrusion with Lisa would be the last irritation he had to deal with at the wedding. He quickly realized he would not be so lucky when he spotted the purpose filled approach of Nick Hartley, a fellow employee at Becky and Colin's workplace. Nick was the definition of what you might call a social connector. He seemed to have no end of acquaintances and no end of casual conversational topics to entertain them with. Nick thrived on maintaining his vast amount of contacts, his greatest joy often seeing the smile in the distance of someone he hadn't spoken to in months.

Colin had no illusions that Nick genuinely wanted to talk to him. He was well aware that Nick saw the interaction as a requirement. The two barely ever spoke to each other during the endless hours they shared at the office. Nick would say hello only when he could muster up the effort to interact with the energy draining form that was Colin. For his part, Colin routinely had even less drive to exchange daily greetings and partings with Nick than with most people because he knew they were issued only to adhere with larger social convention, rather than because he in any way felt like interacting with he whom he greeted. Nick ruined the minute chance he might have had of gaining Colin's affection when he showed tremendous friendliness in their first encounter. Nothing made Colin wish to say hello less than being said hello to when the hello had not yet been earned.

"Hello Colin."

"Hello Nick."

"That was some speech you gave."

"You liked it?

"Yeah, it was," he said nonsensically in an attempt to not actually comment. "Mind if I sit down?"

"I don't mind if you don't."

"Ok great. Some wedding, huh?"

"I suppose it is."

"How does it feel to be responsible for this?"

"What do you mean?"

"They never would have met without you, right?"

"I didn't introduce them or anything. He just met her when he stopped by the office one time."

"Yeah, I know how it happened. I am quite close with Becky, remember?"

"Sure."

"But in any case, if it wasn't for you knowing both of them they never would have met or fallen in love or gotten married and all of us would have been God knows where today."

"Does God know?"

"It's crazy isn't it? The way life and time works. Any little action or path taken by any one of us can affect the lives of countless others. You taking the job at Feldman Staffing allowed Reed to meet Becky. Them falling in love caused this wedding to happen and for all of us guests to be here. Who knows, maybe as a result of this two people, guests, workers, who knows, will meet and fall in love themselves. At the very least, there will be some occurrence at this wedding today that will directly affect the rest of someone present's life. It's like dominoes, life. With each falling event and endless amount of other events are set in motion. Joyous events. Tragic events. All kinds of events."

"I guess."

It was at this point that Nick remembered who it was he was talking to and decided that there was no one less deserving of hearing his philosophical musings. He politely said an unreturned goodbye and ventured out into the waters of those he might soon know.

For the more than four hour duration of the wedding party Colin showed no signs of leaving. To do so would take more energy than staying for he would have to explain his early departure. So he just sat in his seat and ignored.

He ignored the dancing, both fast and slow. He ignored the obnoxious tugging of middle aged party mongers attempting with physical force to make him join the conga line. He ignored the obvious attempts of Lisa to just happen to walk past his table each time the band's crooner broke out a love ballad. He ignored the overloud chatting of senior citizens over his shoulder, who seemed to have lost their concepts of both volume and proximity. He ignored the incessant scampering of children playing who knows what game that always ended with one chasing another on a trajectory that passed directly through Colin's chair. He ignored the polite conversation offered up by one jovial server and the angry stares issued by another when he failed to touch his side of garlic mashed potatoes. He ignored the weepy eyed words of Becky's father, and the flood of tears amongst the crowd that followed them. He ignored the perfectly structured witty words of Reed's father, proving a clear relation to his son, charmingly being at once hilarious and sentimental. He ignored the cutting of the wedding cake. He even ignored his own bladder's ceaseless plea that he use the bathroom. He could not take the risk of exiting the conversational blind spot he had managed to park himself him.

And he waited patiently for the one moment of the night he had unshakeable faith would come. The validation of his reasons for attendance in the first place. And of course, as he knew it would be, his faith was soon rewarded.

"Hey there buddy."

"Hey Reed."

Reed patted Colin on the shoulder and sat down in the unoccupied seat next to him.

"You having a good time?"

"Of course."

A lie to his best friend was more honest than the truth to everyone else.

"Sorry I couldn't stop by until now."

"It's understandable. It is your wedding after all."

"I suppose it is," he said, glancing over at his bride.

"You really love her don't you?"

"I really do."

"Are you scared?"

"Of what?"

"I don't know. That it won't stay the same. That your passion will fade. That your love will die."

It was not a question he had planned on asking, but it was one he had always wanted to ask. Not of Reed. Of himself. But it was impossible to question the lasting quality of love that he had never acquired in the first place.

"You know. I'm not. I really think this is the real thing."

"I'm glad."

"Thanks for being here buddy."

"No problem."

"Reed my boy!"

Their conversation was interrupted by the clasp of thick fingers on Reed's shoulder. Colin recognized the hand. A short time ago it had attempted to clothe him with a plastic flower lei.

"I'll stop back later," Reed assured Colin as he walked off with a man who looked prepared to sell him a toaster. And he would stop back. About that Colin had no doubt.

The smell returned. The feeling returned. It was frustrating. Frustrating that the best he felt in months was the result of an unidentified entrant to his nasal passage. Frustrating that he could not identify the source of the smell, nor the joyous memory connected to it. Frustrating that this brief moment of bliss was tainted by frustration. Frustrating that in a moment it would disappear. He might be able to recall the memory of this feeling, but he would likely never feel it again. Vanished into the haze of small talk, place cards, and bafflingly long lasting eighties dance music.

II.

"I think somebody told me the lobster here is really good."

"It's lobster. The real story would be if it was mysteriously weak."

"Shut up," said Becky, playfully punching her husband.

Lisa smiled at Colin, trying to quickly recycle the playful flirting for her own purpose before it evaporated from the air. Her green efforts were to no avail. Colin remained focused on the menu, hard at work although he had already decided on what he would be ordering seven minutes before.

They were at Light & Dark, a restaurant true to its name, which kept one half of its premises in complete brightness, illuminated by oversized chandeliers, and the other consumed by dim mood lighting, some tables provided with only a single candle.

They were seated in the dark section.

"What does this say?" said Becky, holding her menu as close as possible to the candle without setting it on fire.

"Topped with a mushroom gardenia sauce," responded Reed.

"What do you think that means. It has flowers on it?"

"Hard to say."

"What are you getting, Colin?" inquired Lisa, who wished to be part of the table's conversation.

"Hard to say."

It was Colin and Lisa's second date. Both double. Both chaperoned by Reed and Becky.

The day after the wedding Reed had called Colin to encourage the set-up.

"What'd you think of Lisa?"

"Who?" Colin genuinely had no idea who he was referring to.

"The girl Becky introduced you to at the wedding yesterday."

"I'm not sure who you're talking about." Colin had remembered who he was talking about.

"C'mon. Cute little girl. Shortish brown hair."

"Ok."

"In any case, she really liked you."

"Did she." It was not a question.

"Yeah. You should ask her out. I can get you her number."

"I don't think so."

"Why the hell not? What have you got to lose?"

"I just don't think I'm interested."

"You said you didn't even remember her."

"Exactly."

The next day the newlyweds left for their weeklong honeymoon and Colin forgot completely about the conversation. The following Monday Becky returned to the office and continued exactly where Reed had left off.

"Why won't you ask Lisa out?"

"Who?"

"You know exactly who I'm talking about."

"Maybe. How were the Bahamas?"

"Oh, amazing. Most beautiful beaches I've ever seen."

"That's great. What kinds of activities did you guys do there?"

"Oh, we went parasailing and – Hey you're trying to get me off topic aren't you?"

"I'm just inquiring about my friend's honeymoon."

"What are you so scared of Colin? You have nothing to lose by going on one date with a girl."

"I lose the time I could have spent doing something else. I lose the money that I inevitably have to spend to pay for both of us to eat or see a movie, or whatever other costly activity we do."

More likely a movie so I don't have to talk to her, he thought.

"And what if it works out?"

"That's highly unlikely."

Three days later he received a phone call.

"Hi, is this Colin?"

"Yes."

"Hi. This is Lisa."

"Who?"

"We met at Reed and Becky's wedding."

"Oh."

"How are you?"

"Same as yesterday."

"How were you yesterday?"

"More or less the same as the day before."

"I see. So hey, listen. I was wondering. If you weren't doing anything. If maybe. You'd like to get together some time."

"Well right now I am kind of busy."

"Oh. How come?"

"It's tax season."

"Oh. Well maybe when tax season's over."

"Yeah maybe."

On April 16th, Colin was paid a visit at the office.

"Hi!"

"Hi. How can I help you?"

"It's me. Lisa!"

"Oh right, Lisa."

Colin looked over at Becky who pretended to read a blank sheet of paper.

"Did you get everything done in time?" asked Lisa

"For what?"

"Tax season."

"Oh right. Yeah it was fine."

"That's great."

"Yeah."

"It's real nice to see you again."

Colin nodded. Slipping into silence had been a successful conversation killer at the wedding and it seemed the proper weapon to wield again on this occasion. For a moment his tactic appeared successful. Lisa frantically tried to let words flutter from her mouth but nothing came. Defeat was written on her forehead.

"Look at you two. Chatting in the office."

Becky's intervention extended the nagging pestilence.

"Hi Becky," said Lisa.

"Well if seeing this doesn't remind me of a couple of other people."

"Who's that?"

"Me and Reed. When we first met he used to come in here all the time and talk to me as long as he could whenever our boss wasn't peeking his head around the corner. It was really endearing."

"I always wondered how you weren't fired for all that chatting," interjected Colin.

Becky ignored him. "I was just thinking. There's this new restaurant that me and Reed wanted to try out. It'd be great if you guys came and joined us."

"Oh that sounds really... real fun. Like a lot of fun," responded Lisa excitedly. "Do you want to Colin?"

Colin ignored the inappropriateness inherent in being addressed by name so casually by someone he did not know and assessed the situation.

If he gathered correctly, Becky's spontaneous idea of dinner for four was very much preplanned. Similarly, Lisa's eager response to the idea had been scripted and practiced, yet still stumbled over and delivered wrong. The efforts of his best friend and his best friend's wife to play matchmaker had left the arena of informal good deeds and had turned into an all out crusade, complete with meetings, strategies, and fail-safe battle plans. If he again resisted this union which they were so determined to form, he would only be attacked with a surge of bigger guns, larger forces, and endless amounts of irritation. The effort it was taking to avoid a relationship with Lisa was becoming greater than the effort it would take to be in one. His complete lack of interest in her was powerless in the face of such exhaustion. He raised the white flag.

"Ok," he said.

"Ok what?" replied Becky, sure she had misheard the answer.

"Ok, I'll go to dinner."

"Really?" said Lisa, who raised her hands, foolishly expecting some sort of embrace.

"Yeah. That sounds fine."

"Well great," said Becky, shocked that the battle had ended so quickly and almost disappointed that she would never get to use future brilliant strategies she had already thought up. "I'll call Reed and tell him to set up a reservation for Friday."

"I'm really excited," said Lisa, still figuring out what to do with her hands and showing no signs of going away until she received a response.

"Yep," responded Colin.

By conventional standards the first date might be referred to as a failure, or if one is willing to be liberal with words of extremity, a disaster. It was less a double date, than a date between Reed and Becky, in which they each had a silent observer to their respective sides, watching their every move and listening closely to their conversation. Reed suspected that they might receive a review in the next morning's edition of the paper. "The Marriage Dynamic With a Side of Mozzarella Sticks," cowritten by Colin Benson, an investigative reporter who had gone undercover for fourteen years, posing as his best friend, in order that one day, this article, his masterpiece, might find itself wrapped in plastic on someone's doorstep.

Following the "Deaf Date," as Reed liked to refer to it, making a pun on the classic term "blind date" that he thought was much more clever than anyone else did, it came as quite the surprise to everyone that Colin suggested a sequel. And even though the darkness of Light & Dark made no difference because Colin didn't spend any time looking at his date, and even though in subsequent meetings he never gave Lisa even the smallest reason to consider him a worthwhile beau, the two became a couple. It was baffling to Reed and Becky even though they had fought so hard to put it together. The whole affair seemed odd and wrong and at a certain juncture they chose to remove themselves entirely, feeling stained by some mysterious sin. For Colin, staying with Lisa was barely a conscious decision. It took less effort to stay with her than to end it.

Colin made no inquiry about Lisa's past relationship experience. Actually, he made no inquiry about any aspect of her life. He did not ask about her family. He did not ask about her career aspirations. He did not ask her about what music or movies she enjoyed. He did not ask whether she had any close friends, although he gathered she did not from her universal availability. He once asked her to pass the ketchup. Her compliance with his request revealed nothing about her personality.

Whether her past experience consisted of unqualified monsters who abused her both verbally and physically, or consisted only of a giant lack, she seemed unfazed and even satisfied with a relationship based exclusively around the quality of silence. At restaurants, in their apartments, in stores, in parks, in both private and public places, even on the telephone, Colin would rarely speak a word, and almost never connect words into a full sentence. Lisa similarly allowed her voice to hibernate. She was either content following his lead or found it too awkward to talk with no guarantee of response. Whichever it was, she spent their time together smiling, and for some reason desired their personal spaces be combined as often as possible. He obliged her, having nothing better to do.

Over time Colin realized that he did not find Lisa in the least bothersome. During brief moments her company was even vaguely pleasant. He considered conveying his feelings and giving her what would have been a huge compliment coming from him, if he did not expect she would respond like most of humanity and take it as an insult. And even though he felt no real attachment to her, often forgetting about her existence when she was not in his immediate sight line, he came to find that he did not wish to hurt her.

During the most obscure of instances, Colin would actually feel remorseful that he was unable to develop any feelings for Lisa. By all observations she was a sweet, kind, amiable girl, trapped in an aloof relationship with Colin because of the overwhelming need to be connected to someone, whoever they might be, and because of looks that were not up to snuff enough to have made most men take notice, and because of years of crippling shyness when it might have made a difference to speak up. She deserved someone who felt passion at the mere sight of her. He sometimes wished that he could be that someone. He sometimes wished that he could work up the energy to have an actual conversation with her or kiss her as more than a mere formality of the charade they were putting on. His wishes went unfulfilled. The relationship lasted.

• • •

Nick Hartley had been acting strangely since the wedding. The sound of his unnecessarily loud voice on work related phone calls, amplified in order that every co-worker in his vicinity would recognize how quickly he would climb the company ladder, had become no more than a faint murmur, easily mistaken for the buzzing of an unseen insect that had made its way through the heating vents into the office. His morning greetings, in which he, the optimistic fiery coach, made the rounds inspiring his team of talentless also-rans to fight the good fight, had become a single extended "hello," said only once and miraculously maintained from the time he entered the door until he reached his desk several yards away. Most peculiarly, he had ceased sneaking chats with Becky at every available opportunity. Colin had noticed the radical change in the way the old friends interacted with one another. Constantly to not at all was not exactly a subtle variation. But he did not care enough to inquire as to what had occurred. In fact, he found the new Nick to be far preferable.

Reed, now in his third year of law school, and increasingly overwhelmed with his studies, had as of late no time to visit Becky at work and was unaware of the change.

"We should get together with your friend Nick sometime," he suggested one evening. "He's always an interesting guy to talk to. Got lots of thoughts."

Whatever rift had taken place between Becky and Nick, she

intended to keep it from Reed. She made no indication of any turmoil and agreed that a get together was a fine idea. She would make the arrangements for the earliest convenient time.

It may have been the sound of cascading pins or the cathartic release of heaving a fourteen pound ball, or the all consuming smell of day old pizza that filled the alley. Whatever the deciding factor, if there was one at all, it was the champions' sport of bowling that Becky chose to be the great equalizer and the ideal activity to ease the tension when spending time with a close friend she had mysteriously not spoken to in over two months. Reed and Becky arrived first and reserved lane twenty-three, directly next to a group of scantily clad 12 year old girls, who rolled the ball between their legs after spreading them just a little too wide.

"Well that's inappropriate," said the just appearing Nick, effectively breaking his code of silence.

"Hi Nick," was how Becky chose to respond.

Nick had brought with him two accessories. A personalized Brunswick bowling ball, complete with custom fit finger holes, and a tall blonde companion by the name of Patrice. She brought with her one accessory. Her prominently displayed cleavage.

"Yes. It is inappropriate," added Becky.

Reed extended his hand to greet Nick. He let go of the blonde but hung onto the bowling ball. An outside observer might have noticed Nick preparing to wield the ball as a weapon, almost expecting an attack. Reed did not. He was focused on an awkward attempt at a left-handed handshake, compensating for the giant ball attached to Nick's established greeting hand. The left-handed handshake failed. They normally do. But the valiant attempt eased Nick's tension as he realized that he had been greeted as a friend. He dropped the ball and pulled Reed in for a double back patting man hug.

Reed, a talented bowler who had broken 200 several times in his life, was the clear class of the group. Each time he stepped to the line he unleashed a ball that glided towards the pins at once both poetically and with a furious vengeance. Or at least he liked to think of the ball's movement in such terms. On this occasion, he was more impressed with himself than anyone else was. Nick was busy chatting, Patrice was actively listening to Nick's words, if not actually hearing them, and Becky pretended she was alone, then as a result, was very quickly left so.

"Let me ask you something," Nick said to Reed who went uncongratulated after his second straight strike.

"Sure."

"How do you feel about criminal law?"

"I feel like it's the best way to try criminals."

"Very funny. I meant, as an aspiring lawyer, how do you feel about the prospect of working in criminal law? Is that something you're pursuing?"

"It is actually."

"What aspects of it?"

"All aspects. I want to keep myself open. Although I'd much rather be on the prosecution side of things than the defense side. Especially when it comes to the more reprehensible crimes."

"How come?"

"I just can't stand the idea of being responsible for letting someone go free who's done something horrible, like commit a murder, or even something not as bad, you know? And not just be responsible, but have it be my responsibility to get them off the hook. And even though I'd want to only take clients I believe in, I know its not possible to make a living that way. And if you work for the state you're just assigned to criminals. You have no choice but to defend them the best you can. Guilty or innocent."

"That's interesting," commented Nick as he carelessly released his ball down the lane, knocking down just one pin.

"What?"

"My thinking would be just the opposite."

"What do you mean?"

"It's the thought of falsely convicting an innocent man that bothers me more. Not the thought of letting a guilty man go free. With the guilty man, at least there's the chance he won't commit a crime again. He may. And it may be a horrible tragedy that he was prevented from doing so. But I'll take that any day over the alternative of essentially removing the right to live from someone who has done nothing wrong. See the divergence here is between looking at things from an individual perspective or a societal perspective. When you think of yourself in the position of being falsely convicted, the idea that such a thing can happen is unfathomable. When you look at people as cogs in a larger context, on the other hand, as part of something that will continue beyond when any of us individuals are gone, then it seems the justice system should favor guilty before innocent. It'll do the greater good for the most people. And really it might be beneficial if we could just take on one perspective or the other but we're inevitably and helplessly caught somewhere in the middle. When we accept the idea of capital punishment we justify it for its before the fact reasoning. If someone knows that their life may be taken from them, they may stop themselves from committing a murder. If they have any line of rational thinking in their brains at all when considering such an action. But once the crime is done, doesn't the punishment boil down to not much more than an accepted form of revenge? I suppose the punishment needs to be dealt out in order that the larger societal warning can be enforced but from an individual perspective I'm not sure how I feel about revenge as a government practice."

Reed grinned and turned to his wife.

"I told you your buddy Nick's got lots of thoughts."

Becky thought she had successfully broken from her shell of no reactions and forced a smile. She had not. All Reed saw was an uncomfortable and somewhat confusing grimace.

"Is everything alright?" he asked her.

"Everything's fine," she responded, entirely unconvincingly.

• • •

"Reed, can I talk to you about something?"

They had returned home after the long night of strikes and spares and were preparing for bed. Thus far the only progress they had made was the actual entrance into the bedroom. There Reed had put his arms around the love of his life and had not let go in two full minutes as she affectionately leaned her head on his shoulder.

"Anything. You can always talk to me about anything, you know that."

"It's sort of difficult."

"Whatever it is, I'm here to listen."

"Ok, let's sit down."

They relocated to the edge of the bed. He didn't let go of her. He never liked to let go of her.

"It's about Nick."

"What about him?"

"Well. The thing is. When we first met I had a thing for him. Or more than a thing. I'm not sure what to call it exactly."

"A crush?"

"No...To be honest...I was sort of in love with him."

"I see."

"That was my sophomore year of college and he had his girl-friend, who he had met the year before. So I never said anything. But I kept being in love with him. For the rest of college. And for a little bit after. Really, until I met you."

Reed didn't notice that he was holding her a big lighter. Becky did.

"Do you still have feelings for him?"

"No. Reed, when I fell for you I fell for you completely and my feelings for Nick went completely away. It was liberating. And you felt right in a way that he never did."

"And he never knew?"

"No."

"Why are you telling me this now?"

"I know. I'm horrible. We're in this relationship – this mar-riage, and I'm supposed to be completely honest about things, and there's this one huge aspect of my life that I've deliberately not mentioned. I should have told you the moment I met you. Or if not then at least when things started getting serious. But not any later than that. And I certainly shouldn't have waited until now."

"But you didn't answer my question. I didn't ask, 'why did you wait to tell me about this.' I asked, 'why are you telling me this now.' What prompted you to bring this up at this moment after not mentioning it for so long? Something specific must have hap-pened."

"You're right. It did."

He let go of her completely.

"And what was it?"

"Tonight was the first night I've talked to Nick in two months. I only did because you said you wanted to get together and I was determined not to bring this up. But I realized tonight that was wrong. I love you and I shouldn't keep things from you. Even if they're difficult to talk about."

He held her once more.

"What happened two months ago?"

"It was at our wedding. Towards the end of the night. Nick pulled me aside. He said he had something he needed to say to me, and even though it was only going to ruin our friendship he needed to say it anyway. He told me he was in love with me. He said he thought he was towards the end of his relationship with Kelsey. He said he was sure he was during the beginning of my relationship with you. But he knew that I had waited so long to find someone I was so happy with and he didn't want to ruin it by revealing his feelings and making things complicated. He said he realized that he would never live with himself if he didn't tell me before I got married. He said that he got too scared to anyway. But he was telling me then. Not for any good that it would do me. But for his own selfish needs. He never knew my feelings about him all those years. I don't know if he would have said anything that night if he had. He probably thought I would just brush off his comments. Thought I'd be completely unaffected. But he didn't talk to me after that anyway. I guess the thought of doing so after he had made himself so vulnerable in front of me was more than he could bear."

"And. Were you completely unaffected?"

"Reed, I love you more than I ever thought it was possible to love another person and I want to be completely honest with you."

"Ok."

"There was a moment. Just the shortest of moments, right after he was done talking, when I thought, what if I ran away with him right now? But it passed as quickly as it came. It's no different from any moments I'm sure you've had when you see an unknown beautiful woman on the street and say, I wonder. I wonder if I had met her instead. And it was gone like that. And I knew I was absolutely with the right person and that all those years Nick had a girlfriend were a godsend, because if he hadn't I might not have met you. Sometimes it takes seeing alternate possibilities to know how great what you have is. I didn't even need to see this to know I have it great with you. But it just reaffirmed it once again for me. I love you and I don't want anybody else."

For a moment Reed was silent. He knew the moment was agonizing for her. He thought, this moment will only be as long as the short moment she spent thinking of a life with Nick. He wanted her to feel the wait. And then he did what he intended to do from the moment she had stopped talking. He kissed her.

"It's okay."

"Really?"

"I love you and nothing's going to change that. I'm glad you were honest me. We all have moments that our minds think of alternate possibilities. You said it yourself."

"Yeah. We do."

"If you say that Nick is nothing more than a friend to you now, then I believe you. If you tell me there's nothing to be worried about and you're completely devoted to me, then that's all I need to hear."

"He's nothing more than a friend. And I am completely, completely devoted to you."

"That's all I need to hear."

• • •

Reed trusted his wife. Not for one moment did he doubt the love she felt for him or the validity of her declaration that she no longer had any interest in Nick. For days afterward he questioned whether he would rather Becky had refrained from revealing anything at all and always came to the same answer. It didn't make any difference. Becky had told him to make herself feel more at ease. If the person who could make him happy like no other felt better as a result of her revelation, then he felt better as well. And that should have been the end of it. He had faith in the accuracy of his repeated response. He knew that the conversation should have come and gone and then taken a permanent vacation from his mind. But he was unable to stop questioning his reaction. Even while the answer was unchanging. And it was this that bothered him.

Why wasn't he upset? His wife had shared with him a moment, during their wedding of all times, in which she had briefly considered running off with another man. Any man with his feelings thoroughly invested in another upon hearing such information should feel at least a twinge of jealousy and more likely a furious inescapable anger. He did not. Instead he felt content. He felt even. He felt nothing. And he was able to distinguish far less of a distinction between these three feelings than he would have liked.

It hit Reed suddenly and cruelly that the story of his life up until very recently had been told through the search. The decision he made in his third grade classroom to be consistently happy had been fueled by the push towards things to come. He maintained his positivity throughout the years by consistently crowning every thought with the expectation that somewhere along the line, he would find complete happiness. The journey towards this ultimate elation was a source of incredible satisfaction. Though he never consciously had the thought, it was easier to live believing the high point lie ahead and there was always the danger of a setback once that apex had been reached.

Becky was everything he had always been looking for. Her entrance into his life had effectively ended his quest. All this time he had been too deliriously happy to notice the halt in expectation cautiously tapping him on the shoulder. Suddenly, in the aftermath of Becky's confession, the unsatisfactory calm crept to the surface.

He had nothing left to search for. No goal to reach. No dissatisfaction to defiantly fight against, grinning widely like a movie hero, obnoxiously confident of victory while taunting an increasingly exasperated villain.

Reed's mind made the necessary compensation.

He became jealous. He developed an unspoken anger about the events with Nick, which created a subtle uncomfortable tension in his interactions with his wife. The fact that the anger and jealousy were irrational and born into existence only as a result of unqualified fulfillment, present when there was still so much life left to live, did not in anyway make these emotions false or any less powerful. Reed's conscious efforts to be consistently happy and his unconscious need to have dramatic meaning to his life, clashed, leaving an inconsistent identity, buried within itself and allowing no holes through which another individual could peek in.

Becky sensed the variation in her husband immediately but failed to question him about it. She may have been scared to unearth the hurt. Or she may have also found the newfound tension more interesting. Either way, a separation was created. A cement wall, crushing any feeling which tried to pass through it, only stepping aside for arguments that in no way resembled communication.

"How's Nick doing?" Reed asked, breaking the sound of wordless chewing, a week after Becky's revelation. It was the first time Nick's name had been spoken since. He sensed her tension. The way her fingers clenched the silverware tightly as soon as the taboo subject was broached.

"Fine. I suppose," responded Becky.

That was the extent of the night's conversation.

For now, Reed hit the brakes on the game he was creating, but the taste was a thrill. The pieces were in motion and a sense of progression had returned to his life. There would continue to be change. A higher level to aspire to. The destruction of calm had reinstated calm. His mind had been completely reorganized to please itself and Reed was barely aware of it.

◆ ◆ ◆

Colin had taken up painting. He had no talent, creativity, or artistic drive. He did have supplies. He had bought fifteen brushes, beginner's sets of oil, acrylic, and watercolor paints, and canvases of four different sizes. He got an easel. He set up newspapers on his floor and pretended that he cared if he got paint on his carpet. He organized all his supplies in their precise proper places and waited expectantly for a reaction as if he had bought an amateur chemists set rather than an art studio.

His sudden artistic inspiration was born in an uncharacteristically revealing comment made by Lisa a few days earlier.

"Sometimes I wish I was an artist," she had said, upon observing a drawing of the Parthenon on the menu of the diner where they were dining. "They have such passion."

A wave of curiosity momentarily struck. Who was this person he was sitting across from? It had never occurred to him that the form he was frequently accompanied by had hopes, fears, dreams, expectations, thoughts, feelings, pangs of regret, yearnings for glory, or any number of other unspoken mental patterns, occurring privately in her mind. "Tell me everything about yourself," he almost blurted out, his instinct overwhelming him before rationality could take control.

"I think I'm going to have the grilled chicken sandwich," said Lisa.

Lisa's bland and predictable food choice immediately killed Colin's curiosity. He ceased wondering about the person who had made such an intriguing statement and shifted his focus to the statement itself.

Artists had passion. That elusive quality he had heard so much about. A day later he gladly shelled out a large portion of his recent paycheck on a full set of overpriced artistic supplies for the possibility that he might obtain some inspiration to break the increasingly intolerable monotony of his existence.

And there he stood in his impromptu art studio, perfectly equipped for the task at hand, waiting for inspiration to strike. Waiting. Staring at the blank canvas. Seriously debating whether staring at a blank canvas was more or less exciting than his normal routine. Receiving no inspiration whatsoever.

Colin was not sure what he had expected. He had never so much as doodled on a scrap of paper while being kept on hold for an obnoxiously long time with the electric company. And there was nothing whatsoever to do during those phone calls. He had never had the instinct to express himself outwardly. He had never produced anything of the slightest bit of worth or interest to anyone including himself. And he knew that artistic inspiration could not be forced.

He forced it anyway.

He dipped his various sized brushes carelessly and spontaneously into any color or variety of paint they happened to fall in, splattering oil, acrylic, and watercolors in an unkind mixture onto the canvas in a creation of the first image that had popped into his head. That of a pig. He had eaten ham for lunch. That was his inspiration. All told, he completed his masterpiece in twenty seven minutes, including at least six minutes spent in the bathroom, thanks to the ham, which was two weeks old and not sitting very cheerfully in his stomach.

The end result could barely pass for a children's drawing. He assessed his failure and came to the very logical conclusion, which he in no way believed, that his talents may not lie in creating representations of actual worldly objects. He set to work on an abstract concoction, paying no mind to form or substance or reason for any of his artistic actions. The result looked more like a pig than his first artwork. But even less like a painting.

In a final desperate attempt to find some meaning in what he was doing Colin considered the colors. He had been using the colors only in the manner in which the art store had provided them, an uninspired method of production, he was well aware. So he mixed. He threw blues into reds and yellows into greens and browns into mixtures of red and blue and any color into any other color with little consideration of what he was choosing or why. Before he managed to apply one stroke of paint to his third and final canvas, he looked at his mixing board. All he saw were several puddles of slightly varied grays that had somehow been concocted in the process of his aimless amalgamations.

He vomited. There was something disgusting about those grays that went right to his stomach.

Colin ran. At first to get fresh air and dissipate the nausea.

Then because of inertia. He ran out of the suburbs. He ran into the city. He thought of Forrest Gump. There was a happy man. Perhaps the key to happiness was to be fictional.

Finally he stopped. An image had halted his legs.

A homeless man. Asleep on the cold cement. Clothed only in newspapers and his own feces.

• • •

"I want you to keep an eye on Becky for me."

Reed had recently unearthed his Nintendo. He and Colin were playing their old favorite, Duck Hunt. Nothing relieved unspoken aggression like the ruthless murder of virtual mallards.

"How come?"

"I think there might be something going on between her and Nick."

The night of bowling had reinstated only the smallest amount of communication between the old friends and objects of each other's affections at inopportune times. Colin saw the awkward hellos Nick and Becky exchanged, said on both sides and then immediately received under the enormously false pretense that the words were not quite heard, eyes darting in the other direction, and bodies quickly pulled along. Colin personally found the game amusing and would have thought Reed's suspicions a logical answer to the mysteriously uncomfortable interactions if the uncomfortable aspect hadn't been so dominant. As it was there was not one iota of sexual tension between the two. Only an easily interpretable desire to get away from one another as soon as possible.

However. Far be it for Colin to turn down a request that Reed was specifically asking him for.

"Yeah, no problem. I'll keep an eye out."

Colin kept both eyes out as if each pupil was being paid by the hour. He watched Becky's every move and interaction. He monitored her phone calls. He went through her papers. He followed her home at night and as she left in the morning. He enacted a level of commitment to Reed's request that he would never have expected and could not possibly have desired. He told himself he was doing it for Reed. He didn't listen to himself. It was a waste of thought speech. Colin was well aware he was brazenly burning the line of appropriateness and scattering its ashes as he sprinted past it. Doing so thrilled him. It was the second major exhilaration he had been able to lock down upon in a short period of time. Life was good.

Colin had returned to the feces ridden homeless man. He found himself repelled by the horrid smell, sickened by the visual image. His ears even seemed to take offense, buzzing as if the man secretly gave off a petrifying sound he could hear but not perceive hearing. Yet despite the sensual abhorrence Colin was overwhelmed with fervent tension in the man's presence. Energized by being around someone whose life had met with such destruction. Who, regardless of whether or not this was his particular low point, had surely seen better days. Perhaps not good days. But certainly better.

Colin returned day after day and stared. The man did not eat. But he managed to produce fresh excrement to lie in. He did not interact with anyone. But he talked up a storm. Snippets of a life gone by or never had at all. A better existence. One where turds would or did not serve as his pillow. He cried. For hours. He masturbated. For even longer. He cried while he was masturbating. And he drank. From bottles that there could be no telling how he acquired. He drank himself to death.

It was horror.

It was the type of sight that there could be no answer for. No justification. No analysis. No intelligent thoughts induced. No response that could possibly seem an adequate reaction to that which was being witnessed.

Horror. And Colin was overcome by it.

He had finally located the emotion he had been looking for. It could be found in the unexplainable tragedies of the world, hidden, not too discreetly around every street corner.

That particular homeless man quickly became a bore. Colin had still discovered his calling. And unspeakable horrors were readily available.

His routine became as follows. He would wake up early each morning, and set out at least an hour before work, prowling the streets for fresh meat. People in distress. Tattered clothes. Starving stomachs. Expressions of despair. His engine refueled with the gasoline of suffering, Colin would set off for work where he would watch Becky's every move. Obsessed by the subtlest facial gestures, ready to report any misfire back to the commander and chief who set him on his mission. And his breakless observation was paying off. Becky was losing her happiness. Day by day her face was both hardening and becoming more fragile. Colin waited for her to break. After work he would rush home, anxious to plop himself down in front of the local news. For an hour and a half he was fed by a buffet of domestic abuse, petty homicide, life destroying fires, and fatal traffic accidents. An orgy of meaninglessness. When the broadcasts turned off, there was the marvelous internet, which provided open access to the whole world's senseless calamities.

Colin was not a sadist. He was not even a cynic. He did not enjoy spending the sunrise watching those whose brains were beyond repair, unable to help themselves and completely ignored by society, never offered the slightest bit of help. He found it even less pleasant to watch those in the same position who could still think for themselves but had given up on living, embracing hopelessness. He was not pleased by his inability to help those he watched, nor by the passing notion that he might be able to help one, but would go completely unnoticed, and might be almost insulting the countless others whose pain it was impossible to heal. He hated the endless repetitious stream of human disinterest stories brought to him by the not quite attractive enough anchors on the news each evening and the number of results that popped up on a search engine when he searched for that day's date in conjunction with the word "murder." And he certainly did not take any joy from the fact that in a matter of mere months Becky went from inhabiting the workplace in a post wedding bliss to pulling her hair over her face so that no one would spot her tears. That a hoarse Reed admitted his voice was lost from a several night screaming match with his wife, apparently the new norm. That after a long period of unmanageable stress that was making her spontaneously shake, Becky had resumed regularly talking to Nick. That he saw Nick rubbing her back in comfort. And hugging her tightly. And making Reed's formerly absurd suspicions suddenly warranted. He particularly hated the fact that he was considering telling Reed what he had witnessed. He was prepared to devastate his friend with sights of what might be no more than friendship, not out of loyalty, but out of the thrill he would get from throwing another's life in such turmoil.

He did not like any of it. But it made him feel.

• • •

"It's blinding in here."

"Maybe you should have brought sunglasses."

They were back at Light & Dark. In the light section. The bright lamps reflected off the food's silver platters and directly into the eyes of the feeders. It was impossible to tell the difference between the three different accessible types of chicken under such conditions.

Colin had managed to convince Reed and Becky to join he and Lisa for a reunion of sorts. He had used as an excuse his six month anniversary. It had actually only been five. Lisa, he was sure, was aware of the discrepancy. She said nothing. Perhaps she was expecting a present.

"I don't wear sunglasses at night. I'm not a douchebag."

"Not for that reason."

Reed and Becky's banter had lost much of its romantic flare since the previous dinner.

Colin had become desperate to witness the marital tension first hand. He had seen Becky age ten years in less than one. He had heard Reed's vicious ramblings. He had seen the separation occurring even when they were already physically apart. He had yet to directly observe the hate that became the marriage's significantly vote siphoning third party. He needed it. He needed to watch it burn.

"What are you getting Colin?" inquired Lisa, placing her hand on top of his and eager to disrupt the violence present at the table.

"Hard to say," he responded.

Lisa had lately taken even more of a backseat in Colin's life than that which she had originally been buckled into. Having finally engrained himself into a successful routine of emotional provocation, he had mostly forgotten her existence. Occasionally they met for dinner when she directly requested meal meetings. But otherwise he vanished from her life. Quite the impressive feat to become even more translucent a presence than he had already been. Even more so for the fact that she actually noticed.

"I miss you," she had told him on the way to the restaurant. It was like missing someone who had never been born.

It had taken her weeks of courage to speak those words. He took little notice of the statement. Maybe if Lisa had attempted suicide or been raped she could have piqued his interest. Simple sadness did nothing for him.

Reed and Becky hit just the right note. Their implosion was even more deeply satisfying than he had expected. He had known there would be bickering. He had hoped to see revulsion where love had once rested. He saw it. What came as a shock was that amid the very real hatred, the love still existed. Was more prominent than ever. And would be completely wasted because of pettiness and boredom and the need to keep life interesting.

At home Colin cried at the thought of it. He cried for his friend and for a woman he had never felt any attachment to. He cried for the love which would never reach its potential. He cried that even love so powerful would not remain.

He held onto the glorious tears, dreading the moment when they would soon pass.

III.

The phone rang. It was not accustomed to doing so in the middle of the night. Colin was glad for the intrusion. It had interrupted a rather boring dream about paperwork. He wished he could reassure the phone that he was not angered with its interruption, as he sensed an increasingly apologetic chime in its ring. He took a moment to think about the phone's plight. It was a machine incapable of not doing its duty. It could provide happiness to a lonely soul, desiring only contact, even if was merely conveying the words of a telemarketer. The machine created the comfort, not the individual on the other end of the line. Conversely, the phone might be despised by its owner, through no fault of its own, for allowing the voice of an unwanted individual to violate privacy and enter one's home, or for being the technology that transmits a piece of bad news, or for waking one up in the middle of the night. Colin felt for the phone and its powerless position. The phone could not make choices. It could be a victim and was without the ability to make a decision that might end its victimhood. In his just awoken state he felt for the phone more than for any person he had ever known. Except of course, one. The person who was causing the phone to ring.

"Colin. Thank god."

Reed was crying. Colin had not heard Reed cry in two decades of friendship.

"What's the matter?"

"I need you to come over."

"What happened?"

"Please. Please just come over. Tell me you'll come over."

"I'll be right over. I promise."

Reed was barely able to open the door.

"Hey," was all he could muster before his tears took over for his speech. His bones appeared to be contracting. He was being swallowed by himself. Colin could hardly stomach the sight of him.

"Reed. What happened?"

"Come with me."

• • •

The sight of Becky's dead body shocked him far less than it should have. It almost seemed to be the work of an avant garde interior designer, perfectly placed where a coffee table might normally be. Colin had never noticed the absence of a coffee table in the room before. The need for one seemed so obvious now.

"I hit her. She died," Reed managed to squeeze out of his vocal chords, each word causing him more pain than the last. "I hit her and she died. I've never hit her before."

"Why did you hit her?"

"She slept with Nick."

"She told you that?"

He waited some time for the only response Reed could muster.

"Yeah."

Reed collapsed on top of Becky's body. He wailed. He cursed. He moaned. He came apart. And he did not yet even fully grasp what had occurred. The inner arson of having ended another human being's life. The unequaled horror of having lost the person he most loved. A person who had become an integral part of his identity. The unspeakable correlation between these facts of anguish. Himself, responsible for all of it. Right now all he could feel was pain. All consuming. Unidentifiable, unstoppable pain. When he did grasp the full reality his life would, for all intents and purposes, be over. He would never recover from this. No one could.

Colin knew this. And it informed his every thought as he attempted to calmly assess the situation, all the while trying to quiet the twinge of excitement that crawled up his spine.

• • •

Colin took his time cleaning up. Not one step in the process was performed mindlessly, as a force of habit, or because it seemed natural. There was not a hint of autopilot. He scrutinized over every detail.

The task at hand was the removal of Becky's body. The successful clean up of the apartment such that friends and family would believe Reed was innocent when phone calls to Becky stopped being returned. So clean that spectacular crime scene investigators who may or may not only exist only in the annals of the nightly CBS primetime lineup would never even suspect that Becky may have died in her own residence, and certainly not at the hand of her husband.

Colin began with the body itself. Transferring it was a tricky proposition. Reed's apartment contained no body bags, or large sports equipment cases, or human sized trunks. He located a box of double thick Hefty trash bags, designed for those whose garbage needs exceeds the norm. He pulled out six bags. Two sets of two he opened up within themselves. He wrapped one double coated bag around her upper body and the other around her legs. The remaining two bags he cut up just thick enough to cover any of her still showing torso, and wrapped it around her. Both duct and packing tape were accessible and so he used both to wrap her. Cleaning up the carpet was a bit trickier. In the linen closet he found an assortment of cleaning products with overly optimistic names like Fantastik and Awesome. He also found a specialized carpet cleaning solution that proved to be highly effective if not specifically designed for the removal of human blood. He continued scrubbing with club soda and a toothbrush. This dulled more of the subtle specks.

It was a game. He could almost hear the ticking clock and the murmur of an audience, watching behind two way glass, pointing anxiously to a crucial spot of evidence he had up till then missed. Colin shielded himself from the reality even as he tried to immerse himself in it.

Becky is dead.

In an acute display of the fragility of life, one punch with slightly too much force to a specifically tender region of the head had erased a person from existence. And not one of those impersonal foreign images attached to a name, whose death Colin viewed on the news each evening, but an actual individual he had known. A person without whom his life would be drastically altered. Yet there he was, Becky's lifeless limbs in his hands, finding her fatality to be far less realistic than an obituary notice containing nothing but names, dates, and the location of memorial services.

It was easy to believe that someone he had never met had died. People died all the time. By their own hands, by the hands of others, as a result of unstoppable accidents and catastrophes of nature and technology. Sometimes even of old age though that was rarely reported unless they were a personality of note to the collective conscious. It was far more difficult to accept as truth the disappearance of a major character in his own life.

Colin wished to fully take in what had happened. Tragedy was his drug and sitting in front of him was the largest shipment he had ever come across. His mind was acting as an impenetrable adhesive tape, preventing the product from use for fear of the danger of its potency. He was anxious. He kept his mind focused so as not to lose sight of what had happened. Not to forget the platter of meaningless horror delivered to his doorstep. Not to be so shielded from pain that he slipped into dullness. It was like having a fear of heights and a love of falling. He strained to slip himself over the edge.

Reed held himself. Colin had not offered him a hug. No embrace. No physical or verbal comfort. Nothing to soften the blow. He deserved the pain but that had little to do with the inaction. The inconceivable reality was elucidated most by its still breathing casualty.

• • •

"Let's go."

"Where?"

"To your family's cabin. We're going to bury her in the woods."

• • •

Colin had first been invited to the cabin at the age of twelve. He stayed for a week over summer vacation. It was a relic. Hardly a luxurious getaway from the struggles of the everyday world. His first impression was that it resembled the house built by the second of the three little pigs. Or that some trees had fallen one night in a storm and inadvertently formed a shack that one could reside in if they abandoned all notions of comfort. Even the mattresses left year after year under the flimsy rooftop felt like they were made out of wood. It was a poorly made structure built in a visually unappealing spot of the forest. And Reed's family loved it. His father spent the days frolicking through the woods with his shotgun, claiming he was enjoying the sport of hunting. The forest contained no animals bigger than a chipmunk, and he never fired his gun though he returned to the cabin each night from his expeditions, peaceful and content that his day could be spent in no better way. His mother would waste away the hours reading romance novels against the rough bark of the nearest tree and overcooking homemade cookies in the cabin's shoddy oven. As for Reed himself, there was no other location where he felt more at peace. He would tag along with his father, delve into the joys of cooking with his mother, and spend hours alone just wandering the forest. Getting lost. Finding his way again. During his brief visits, Colin often saw Reed vanish into himself as he scampered from tree to tree spontaneously, oblivious to the fact that he had company. He could see the liberation. The freedom from having to be socially impressive when there was no one around to talk to. Reed's highest elations did not take place at the cabin. But his moments of greatest contentment did.

Colin was sorry to forever taint Reed's association with his spot of childhood serenity. He did briefly consider choosing another abandoned spot or leaving Reed and enacting the burial on his own. He could not, however, shake his initial instinct to amplify the heartbreak as much as possible. In a long, slow, silent drive, the unspoken laying in the trunk, to the woods they went.

• • •

"How did this happen?"

Reed's tears halted for a rare instant. He asked the unfathomable question of himself.

They were sitting in the cabin. Colin was clutching a shovel. The shovel seemed anxious to be plunged into the ground. To feel the dirt. It was a dog leading its owner. It might urinate in the house if it was not let outside soon enough. They had been sitting there for over an hour. Colin watched his friend cry. Neither said anything. Colin wasn't sure why he hadn't ventured outside and started on the task at hand. His feet hadn't moved. The rest of him remained with them.

Reed continued.

"She shouldn't have died from one punch. How could that have killed her?"

He waited for a response. He received none. He continued.

"Why did I hit her in the first place? I've never hit her before. I love her, why would I have hit her?"

Nothing.

"She fucked Nick. And that hurts. But I still shouldn't have hit her. I should never have hit her."

Nothing.

"What happened to us? What happened to me? We were so happy and then..."

Something. Reed stood up. He left the cabin. Colin followed.

Outside Reed turned around. He was resolute. It was like looking at the last page of a book.

"I'm going to turn myself in."

"You can't do that."

"I have to. I set myself on a path for this. And then I did it. Don't you see? I lost myself. I did this. This is the worst thing I could I ever imagine doing and I did it. I have to be punished."

"I can't let you do that."

"It's the only thing to do."

"You'll never survive. A trial. Years in jail. Worse."

"What would you suggest?"

"I don't know. You move on, I guess."

"To what? I have no life left to live."

A long silence followed.

Colin returned to the cabin.

A million thoughts ran through his head. Most of which only skirted the outermost edge of truth. Worry for Reed in prison. The shell of a person he would be debased to. Reed's lack of life even in the outside world. An event he would never recover from. The thrill of finding himself deeply entrenched in a story fit for the nightly news. Boredom. Fear. Sacrifice. Old Yeller. The memory of where Reed's father kept his gun.

◆ ◆ ◆

The front door creaked. Reed turned. One click and a blast and his physical condition matched his mental one.

As he watched Reed's blood seep from his mangled head onto the porch, Colin's first thought was of how impossible it was to ever really know another individual. His second was a sensory notation of how the shotgun felt in his hands.

The shovel got its wish. Twice over. Several hours of immersion in the Earth's clay. Powerful heaves as it cleared a deep impenetrable hole in the forest's floor. Sharp cuts as it destroyed the ground. Raising of soft grains as it refilled it.

Colin spent the night at the cabin. He had murdered his best friend. He became lost in the thought. He was full.

• • •

The doorbell rang. Colin had no sympathy for it. The high pitched clang he had once tried and failed to disable (succeeding only in permanently darkening the alcove of the kitchen sink) was nothing but a nuisance. Each successive echo of this satanic bell reverberated the maniacal joy of a practical jokester. It built anticipation as he made his way to unlatching the door and revealing a small portion of his house to whatever unwanted guest stood behind it. The telephone was at least capable of bringing good news. The doorbell never did. It brought solicitors and religious fanatics and long lost cousins looking for money. Friends knocked. All others rang the door bell. There was a reason the children's' jokes did not begin, "Ring Ring, who's there?"

"It's Nick Hartley."

It was a weak punchline.

Colin was not pleased but also not surprised to receive this visit from Nick. He had been anticipating it even though Nick had never before been to his house, nor so much as asked where he lived.

He had seen Nick glancing at him at work twenty times an hour for the past week, trying to start a conversation without the hassle of using words. He wanted desperately to learn if Colin had any knowledge of the reasons for Becky's disappearance. He certainly would have called Reed and Becky's house and received no answer for several days straight. He surely would have visited their residence, finding the lights dark and no one responding to his pounding at the doors and windows. He probably had yet to alert the police, perhaps out of fear that his necessary precautionary secrecy about his affair with Becky would only be taken as ambiguous nervousness and shoot him right to the top of the suspects list. Perhaps he initially feared Colin would jump to the same interpretation and refrained from introducing the subject, hoping he might similarly be questioning the absence of his friends. Eventually Nick would conclude that his silence meant he must know something, Colin's attempts at looking over at Becky's desk and furrowing his brow in confusion a miserable failure of acting. He would track down Colin's address and surprise him at home where his guard might be most down, ready to pry out what he surely suspected was a secret Colin had been asked to keep quiet. Thus, maintaining its status as a secret.

"Can I come in?"

"Sure."

Colin almost laughed as he watched Nick carefully determine how at home he wished to make himself. He was walking a delicate balance, friendly enough that he could woo Colin into unlocking the information he desired. Not too familiar that Colin might toss the overzealous asshole out of his house. He left his shoes on and sat on the more uncomfortable of the living room's couches.

"I'm not sure if you know why I came here today."

He waited for a moment, not knowing Colin well enough to realize that he did not see being directly addressed as an adequate reason to form a response.

"It's because of Becky," he continued. "She hasn't been to work all week. I was wondering if maybe you knew anything about it."

"Yeah I was wondering about that myself. It's weird."

"So you don't know anything?"

"No."

"Have you talked to Reed?"

"Not recently."

"Because he's gone too. I've been calling them up. I went over to their house. Nothing. There's nobody there."

"That's weird."

"Doesn't that concern you at all?"

"I don't know. They must have gone somewhere together."

"Yeah, I suppose."

Nick stood up. He paced around. This unearthing process was going be more difficult than he had prepared himself for. He was feeling less patient than he had planned.

"I don't believe you."

"What?"

"I think you're lying. I think you know something."

"What makes you say that?"

"I've seen you around Reed. You worship him. I don't believe for a second that you didn't know he was gone. You would have jumped out of your pants in concern when I told you he'd disappeared if you didn't know anything."

"Why don't you just shut the fuck up?"

Nick was taken aback by the forcefulness of someone he had never seen become so much as mildly peeved.

"Looks like I hit a sore spot. Pissed off that your man ran off with his wife are you?"

Colin's coffee table was the resting place of a ceramic cow. The cow was of the anthropomorphic variety. It stood on its hind legs, wore an apron, and was hard at work churning a bucket of milk into butter. It had been a housewarming gift from his mother. He had received it three months after moving into his place. This unwanted gift had passed through three unappreciative generations of the Benson family, each wanting it less than the one before. Nick may have heard the shattering of tradition as the cow smashed against his ear lobe. More likely he was distracted by the pain.

"What the fuck was that for!?" Nick screamed as he clutched the bleeding side of his head.

"Don't you talk about Reed. It's your fault all this happened."

"All what happened?"

"You slept with Becky."

"You know about that?" said Nick, after a moment of hesitation.

"Yeah."

"I love her."

"I'm sure that's true."

"She's been really unhappy."

"And isn't it good that she has you to cure her depression?"

Nick stood up. He wiped his ear with his hand.

"Do you have some paper towels or something? My blood's getting on your carpet."

Colin retrieved a roll of Bounty from the kitchen. When he returned, Nick was fighting back tears.

"She felt worse afterwards," he said. "It was the most terrible moment. Sharing such intimacy and being greeted with coldness and remorse. I felt awful."

He sopped up his blood and continued.

"I didn't want to be there either. Not like that. Not as emotionless physical comfort. Revenge almost. She just wanted to prove something to Reed somehow. I think I knew that. And I helped her along. I encouraged it. I couldn't stop. I do love her. But I don't even think it was love that was pushing me along. It was lust. Or pride. Or something."

Colin was only half listening. He was distracted by a knife he had left on his windowsill. He had been eating an apple earlier. He hated the skin.

Nick went on. "Do you think I like this? Do you think I like what I did? Do you think I'm happy with being fully aware that my feelings have been wrong or irrational or harmful and yet they control my actions anyway? It's fucking frustrating. The lack of control I have over myself."

"It's a poison."

"What?" Nick had forgotten he was speaking to a specific individual.

"The need to feel. It's a poison. It consumes you. It takes away all hope of being a thinking, rational human being. Of doing any good. It's the only thing there is. And it poisons you until there's nothing left."

Colin picked up the knife.

"I'd like to think that I can overcome my rotten instincts," Nick responded. "I'd like to think that I can sculpt myself. Make myself the best person I can be. If there's any meaning to life, it's got to be that." For a moment Nick was his preferred rational self. He had regained the philosophy by which he lived his life. Then he remembered why he was there in the first place. "But right now I just want to know Becky's okay."

"She's dead."

Nick looked up. "What?"

The knife's first slash proceeded diagonally down his face, slicing his nose in half. The second was directly perpendicular. After, it was less neat. Colin left the knife guide him. Chaotically piercing Nick's flesh in a hundred different places. Continuing well after it had drained all the life from his body. He analyzed the destruction. He cut the body open. He felt the brutally damaged insides. He had removed the personality residing. He had mutilated. He made sure to note every result of his action.

• • •

"Colin."

He hadn't seen Lisa in a month. They had never officially broken up. They had never so much as spoken about the status of their relationship. And she had never inquired why he had removed himself from her life. But she had stopped contacting him. She had ceased asking him to join her in silent food consumption. And the look on her face said quite clearly that she had never expected to see him again.

"Lisa. Can I come in?"

"Of course."

She offered him tea. He accepted. Despite everything, she was glad to see him. He could tell. She tried to hide it, presumably of the opinion that she should display irritation or anger over his abandonment. She was unsuccessful.

"How are you?," she asked, instead of the "Where were you?" she had planned.

"Better than I should be," he replied.

"That's good."

They quietly drank their tea. It was like old times.

"Come away with me," he said.

She choked on a gulp of tea.

"What?"

"I want to get out of here. Far away from this place. I want you to come with me."

"Are you serious?"

"Completely."

"When?"

"Right now. My suitcase is already in the car."

She ran over the words she had just heard in her head, making sure they signified the meaning she had interpreted.

"But everything I have is here. My work. My family. All my

stuff."

"You can find a new job. You can talk to your family on the phone. And I bet you don't really need more than one suitcase of all your stuff."

She listened to the room's ticking clock. A small detail of the sort that confirmed she was not having a dream.

"I don't know."

"I want you to come with me," he continued. "I love you."

She put down her tea. Her hands shook.

"I love you too."

Colin didn't know whether she meant it or just wanted to say it. It made no difference.

She was packed within an hour. She shut down all her electric appliances, unplugged every outlet, not wanting to feel guilty about unnecessary energy consumption in her soon to be abandoned house. She quickly made the decision of what was essential and what was not. Each severance caused her a jolt of pain, but it was washed away by her passion over what was to come.

Finally, she joined Colin who had been waiting in his car.

"So where are we going?" she asked.

"I'm not really sure. I think we'll just see where the road takes us."

"It's quite the adventure."

"I suppose it is."

"I love you," she said.

"I love you too," he replied.

He started the car. He took a long look at the smile on Lisa's face. He drove off.

BOOK II

THE POLICEMAN

I.

He stumbled. He tripped. He hit his head against the wall. He injured himself but hardly noticed. The two bloods mixed without much discord. On the right route to home purely by instinct, all memory of the route erased. No hope of finding the right path but pulled along it anyway.

• • •

Thomas Giacorozzi preferred his eggs scrambled. Actually, preferred is misleading. It was not a preference. It was a necessity. He would not eat them any other way. Hard boiled were hard to swallow, sunny side up were a thunderstorm of unpleasantness, and over easy were well under delicious. Minimal distinctions, most would say. Scrambled are scrumptious, Thomas would respond.

He was preparing this decidedly yellow of dishes, rapidly rotating his fork in the egg yolk with a mechanical fluidity to his movement, on this particular morning. The morning he would learn of his child's death.

Neither of his sons had returned home. He wasn't aware. It was long past the point that most parents would stay awake, a single light in the window, restless until they could peek into their children's rooms, finally serene as they saw them tucked under the covers. Thomas had never done this, so it was completely without feasibility that he would have found any reason to worry about their whereabouts or condition. In fact, Thomas regularly went days without seeing either of his boys. He would go to work as they slept, return when they were out, sleep as they returned. Even their occasional crossovers in the house were defined by a room segregation, rarely breached.

His biggest surprise, as Justin stumbled into the house, hobbled by an emotional limp, bruised by a physical one, was that he was interacting with Justin at all. Not that his son was covered in blood. Or that he saw him crying for the first time since he slept in a crib.

Thomas overcooked the eggs. Justin's cry that his older brother was dead was enough to make him forget they were in the frying pan. He mustered the strength to turn off the flame before the house burned down. Justin would have been glad to be erased by the fire.

Thomas did not embrace his still living son. It was not due to disbelief. Justin was often untrustworthy but there was no doubt in the truth of his wails. It was not because he was angry at Justin for delivering the news, even though hatred for the messenger was Justin's initial interpretation of his father's behavior. Thomas did not question his reaction. It was simply how he reacted. There was no need to analyze it. At that particular moment he felt no love whatsoever. Not for his deceased son. Not for his living son. Not for himself.

Justin desperately searched for the answer of what to do with his body. Overwhelming restlessness prevented him from sitting down. Uncontrollable weakness sapped the strength needed to hold himself up with his legs. He settled into a one hundred and eighty degree rotating squat, wishing his brain could awkwardly bend itself in such a way. As he rotated he caught glimpses of his blank faced father, angry that he did not even have the emotional satisfaction of the embraces that come with shared grief.

The next few weeks were a haze. The Giacorozzi party of two drifted half present through the crime scene. They participated in a blurry morgue identification. They had to keep their eyes open as Justin managed to escape being identified as present at the manslaugterer's house, his facial features presumably shielded by the mask of blood pasted on him, avoiding a term in a juvenile detention center that may have left an emotional scar even deeper than the current gaping wound. They were barely awake at the poorly attended funeral, absent of Adam's so called friends who must have viewed their absence as a pride boosting act of defiance against a figure they would never dared have crossed had he been alive. They slept for weeks on end. Justin occasionally spoke to his father. Not because he had any desire to or even because he really intended to. He would notice he was speaking in the middle of a sentence, apparently drawn to talk with the only person near him, needing the social interaction even if it lacked any content, substance, or love.

• • •

Imagine a scab. A festering sore, manifested in an incident of burning pain, and a constant reminder of the pain that has been suffered.

Imagine a scab that reopens every morning. An unpleasant alarm clock, shocking the sleeper into the morning with a hot jolt of suffering and a new coating of blood on their sole set of bed sheets, washed daily and still unable to remove the stench.

Imagine a scab made purely of thoughts. A mental hole plug, preventing every thought from reaching consciousness, with the exception of thoughts about the scab itself.

The loss persisted.

Justin sat around the house. He thought about his dead brother.

Justin lied in bed. He thought about his dead brother.

Justin went to school. He thought about his dead brother.

Justin brought groceries. He thought about his dead brother.

Justin watched TV. He thought about his dead brother.

Justin found a five dollar bill on the street. He thought about his dead brother.

Justin urinated in a public toilet. He thought about his dead brother.

Justin prepared himself a pack of instant macaroni and cheese for dinner. He thought about his dead brother.

Justin looked upon his cold father who had forgotten how to love and that he was even supposed to, to begin with. He thought about his dead brother.

Word of the loss spread.

Each successive student, aware of Justin as an individual or only as a perception of visual frequency, slowly then quickly learned of the death of someone whose life existed for them solely as a description. Each one reacted. Variations of genuine sadness quickly replaced by a return to the tragedy bare comfort of their own lives. Reactions of mild surprise and words of empathy not really felt but spoken because they were morally right. Responses of true identification from the few who had faced similar loss, still unable to squeeze their feet into these particular shoes.

Justin was blindsided by an air raid of comfort bombs. Some directly addressed the issue. "I'm so sorry about your brother," spoke an unnecessarily popular girl as she passed him struggling to swallow even a small bit of an already hard to stomach Sloppy Joe's sandwich in the cafeteria. She angered him. Not only because she had never spoken to him previously and was incredibly presumptuous addressing him about something so personal. But also because had she known Adam she may not have been sorry about his death. She may have secretly rejoiced.

He was even more angered by the parade of unspecified "I'm sorry's" that were fired at him in the hallways. Baffling declarations confident enough to address the pain but not the cause of it, succeeding only in raising the orator's self esteem and in further isolating Justin from the rest of humanity. Vague apologetic statements that could be referencing any topic. Justin took some satisfaction in bitter responses, intending to make the sorry speakers sorry for saying sorry at all. But the satisfaction turned to frustration when his victims brushed off his viciousness as a byproduct of his loss, and the frustration turned to paralyzing pain when he thought about his dead brother.

One student, Harry Barnes, who had lost his mother in a car accident the previous fall, addressed the issue directly.

"I know we've never really talked before – "

"No we haven't."

"– but I just want to say that I've been through something very similar and I know how it is. I know everybody is trying to comfort you and you don't want to be comforted. And it's frustrating because everyone seems to think you should immediately feel better and they're the ones who can make that happen and all you want is to feel that pain for a while. I'm not over my mother's death. Not even close. I don't think I ever will be. But I have to think that one day I'll be able to live my life again. Right?"

Harry was being realistic. He was providing a different perspective. But he was just as unhelpful and just as infuriating as all the others. He was trying to comfort himself through identification. Knowledge of the shared experience of pain did not make Justin feel better about the pain. It made him feel worse. It made him feel hopeless about the prospect of living.

One person who did not address Justin was Jimmy Fordham. He did not say a word. He kept from Justin in the hallways. And only during the very briefest of moments, when they made split second eye contact because it was impossible to turn their heads without doing so, did Justin see any indication that Jimmy even knew what had happened. During these brief moments the pain was immediately readable. It was like looking in a mirror.

Justin barely attended high school. It was miraculous that he managed to finish with a degree at all. He had no plans to enter higher schooling and graduation was merely a continuation of the already present question of how to spend his unceasing, throbbing, angry days.

Thomas was no help in providing activity for his son. His life had transitioned into one impossibly extended scrambled egg cooking session. Justin passed his father in only one room, the kitchen, and was only responded to when he brought up one topic, eggs. The relation of the shell to the yolk. Whether or not they came before the chicken. And why scrambled was the only proper way of turning past future chicken babies into a delicious meal to start the day. And continue the day. And end the day. The smell of scrambled eggs pervaded the entire house so consistently that Justin did not even smell it. It leeched itself on to him, part of his natural smell that made passersby mysteriously hungry.

He had nothing to produce. Nothing to accomplish. Nothing to offer. Only aggression. And no outlet to release it.

"You should try cooking."

"Fuck you Dad."

Thomas was unfazed by the comment. Didn't even seem to notice it. Justin's anger grew.

Justin destroyed a mailbox. He wandered the streets with a baseball bat, ready to swing. The mail box was the first thing he came across. The side was severely dented on the first swing. The whole structure collapsed to the ground on the second. Letters flew out. They deserved to lose their mail if they weren't going to collect it, Justin thought. He had half a mind to smash their windows. Later, he did. He stole beer. Drank it. Smashed the bottles in excessively clean public places. He tried to rip a park bench from the ground. He failed. It was bolted tight. He kicked a man who was walking too slowly in the shins. Then ran away quickly.

Months passed. Justin left home. It would be less frustrating to live with no one when he was actually living with no one. His father had disappeared so far into himself that he hardly believed Thomas remained aware of his own consciousness. Thoughts of selfhood had been replaced by a tower of scrambled eggs. He was waging a battle against the chicken population and winning. At times he would return home without even a carton. Just a pile of eggs cupped in his arms, mumbling words that couldn't possibly be English, barely noticing his surroundings as eggs fell, cracked, and stained the floor with a rotten stench for weeks at a time unless Justin saw fit to clean it up. The lack of love was a good reason to leave. The rotten smell was a better one.

Justin took a job in a keys and locks store. Randy's Keys and Locks. There was no Randy. He spent his days making copies of people's keys in an impressive mold machine. The most modern key making chiseler, his manager would brag. Producing keys in thirty seconds flat. So fast in fact, that he would often make a copy for himself directly under the customer's nose. He never intended to use the keys. He hadn't any idea of the location of the locks, or what they might unlock, whether a house, a car, or a safe locking up family heirloom mittens, a treasure to their owner, worthless to Justin who already owned a pair of very warm gloves. He made the keys because they were a physical object of connection. If only to strangers. He owned an important piece of their lives, or at least a replica of one. The collection that piled up on his night table helped him not feel so alone.

And he was alone. Not just alone, but lonely. Lonely for a very good reason. Lonely because he was alone. He had lost the person he had most loved. His brother. He had lost his best friend who had suddenly reappeared in his dreams, talented understudy who periodically gave Adam the night off. He missed Jimmy. He felt selfish for starting to miss him only when he had reached such a point of solitude. He had lost his sorry excuse for a father who was nonetheless a human figure, helping to soften the full force of loneliness merely by the fact that he was not literally alone. But the pain of being around this badly crafted father figure with nothing to teach or offer, other than life itself in some long distant past, had become too great. Particularly because he made it impossible to take even the shortest break from thoughts of Adam. The move was necessary to have any hope of ever finding his own life. To exist as something other than a victim of loss.

He rented a room in the city. It was a strangely designed old tenement. The toilet was directly next to the stove, painting a full portrait of the circular feeding process with one quick view of two eyes. The mattress was made of very strong springs and very little mattress. He woke up each morning surprised that he had fallen asleep at all. He underestimated the lethargy that comes with having nothing to do.

He was kept alive on a steady diet of suffering. In the morning, afternoon, and night. It was endless and had nothing that counterbalanced it. He watched television programs he didn't like on fuzzy feeds of channels he didn't receive. He ate meals he wasn't hungry for and didn't enjoy the taste of. He walked. Long walks, hours at a time, with no planned destination, but always along a different route to avoid the pain of repeating himself.

In desperate need of a vice to occupy himself Justin found it frustratingly difficult to latch onto an addiction. He puffed away on packs of cigarettes that cut a gash into his budget and failed to provide any relief. He hated the taste, he hated the smell, and they did not even provide him with a much needed craving. The sole satisfaction they offered was in taking his mind off his brother's death long enough to stew over being a medical anomaly to those alleged highly addictive killers. He considered suing the cigarette companies or the surgeon general for failing to deliver on their promise. Instead he turned to alcohol. Even without having been alive twenty-one years or having a falsified document claiming he had been, he was able to acquire beers, liquors, wines, ales, rums, scotch, brandy, and any number of intended liquidized sorrow enhancers that he believed would drown his troubles away. It would have been just as well to tie a rock to his leg and jump in the shallow end of a public kiddie pool.

He drank alone, somehow amplifying the loneliness even more than days of solitary confinement already did. As if the walls themselves had left him and all that was left was a characterless white void, similar to certain artistic depictions of heaven. If the religious were right he saw no hope in venturing to such a place.

He relocated himself to bars, either so lax they paid no mind to the fresh faced kid growing his first beard, or employed by far sighted and mentally deficient bouncers, or those who believed he was of age merely because he put on a squinty eyed look of intimidation. He would sit at the counter downing drink after drink, waiting to be questioned about his troubles by the uninterested bartenders, flashing looks of despair to assorted strangers who paid him no mind, getting far too drunk to the concern of no one.

When he was turned away from the bars he displaced himself

to any of a series of sleazy strip clubs, mixed in on the waterfront between discounted warehouse stores that sold tattered shirts and for some reason advertised their weakness in comparison to real stores where those not in the grips of poverty might shop. The strip club employed unattractive girls who gladly shared their nipples with Justin regardless of whether or not he had asked for them. They were unfazed by words telling them to halt, confident that their breast would persuade the customer otherwise. Their lack of appeal and the buildup of grime in his integrity did nothing to curb his lust. His lack of a car did not help. These houses of sexual implication and the dive bars with women who had never ventured across the train tracks were the first buildings he came to as his feet got tired from overuse.

His libido swelled. Each semi-attractive buxom female he passed was an object of prey. Even if he did find them at a dive bar, wearing too much makeup, and speaking in a vernacular so poor it could hardly be described as English. Sticking to these locations he managed to lure an intoxicated parade of willing girls into his bedroom. Justin's body falsely persuaded him that each climax would cease his suffering. Each time he was met with crushing and depressing disappointment as the buildup ended and the briefest moment of pleasure had given way to overwhelming emptiness. And each time his libido would recharge, convincing him once more that it was the answer to his troubles, only to fail at delivering on its promise once more and burying him in a deeper emotional hole. He parted from these women quickly, disgusted with himself for the complete isolation of a fellow individual he had just enacted. For sharing such presumed intimacy with someone with whom he hadn't even dipped his toes in the surface of connection. They were completely separate as was everyone. His anger grew. He thought of his dead brother.

Justin fantasized of violence. He imagined getting into an argument on the street with any random stranger about any random issue. He pictured himself pummeling his adversary with an unparalleled sequence of punches and kicks, eliciting tremendous pleasure as he asserted himself as the definition of fear.

He was bad news. A threat to every face he passed. They looked forward, viewing him peripherally or out of focus, dangerously uninformed of the damage this unknown individual was capable of. He prayed that someone would cross him, test his volition to do what he could. Disposing of even the smallest harness built for his anger, letting the molecules of fury explode wildly, putting pain to others and a solid definition of toughness for Justin to associate himself with. He was a rock. A mountain. Unclimbable.

His fantasies became increasingly brutal. In one a man who pushed him, believing he had chose a harmless bystander to clear his way from on a stressful day rather than a pot of boiling water. He changed the man's face. Beating him until he was nothing but a giant scar. In another, he was given horrible service by a bartender, treated as a dirt rag who did not deserve to live. He took the man out back and shot him five times with a gun than he did not actually own.

He fantasized about violence so much that actual confrontations creeped into his daily interactions with little warning. A cashier at the market, too slow in ringing up the box of crackers that would hold him over for a week. She was told of her worthlessness. Later Justin felt terrible. Like each word he had spoken had burned off a piece of his skin. He washed his hands, lacking any soap, hoping to clean himself off from the incident, only to find himself screaming "fuck you" to a stranger hogging the hand dryer in a public bathroom. Each time he imagined the potential blood on his hands, produced by an imaginary onslaught of his physicality, while the inside of his eyes produced tears that his lids would not dare allow to taste the air. He was ashamed of the pain he caused to these strangers, even if only in fantasy. He shook.

He lost his job. Due to chronic lateness and a general lessening of the customer's well being. He cursed himself for not being able to hold a position for more than a month until he realized he had been doing it for a year and a half.

• • •

"Fuck," Justin blurted as he jumped into his bathroom with a baseball bat, ready to attack the intruder he had glanced in his bathroom mirror.

No one stirred.

"I know you're here," he said.

He flipped on the lights. The bathroom was empty. He paced around it slowly. There was nowhere to hide.

"Am I imagining things?" he whispered to himself, refraining from full volume for the concern that somehow the intruder had managed to hide in the medicine cabinet.

He looked up and saw himself. He had passed his own reflection and thought it was a stranger.

Justin wondered why it was he had mistaken his own likeness. He looked closely at his image. He was not emaciated. Neither had he put on any pounds. He looked precisely as he remembered himself and yet there was a disconnect.

"I don't know who I am," he said out loud, synchronized with the stranger in the mirror.

He wasn't sure why he hadn't recognized it before. He had

become a stereotype of out of control grieving. Barely a person at all. A year or more without real communication, interacting only with others as physical objects, servants delivering unfulfilling fixes of alcohol, or customers instructing him to construct copies of keys, had left a serious gash. His suffering had drained him of a personality.

He hadn't realized it at first because he had taken on a persona quite familiar to him to make up for the deficiency. He had become Adam. Except that he could not fully commit himself to the part. Justin fantasized of violence. Adam enacted violence. The thought of actually going through with many of the scenarios that ran through Justin's head made him sick. He lacked Adam's natural bloodthirst, the joy his brother had gotten from the simple act of eliciting physical harm, his sociopathic tendencies, and the inability to feel guilt. With every daydreamed unnecessary punch, with every visualized divide of hurt forged with a stranger, carved into a relationship of hatred, his suffering increased. After a year of drifting translucently through life, not much sure of anything except loss of what had been and fear of what was to come, he had felt comfort from being something real, something his own, even if it exacerbated the pain.

But the sudden realization that half successfully pretending to be his dead brother was the only thing keeping him anchored killed all that.

He tried to think of one thing that he liked. Of some activity that gave him joy. Of one characteristic with which he could describe himself, stripped from the circumstances of what had happened to him and the influence of his brother.

He came up with nothing.

He tried to think of some characteristic that was unique to him. Something he did or said or wanted that he hadn't borrowed from his brother or from what he knew of others.

Crickets echoed in the background. His apartment had an infestation problem.

He fell to the floor and cried.

"I'm not anything," he said.

Just a series of actions. Of drinking, of fucking, of indulging. A series of fantasies about violence that somehow reinforced an image of unbreakable toughness which never made its way fully into reality.

He stayed on the floor. Paralyzed. Confused over how someone with such little definition could even continue to breathe.

• • •

So he stopped. He stopped drinking. He stopped fucking. He stopped indulging. He stopped fantasizing about violence. He stopped doing anything in which he could not locate some basic instinct that caused him to act. Not influenced by what others thought he should do. Or by what others were like. Or what others actually would do in his situation. And he was left inactive. Because as long as he searched he couldn't locate this integral part of himself, separate from all else he knew.

Jobless, about to be homeless, he wandered the streets and tried to find some semblance of who he was.

He was immediately jarred by how different the world seemed when he entered it as an observer rather than a participant. People seemed strange. Every interaction was like a game. Each participant asserted their persona at every available opportunity. The humorous waited for a lead in to a joke. The intelligent waited to make a comment that was over everybody's head. The manly waited to mention how much they lifted at the gym or what they would do to a female who had just passed. The kind waited to reassure and offer helpful advice. And the violent waited for a moment to destroy.

Even the physical appearance of humans seemed odd. Strange, variously lanky and stumpy creatures, with curiously toned skin and branch like hands. And the face, the source of all human connection, was the strangest of all. A peculiarly arranged set of holes and juts contained in between protruding skin patches with a seemingly unnecessary amount of folds that we call ears and the center of our person, part translucent orbs we call eyes, that are the supposed "windows to the soul," but when looked at up close look as bland and emotionless as your average rock. "Everyone knows that we are really just animals, although most frequently forget it," thought Justin. "But I think we look more like aliens."

Justin wandered through the slums and saw some drug addicts hidden in crannies who were freshly dead and some just waiting around to be. And he took a long five hour walk into the surrounding suburbs and saw various members of the middle class leaving the mall with newly acquired purchases. And he stopped in convenience stores and flipped through pages of magazine photographs of celebrities and politicians and all those who everyone was supposed to know, and looked at all those who passed him on the street who might want to be known or might want to be ignored and he tried to figure out where one person's life ended and another person's began.

He thought about suicide. He looked into the future and could find nothing to look forward to. Only questions and struggle. At least when he was indulging he had some semblance of purpose, some point to his existence. Something to do. He had been on autopilot, for sure. And he felt much clearer now about his previous actions. But the clarity didn't bring peace. Just the opposite. It was the guide on a sight seeing tour of meaninglessness. Of people parading around personalities they thought they had, just trying to enjoy themselves as others suffered, unable to afford a meal or walk out of their house without the threat of being shot.

He bought out the common cold section of the convenience store, locked the door to his shithole of an apartment on one of the final nights in which he could afford it, and decided that if by the end of the night he had not figured out a good or even a practical reason to live, he would swallow pills until he never woke up.

He contemplated the reasons that others found life meaningful.

Some people lived for family or friends or hobbies they enjoyed but he had none of these.

Some people lived for money or power or fame but Justin couldn't possibly imagine any of these things bringing him satisfaction, let alone having enough talent or ability to achieve them in the first place.

A lot of people lived for love. It seemed a justifiable reason. But the idea of finding love was so foreign that it wasn't any of comfort. It was an idea. Nothing he had ever known through experience. And he couldn't quite grasp on to it enough to save him from feeling purposeless.

Then there was God. A lot of people talked about God. About some higher purpose and everything happening for a reason. But where was God when his brother died? Or, for that matter when his brother was born? Why would God allow such a violent human being in his midst? Or any number of violent human beings? Or such poverty and suffering? Maybe people had to prove themselves to God, so that they could be accepted into heaven. But why would God even set up a world where people were capable of doing the wrong thing? Was this all a big game? Like God's version of solitaire but with murder and rape and depression and disease and natural disasters that wiped out entire cities? And the biggest question of all – Where was God? Where was he to be found in anything? Where was any evidence at all that people don't just die when their bodies give out and that there's some sort of higher being running everything? Sure, everything had to come from somewhere, but even if there had been some God that created everything, where was the evidence that he hadn't just abandoned the universe after he made it? He picked up a copy of the bible that the previous tenant had left in the closet, likely hoping to convert or inspire future residents, and found the array of stories and rules both followed and not, and found it about as helpful as the comics section in the Sunday morning paper.

He poured his pills on the table.

Suicide seemed like such a rational option. If living was nothing but suffering why should he even bother? Why continue to put himself through pain unnecessarily? And what was the drawback? Facing a sentence in hell from a God he had just decided he didn't believe in? In this moment he felt quite confident that the only hell that existed was in the life he was living now. And when this life ended he would stop being anything.

He stared at the pills.

It all made perfect sense.

So what was the hesitation he felt?

A scream sounded through the alleyway next to Justin's apartment. He turned to his window and opened the blinds.

Directly below him a woman was being thrown down against her will by a man whose face he could not see. Each time she screamed the man punched her as hard as he could. She continued screaming so he stuffed her mouth with a piece of garbage he found on the street. The man held a knife up to the woman's neck and forced her to lower her pants.

Justin could see another pair of eyes across the way. No indication of moving. Watching the incident. Perhaps calling the police. Perhaps not.

It required no moment of decision for him to grab his baseball bat and make his way down to the alley.

The man didn't hear him, too caught up in lowering his own pants with one hand. One hard swing to the side was enough to knock him over.

Justin promptly instructed the woman to grab the dropped knife. A second harder shot to the man's just exposed penis contained all the anger against life Justin felt boiling inside.

The man was still wailing in pain when the police arrived. Justin was brought in for questioning and when the woman confirmed his story he was praised for his heroics.

On the way home he thought of the pills still spread out on his table. He wouldn't take them tonight.

For a moment at least, he felt some purpose. So much suffering in the world. So many people even worse off than him. So many people selfishly turning a blind eye. The least he could do was help.

II.

"What have you been doing?"

"Nothing worth talking about."

Justin was sitting in Jimmy Fordham's apartment. Two years had passed since his act of heroism with the woman.

"I don't mean that," Justin corrected himself. "What I mean is nothing worth reliving."

Justin regretted shooting down Jimmy's question so quickly. It was the first sentence he had managed to form. When he opened the door all he had muttered was, "Justin." And then silence. Justin had waited as Jimmy had tried to figure out the correct question to ask and the right way to phrase it. Why are you here? What are you doing here? Who are you, passing as my former friend who would never come to my door?

Even the way he spoke Justin's name had the hint of a question mark.

When Justin finally broke the wait by asking if he could come in, Jimmy nodded in agreement. His face ruffled and he was still trying to figure out how to deal with the shock of the moment that had just passed.

Justin took a look around the apartment, wanting the residence to explain how Jimmy's life had progressed without him actually having to ask.

There was a definitive lack of trinkets. Jimmy was neat. He allowed for some open patches of space and it was clear the few objects he possessed held an actual value beyond the basic need of possession. A photograph of him with his grandfather. A baseball signed by Ted Williams. A copy of The Catcher in the Rye.

Jimmy held few things sacred.

And then there were the signs of a female. A purse on a counter top. Several pairs of shoes in the slightly open closet. And a framed piece of orange and pink artwork that no male would ever pick out.

"Are you living with someone?" Justin inquired, trying to give the falsely started conversation a second go.

"My girlfriend. Sarah."

"How'd you meet?"

"At school."

"In a class?"

"Do you really care?"

"Yeah. I do."

In reality he didn't. It made little difference to him what was actually being said. It was the conversing itself that pleased him. The particular words were unimportant.

"What are you doing here?" Jimmy asked, no longer refraining from the thought that had been on his mind since he opened the door."

Justin took a deep breath. He dove in.

"I wanted to ask you to forgive me."

"Are you in some program or something?"

"What?"

"You know, alcoholics anonymous or something like that? Is this a step requirement visit? Ask forgiveness of anyone you've ever wronged? I'm not saying it's bad if it is, I'm just...asking."

"I'm not in any programs."

"Oh."

"I wanted to ask you to forgive me because the way I treated you when we were kids was horrendous. I spent my childhood worshipping my asshole of a brother and instead of listening to you, the one good person I actually knew, I took his side. I've been trying to figure out why it was I loved him so much. I think he was just so confident about who he was and I wanted to be that confident. But the truth is he didn't give a shit about me. I realize that now. You're the only person who ever really cared at all. And I spit on our friendship in the worst way. I'm so sorry Jimmy."

The faintest reflection of light shined off the tear Justin was attempting to hold in.

• • •

"Justin."

Two weeks had passed. Justin was back at Jimmy's apartment. This time he brought with him a box of chocolate chip cookies he found at the supermarket. And his name was said without any hint of a question mark. It was said with warmth. And maybe relief.

Jimmy invited Justin in to his apartment which was miraculously even neater than on his previous visit. The kitchen table was covered with a table cloth and properly arranged place settings. A wonderful smell was coming from the kitchen. And a beautiful girl was standing behind Jimmy.

"Justin, I want you to meet Sarah."

Sarah extended her hand and Justin shook it. Touching was almost inappropriate. It took only the briefest sight of Sarah for him to want her and when they made physical contact in an unquestionably common handshake he was overcome with desire.

"It's really nice to meet you," she said.

"You too," he replied.

By the time the handshake ended he was already missing the feel of her skin.

"I brought these cookies."

"Why thank you," she said. She took them from him and

smiled delightfully.

He watched her retreat into the aroma of the kitchen. Finishing up the chicken or roast or whatever it was they had prepared for this official reunion of sorts. It wasn't that Sarah was the most attractive girl he had ever seen. She was more pretty than hot. He could think of plenty of women he had seen whose appearance just taunted men to desire them. Sarah was not like that. She had more of what could only be described as the girl next door look. But Sarah invaded Justin's mind because she was the exact image he had always been looking for. She was the precise definition of his type even though it had never occurred to him that he had a type.

When they sat down to eat Justin was very conscious of the direction of his eyesight. Taking control of what was usually an automatic task, he let his eyes rest on Sarah only briefly when they spoke to each other, afraid of lingering too long and revealing himself, but also making sure to look at her long enough that nothing out of the ordinary was deduced by him completely ignoring her.

"So Justin," Sarah inquired, "tell me about what you're doing with your life. Jimmy seemed hard pressed to answer about your current whereabouts when I asked him."

"I realized that we didn't really get into the present last time you were here," Jimmy admitted. "Too focused on the past I guess."

"I guess so," Justin said. He felt the heat of Sarah's stare. "I moved back home. With my father. Though it's more of a roommate situation. We buy our own food. Stay out of each other's way. Don't talk much, except for practical matters like if the toilet's broken. You could say it's the best we've ever gotten along."

Sarah laughed. Just enough to compliment him on his joke

without disregarding the obvious pain behind it. He wanted to look at her but he kept his eyes on Jimmy.

"I've been working at a small market," he continued. "But I just got accepted into the police academy. I start Monday."

"You're going to be a cop?" Jimmy asked, letting on more surprise than he intended.

"That's the plan." Justin responded. "It's a big turnaround I know."

"No, I mean, I don't think –"

"It's okay. I wouldn't have thought it was where I'd end up either. But I want to do some good. There's so much pain in the world. So many people suffering. I want to do my part to make it a little bit better."

"I think that's great," said Sarah.

"I know I can only make so much difference. But it's better than doing nothing. Or contributing to it."

"Seems like he's really got his act together, doesn't it?" she said, putting her hand on Jimmy's.

He nodded.

"How about you Sarah?" Justin inquired. "What's your story?"

"My story," she smiled, "Is likely not a very interesting one. But the current chapter, besides shacking up with this guy over here, is that I'm teaching at Frederick Bachman Elementary School."

"On Marvin Street?"

"Yeah, that's the one."

"That's a rough neighborhood."

"She's deceptively tough," Jimmy interjected.

"I'd like to say that my intentions in working there are as admirable as yours in becoming a police officer," she said, "but the truth is my justifications of every child deserving a proper education is really secondary to the fact that right out of school it was the only place I could find a job."

"Don't sell yourself short," said Jimmy, "you're very admirable."

"Thanks," she said, touching Jimmy's hand under the table as Justin watched closely.

"What grade do you teach?" Justin asked.

"Third."

"How are the kids?"

"Difficult," she responded, as kindly as possible.

Justin forced himself to turn his attention to his old friend.

"And how about you buddy? What're you doing for work these days?

"I'm working as a Logistics Analyst focused on supply chain initiatives for a company called Frederickson."

"I see."

"He's very smart," Sarah added, indicating how little she understood Jimmy's profession herself.

"And how do you like that?"

"Oh it's great. Its super engaging and the people who work there are all really nice. And I have good management which isn't always easy to come by."

"You guys seem like the all American couple," said Justin.

"Well I don't know about that," said Sarah. "My mother is French."

Justin was invited back the next Sunday at the same time. He readily accepted the invitation.

• • •

The police academy was filled with pushing, shoving, verbal

aggression, psychological analysis, physical and mental hardship, memorization strain, and ten guys named Joe who were all bigger than Justin and all seemed to feed on a steady diet of bench pressing.

"I'd bang the shit out of her," one Joe would say to a magazine clipping another Joe had brought in.

"I'd fuck him up," a third Joe would say speaking of a particularly irritating mobster on a direct to video DVD a trainee named Tony had lent him.

Justin stayed out of the conversations. He ate lunch with others who kept to themselves, sharing only the sound of their loud chewing. It was easy to sift through those who were joining the police force because of some sense of morality and those doing so in order to legally carry a firearm they might actually be able to use on someone who wasn't made of cardboard.

He spent every moment away from the academy training himself. Hundreds of pushups and crunches. Endless repetitions of squats and lifting of dumbbells and runs of up to four miles each before retiring to bed, only to have to go the same distance within the context of the academy the next day.

He watched as fellow trainees broke down. Collapsing under the weight of acquiring knowledge, or the one hundred and ten percent of their body weight they were required to bench press, or the boot camp like instructors tearing into their ego as their screams left spit on everybody's faces.

When it came to studying and remembering crucial information Justin had less confidence than he would have liked. "I know I'm not very smart," he would say to himself. "So what I lack in smarts I have to make up in effort."

He took notes religiously, writing down every word his instructors said about laws, procedures, and even the rare anecdote made seemingly just to lighten the mood. He wanted no margin of error. No possibility of drifting the way he always had as a student.

He was determined to make something of himself. The surprising joy that came from those lowest moments where he couldn't find any basis to his identity, was that through enough resolve he could make himself into the person that he wanted to be.

The laws he learned sometimes seemed a bit arbitrary. They had less to do with the protection of the common good than with appeasing particular groups or with the city looking for added revenue or with seemingly nothing in particular, but perhaps they had existed too long for anyone to question. For the most part though, Justin felt the strongest assurance that every morsel of information and training filtering through his system was fundamentally good. Worthwhile. That everything he was learning would actually help him to make a positive difference. And though the academy was strenuous and challenging, and he started each day sore, and his brain hurt from all the information he was trying to jam in it, for the first time in years he woke up in the morning feeling good about the day that lie ahead. And that made it all worth it.

• • •

Sarah Kalick didn't know quite what to make of the sudden injection of Justin Giacorozzi into her and Jimmy's rather quiet life. The route of tragedy Justin had taken to end up in the current circumstances had obviously softened him, but with each social interaction the natural charisma buried under his bruised exterior peeked out just a little bit more. He brought a certain excitement every time he appeared. Like a newborn child just learning about the world. Most fascinating of all was the fact that his particular magnetism seemed to be rubbing off on Jimmy. During and just following interactions with his old friend he seemed more outgoing, enthusiastic. Even their sex life had improved, Sarah admitted to herself.

Prior to his recent reappearance Jimmy had mentioned Justin only once. It was during a particularly intimate conversation early in their relationship that in great part was responsible for fully winning her over. They had been dating for about a month. At the time she had quite liked Jimmy. He had an undeniable sweetness. He opened doors for her and complimented her regularly and there was no indication that these actions were part of any strategy or preplanned behavior. Just a built in chivalry when it came to minutiae. He was also quite smart. He rarely raised his hand in their shared medieval literature class, but when he did he always had something insightful to add. He was fun to spend time with. Humor might not be listed as one of his defining characteristics but he was skilled at inserting a well delivered joke when the conversation called for it. But she was still waiting for some moment to knock her off of her feet. For some turning point that would shift her from pleasant post date smiles to passionate pining. Sarah was a self-admitted romantic. Not the she wasn't in keeping with the stereotypes of females, she thought, but observing most of her friends at the university, who had less desire for love and more for a series of sexual gratifications and brief flings always described as "just having some fun," she often felt atypical in her continuous desire to find "the one." And so every relationship reached a point very early on where she felt the need to assess whether or not she had the potential to be hooked. Whether the romance she always wanted was lurking just over the horizon. A month in, she had reached that point with Jimmy. And although she felt a nice affection for him, she was beginning to doubt that he was the person she had been waiting for.

All of that changed after a low-key winter night in Jimmy's dorm. They lied on his bed and flipped through various television channels showing the horrible Friday night programming of the cheesiest of seventies game shows and even cheesier infomercials and one hour dramas that the networks were trying to get rid of. And they chatted, playfully making fun of each horrendous program they passed. In between chatting, Sarah brainstormed on questions she could ask to figure out who Jimmy really was beyond a kind college student obsessed with baseball (both watching and playing), naturally gifted at math, with a family he seemed to like, fairly intelligent comments to make about movies and books if asked but never volunteered, and boyishly handsome looks that were certainly appealing enough for her to fall for should there be something more to him that could trigger an addiction. "Do you dream a lot?" she asked.

"Sometimes. I had a dream last night that I owned my own hot dog stand."

"Really? And how was business?"

"Probably not very good because I think I was eating most of the hot dogs."

She shifted the conversation. Somehow she didn't think a discussion of hot dogs would lead to the emotional catharsis she was seeking.

"I had a dream last night that I was home," she said." "Do you miss home?"

"Not really," he replied. "I mean I miss my family sometimes but we have a lot of breaks where I can see them. And honestly I feel closer with the friends I've made here than anyone I know at home."

"I didn't know that. Do you have any friends at home you miss?"

"A couple."

"Who's your best friend?"

"I don't really have a best friend."

"Everybody has a best friend. Or at least a favorite friend."

"Who's yours?"

"Susan Milecki. We've been best friends since second grade."

"What's she like?"

"Well she's always smiling. Which I love about her. Nothing gets Susan down. She has this absolutely irrepressible spirit. Of course it sometimes gets her in a little bit of trouble. She can go a bit more wild than I necessarily approve of."

"So, she's a big slut?" Justin joked.

Sarah playfully slapped him on the arm. "That's not what I said! She's responsible when she needs to be. Or at least I hope she is. But anyway, I can talk to her about anything and she's always there for me."

"She sounds nice."

"She is. Okay, your turn. Tell me about a favorite friend."

"I don't know. I mean there's my friend Charlie. I like Charlie quite a bit. He's the funniest guy I know. But it's not like I ever have deep talks with him or anything. Honestly I haven't had a best friend since I was fourteen years old."

"And who was your best friend then?"

"Justin Giacorozzi."

"So what happened to Justin?"

It took Jimmy a moment to respond. Sarah noticed the uncomfortable hesitation.

"That's a good question. I haven't talked about Justin in a long time."

"Did something happen?"

"Yeah. Something happened."

"What?"

"I don't usually like to spend too much time reliving things that are in the past."

"Well if you really don't want to –"

"His brother was killed," said Jimmy, almost to himself.

She paused the conversation. She could tell he had more to say but was digging delicately for it. She gave him the time he needed to respond.

"His brother was killed and I wasn't there for him. Because we'd drifted apart. And because honestly he'd become a giant asshole. But that's no excuse for me not being there for him. He had nobody good in his life. Especially not his brother. But I'm sure the death absolutely destroyed him. And I don't even know what ever happened to him. I hope to God he's still alive."

"We don't have to talk about this if you don't want to," she said, although all she wanted was to continue talking.

"No it's okay. I like talking to you."

"I like talking to you too."

She waited.

"It just annoys me sometimes. I have this great, easy life. But I can't seem to consistently feel grateful for it. I don't mean that I'm down on things or anything, although the occasional set back probably does frustrate me more than it should. But I just mean that you see all this news and even know all these people who just have these horrible lives and I know how lucky I am and for a moment whenever I hear about anything bad I feel really grateful. But I can never hang onto that feeling. I always just go back to living life, not really thinking much about it, perfectly happy, but you know, not as appreciative as I should be."

Sarah felt selfish. All she ever thought about were her own emotional needs. Her intense desire for romance. She never took the time to think about how good she already had it. She was blown away by the principled simplicity of what Jimmy had said. And with that, she fell for him.

• • •

Justin graduated from the academy without any setbacks. He impressed each of his instructors, who saw him as a rule abiding, determined young man filled with character. They all told him he was going to make a great policeman. He took the compliments guardedly. He was wary of feeling any undeserved pride.

Despite his caution towards praising himself for what he had yet to do, Justin left his commencement ceremony with the sudden uncontrollable urge to inform his father of his accomplishment. He hadn't spoken to his father in two weeks. The last words they had exchanged involved a statement about the house being empty of soap. The amount of sentences spoken between one another since he had returned home, might, if written down, fill a single piece of paper. Wide ruled, not college. Margins left open. But he had finally done something positive with his life. And he wanted his father to know about it.

On the walk home he felt the rare hint of pleasure creeping up through his body. The day was gray and he hardly cared. Each crack in the sidewalk, each graffiti marked building, were only a friendly reminder of the complications of humanity. Serious, but not broken. This world was good at heart, he thought. And he was prepared to be sprung on it as an effective force.

He located Thomas at the kitchen table, staring at the wall.

"Don't bother pop, it's all re-runs" he joked, deliberately trying to create a rare light mood between them. "Do you mind if I join you?" he continued.

"That's fine," Thomas said.

Justin sat down at the seat next to Thomas on the circular table. He did not wish to be rude and block his father's view of the wall.

"I have some good news." He waited for a response. He received none. "I'm going to be a cop."

Thomas turned his head. "Really?"

"Yeah. I graduated the police academy today."

"They're letting *you* be a cop?"

"Uh. Yeah, I mean, I passed all the tests."

"Well. I guess the city's going to shit anyway."

Thomas turned his head away.

Justin was abruptly full of all sorts of nervous energy. He couldn't sit still. He stood up, paced around, tried to stop moving and couldn't, considered leaving, but discovered it was equally hard to exit the kitchen.

"What the fuck Dad?"

No response. He slammed the kitchen table with his hand. Thomas looked over.

"Listen to me when I'm talking to you! I'm finally doing something good with my life and that's all you have to say to me? The city's going to shit anyway? I deserve better than that."

"You're living under my roof aren't you?"

"What happened to you that was so awful that you're willing to throw away any chance of happiness?"

"Happiness?"

Justin wasn't sure where it came from. The notion certainly hadn't crossed his mind in a long time. Possibly never. He had managed to fight off crippling purposelessness. He found some meaning to get him through the day. But this altogether higher aspiration had not sprung up once. It was too unfathomable. He was not even sure that his sudden accusation towards his father was not really an indictment of himself, lashed out at this conveniently available opportunity. Happiness. He didn't even really know what the term meant.

Thomas stood up. He was clear. The usual half asleep tone of voice, the slumped body posture, momentarily vanished.

"Happiness? What do you know about happiness?"

"I know that it's something I'm willing to fight for," Justin said with sudden conviction.

"You'll lose."

"And why are you so sure of that?"

"Because it doesn't exist."

He tried not to be defeated by the certainty with which his father spoke. "And why do you say that?"

"Because some people are happy and some aren't. Some people are born into poverty and are uneducated and spend their lives getting shot at. Some are born with silver spoons in their mouth and never have to worry about how they'll pay for their next meal or even how they'll pay for their next high definition television set. Some are born in countries where they can say whatever they want and some are born in countries where they get sliced up with a machete just because their ancestors were born in a particular province. Some manage to find someone they love and who loves them and others fall in love only to watch the person they care about more than anything else in the world drift away day after day until she disappears, probably because she's fucking some other asshole she's actually in love with, and leaving them with two idiotic sons, the more worthwhile of whom goes and gets himself killed. Happiness doesn't exist because only the rare few get to have it. And if it's not available to everybody it doesn't exist like they say it does. People are happy because they're lucky. That's all. That's all that happiness is. Luck. You found the right person. You were born in the right place. And the rest of us unlucky sons of bitches for some reason keep living, because we're too fucking scared to end it all."

Justin looked at his father for a moment, then walked away. Up the stairs. To his room. To his closet, where he kept his suitcase. It took him less than ten minutes to pack. He was used to having few essential possessions.

On the way out he stopped back in the kitchen where Thomas had returned to staring at the wall.

"I'm sorry mom didn't love you," he said.

Then he walked out of the house forever.

• • •

"I don't know what I'm going to do." Justin said. "I don't have any money. I just couldn't stay there anymore."

"And you shouldn't." Sarah approvingly responded.

"I'm so sorry man," said Jimmy.

"It's okay. He's always been like that. I just feel like if I'm going to be the person I want to be, I can't be around him."

"That sounds like smart thinking," said Jimmy.

"Now where the hell am I going to go?"

"Well you're going to stay here, of course," said Sarah, seemingly surprised it was even a question.

Jimmy looked at his girlfriend. Justin felt that he caught the most fleeting look of annoyance. Probably at not having been consulted. But just as quickly he turned to Justin, reverting back to his classic comfortable demeanor.

"Like she said. Of course you're going to stay here."

"I really don't want to impose."

"We're not giving you a choice," said Sarah.

"That's right. We're requiring you to impose," said Jimmy.

Justin laughed. He wanted to prove his father wrong. Show that happiness could be wrenched out from any wreckage it found itself in. But at this particular moment he identified with part of what Thomas had said. Because right now, he looked at the welcoming faces of the couple sitting across from him and he couldn't help but feel extremely lucky.

III.

"Sons of bitches."

To Eddie Santore, everyone was a son of bitch. The drug peddlers waiting on the corners were sons of bitches. The cops he worked with were sons of bitches. Some bartender who had pissed him off was a son of a bitch. He best buds were sons of bitches. His mother was a son of bitch. Justin found it hard to tell if the phrase maintained any meaning at all in Eddie's use of it. Whether it was even supposed to be negative. Eddie threw "son of a bitch" out there like most people used the word "the."

"I'm telling you, we're never going get rid of these sons of bitches. You remove one son of a bitch and another son of a bitch just comes and takes his place. It never fucking ends."

Currently, he was referring to the drug dealers.

Eddie Santore had been assigned as Justin's designated partner. Following the academy, rookie policemen were put on a foot beat for a period of three months. Assigned to patrol a particularly dangerous, drug overrun, and inevitably poor neighborhood. The point was to cut down on criminal incidents through police presence alone. Statistically, having a policeman patrol a neighborhood made a significant difference. But as Justin and Eddie repeatedly watched teenage drug dealers peddle crack right before their eyes, it was hard to believe the positive stats.

"Fucking pigs," shouted a youth of no more than thirteen, riding by on an abnormally low bicycle.

"How about I come stick my fucking cigarette in your eye, you son of a bitch!"

Justin liked Eddie. His fuse was longer than one would think. He genuinely cared about his new profession even if he was a bit cynical about the difference he could make. He was hilariously vulgar, stepping over the line and daring anyone to pull him back to the other side.

"Kid won't keep laughing when I rape his mother," Eddie joked, lighting up a new cigarette.

He was a chain smoker. He wasn't supposed to indulge his addiction on the job but he whisked through each cigarette so quickly and seemed so empowered from each successive smoke that Justin hardly thought it worth betraying his partner over such a meager offense.

They had been on the job for a week. Already they had become acquainted with many of the neighborhood regulars on the five block radius to which they were assigned. Teenagers never in school, always stinking of marijuana, who barely paid the policeman a second glance, except when they were searched. They would blatantly transfer their bags of weed, or often crack cocaine, and Justin or Eddie would cuff them and hold them and throw them in the paddywagon to the jeers of the watching crowd. They had been lucky enough to avoid witnessing any acts of violence so far, but the area was plenty prone to them and it was only a matter of time before they came across some victim of assault or worse.

"I swear to God, these kids are gonna get themselves killed," said Eddie as he whiffed through the remains of his cigarette. "And for what? So some other son of a bitch can take their place."

Justin had to admit, what he saw was a bit discouraging. But he was not too dissuaded. As everyone always said, if you can improve the life of just one person, you have made an important difference. It wasn't just a cliché. It was true. And somewhere along the line Justin would save one of these children's lives. He was sure of it.

"Whatcha drawing there?"

Justin had decided to speak to a child sitting on the stoop of his dilapidated house. He was drawing on construction paper with a set of colored pencils. It was nice to see some creativity amidst the junkies and persistently angry youth.

"My dog," the child responded. "The dog I'm gonna have someday."

"What kind of dog is it?"

"He's a pit bull. He's gonna be my guard dog, so nobody can get in."

"What's his name?"

"A-Killer."

"A killer?"

"Yeah. Asshole killer."

Justin smiled. "How old are you?"

"Eleven. Imma turn twelve next week though."

"Well happy birthday?"

"Ain't my birthday yet. It's on the twelfth. Tell me happy birthday then."

"Maybe I will," said Justin.

◆ ◆ ◆

Sarah was torturously beautiful. Each morning when Justin woke up he imagined her lying next to him on the sofa bed where he slept. He stared at her at every available opportunity when Jimmy was not around. Her adorable smirk. The way the front strands of her blonde hair often ended up in her mouth. She got more attractive by the day. With or without makeup. Just as attractive in baggy pajamas as in a t-shirt.

"She's definitely better looking than when I first met her," Justin said to himself in the shower, trying to get her off his mind, which was particularly difficult when she was in the next room over. "Not that she wasn't gorgeous then," he self-countered.

Occasionally his erratic work hours would leave him time to masturbate when both Sarah and Jimmy were out of the house, but these fantasy sessions provided no real release. They only made him desire her more. Frustratingly unsatisfied that he could never have the real thing.

Jimmy had been so kind to him since he had come back into his life. Justin felt horrible about the thoughts he now had about his girlfriend as a matter of routine. But he couldn't help himself. He had never wanted another female so much.

Outside of his gnawing desire for Sarah, Justin's new living situation was the happiest he had ever been. Instead of sharing an abode with a distant sociopath, an even more distant vessel of bitterness, or complete silence acting as an ever present reminder of his own solitude, Justin now lived with friendly, well adjusted human beings who would ask his how his day was, if he returned home at a reasonable time, and would even cook him meals should the opportunity arise.

"I made spaghetti!" Sarah enthusiastically alerted him when he walked, exhausted, through the door.

Nothing like the comfort of pasta and someone who actually cares about you.

Justin made a regular habit of thanking his guests for their hospitality and insisting that as soon as he had enough funds he would pay them back and move out on his own. Obviously, his hosts did not want a permanent usurpation of their living room couch, but for their part they responded to Justin's routine sentence with one of their own, insisting that he take as much time as he needed, and that there was no need for a reimbursement. They were taking him in because he was a friend in need.

Even more incredible, they actually seemed to mean it.

Jimmy delighted in having a sports watching companion, a male sensibility he could play off of. He didn't expressly admit it. Jimmy was not the type to vocalize how appreciative he was of the things that made him happy. He kept quiet about his feelings. But Justin had no doubt that all past bitterness had been completely forgiven and Jimmy was deeply pleased by the reinstatement of his old best friend.

Sarah, as Justin learned to expect in every situation, was particularly wonderful. She had only met him a couple months before but she treated him like someone she had known her entire life. She was a natural caregiver, constantly searching for some service she could offer to her men, lessening their burden after a hard day at work even though her own day was just as arduous. She regularly did Justin's laundry even though he repeatedly insisted that the favor was not necessary.

"Sarah, I'm going to start hiding my dirty clothes bag from you," he said.

"You can try, but I'll find it. I'm quite the detective," she responded, smiling delightfully.

I love you, he thought.

Justin imagined that Sarah would make the perfect mother some day.

When he drifted he saw images of her holding a newborn baby, singing softly. He saw himself standing behind her.

He had never even realized that he wanted children.

The three spent all of their time together whenever their schedules meshed. Justin had been freely welcomed in to Jimmy and Sarah's favorite activity of watching horrible television and mocking it. He was invited along on Sunday morning brunches and Saturday evening dinners and Friday night movies.

Most pleasingly of all, Justin was laughing. And frequently. They all were. Justin hadn't even realized he could be funny, but living with actual pleasant people was allowing him to discover all sorts of positive aspects of himself he had never known existed.

"You've really never washed dishes before?" Jimmy asked.

"I don't know that I'd ever used dishes before," Justin responded.

They all laughed. Justin watched Sarah's smile.

"Looks like our boy's growing up," she joked, putting her arm around Jimmy.

"Yeah, we should really raise his allowance," Jimmy responded.

Justin closely watched Jimmy and Sarah look into each other's eyes. His stomach gave out. He focused on the dishes.

"Fuck you Dad", he sometimes said in a running dialogue with his not present father. "Look at me now. I'm happy."

Now if he could only ignore the painful throbbing of his heart whenever the couple who had opened up their home to him retreated to their bedroom.

• • •

"Hey kid."

The child looked over. Justin had hoped that he would find him today once again sitting out on his stoop.

"Hey," said the kid.

"How you doing?"

"I'm alright."

"I seem to remember it's your birthday."

"Yeah, that's right."

"Happy Birthday."

"Thanks."

"I got you something."

Justin reached into his pocket and pulled out a set of markers. He handed them to the child.

"I remembered you like to draw. I thought maybe you could use these."

The child looked suspiciously at the markers.

"Is something wrong?" Justin asked.

"Why you giving me this mister?"

"I don't know. It's just nice to see a nice kid around here."

The child continued to stare at the markers as if they were hiding some dark secret.

"What's your name kid?"

"Lashaun."

"You go to school Lashaun?"

"Yeah."

"How are you doing in school?"

"Alright. Teachers like me I guess. I do my homework sometimes."

Justin chuckled. "Yeah that might put you in good with them."

Lashaun looked at Justin's gun.

"You ever use that?"

"No," responded Justin, glancing down at the weapon. "Let's hope I don't have to. I've only been a cop for a couple of weeks though."

"How you like it?"

"I like it. I mean it's kind of scary to be honest, but it's important. I want to do something good with my life. Make some sort of difference."

"I want to be a football player."

"Oh yeah?"

"Yeah. A football player or a basketball player. I don't remember which one."

"You don't remember?" Justin asked, smiling.

"Well I'm good at both," said Lashaun, who smirked with a sudden self assured confidence.

"Right."

Justin looked up. At the end of the block two teenagers were standing closely huddled together. One of the teens passed a large handful of money to the other. The other passed back a manila packet, carefully taped.

"You gotta be fucking kidding me," said Justin. "I'm standing right here." He turned to Lashaun. "I gotta go kid. Have a good birthday."

"Thanks mister."

Justin made his way over to the teens.

"You gentlemen mind telling me what's going on here?"

"Nothing."

"Nothing. So you didn't just take money from him and give him some sort of packet in exchange for the money? I'm just imagining that?"

The dealer held strong. He looked like he was about to spit in Justin's face. The teen who had just bought the drugs was shaking, looking around, halfway between moving and not.

"You're making shit up." said the dealer.

"What did you just buy?" Justin asked the purchaser directly.

He only shook his head, unable to speak.

"Jesus Christ. Okay, I'm taking you in."

"Fuck you." The dealer made good on his expression and spit in Justin's face.

Justin flipped. He lunged forward, pushing the dealer against the wall by his neck. With his other hand he took out his gun and pointed it directly into the dealer's face.

"Turn around and put your hands behind your back."

Justin radioed for the paddy wagon. A crowd gathered to watch. They laughed, taunting their peers who were being arrested.

• • •

"I'm just not sure I know how to deal with these kids."

Justin threw his hand up and caught the high fastball Jimmy had whiffed his way. There wasn't a lot of yard space in Jimmy's neighborhood so they had to go on the street to have a baseball catch. They had to move for the occasional car and pay careful attention to just how hard they threw the ball, cautious that it not get away from each other's gloves and ricochet into a random window. Jimmy's last throw had been a bit on the risky side.

"Sorry," he said, "Sometimes I just like to throw it as hard as I can."

Justin glanced upwards. An old woman had been staring out of her window for the entirety of the catch, looking equal parts terrified that a ball might come her way and indignant that two idiotic youths would even think of taking such a risk on her street. Justin imagined that she had one of her hands on the phone receiver, just waiting to call the police should a single throw go awry. He imagined showing up himself with his badge, nearly sending the old woman into a seizure from the shock.

"It's okay," he responded to Jimmy. "The risk is part of the fun."

He threw the ball back rather hard himself. He looked up and stared down the old woman. It wasn't like him recently to be so malicious. It was a part of his old self creeping back to the surface. "This job must be starting to get to me," he thought.

"So you were saying about the kids?" asked Jimmy, continuing the catch.

"It's just so sad man. They get roped into this whole drug dealing thing at such an early age and they just accept that it's their life. They all have this attitude towards everybody that surrounds them. Like they just don't want to be helped and they won't listen to any reason."

"I see what you mean. That's pretty sad."

"Yeah. It's frustrating. I feel like if I lock them up for something, they're just going to come back and do it again."

They tossed the ball back and forth for a few minutes without speaking. They were both completely engaged in the catch. Both delighted to be reliving a childhood activity neither of them had ever thought they would share with each other again.

"Hey Jimmy."

"Yeah?"

"I'm really happy that we're friends again."

"Yeah. Me too."

Justin glanced up at the window to Jimmy's apartment. For a brief moment he caught Sarah looking at them, but she scampered off immediately upon being spotted, as if she didn't want them to know she had been watching. He thought it was strange but he was always happy to see her, if even for a moment.

"Justin?"

Justin looked over at Jimmy. He had not realized he had not thrown the ball back.

"Sorry," he said.

He resumed the catch.

• • •

"We've received a 911 call coming from 6741 Hightop Rd. Say they heard a gunshot next door," the radio relayed.

"We'll check it out," Eddie quickly responded.

Three o'clock in the morning is a frightening time, thought Justin as he listened to his partner for directions. He was bothered by the eerie quiet, broken up only by sporadic screams and moans. Empty streets occupied only by the occasional drug addict. Quiet nights that gave his mind far too much time to ruminate over painful memories and unpleasant anxieties he still hadn't completely erased.

"Follow me," said Eddie.

The two men made their way quickly down the block. They wished to arrive quickly to their destination without drawing any unnecessary attention from criminals peering nightly through their windows, waiting for unguarded streets and a chance to strike.

"This is the place." said Eddie, stopping at a barely held together structure that Justin supposed could be called a house.

Eddie knocked on the door. No answer. He pounded at the door.

"Police! Open up!" he shouted. They waited a moment. Eddie gave Justin the nod he was expecting.

They took out their guns and kicked down the door.

The first floor was vacant. Only a pile of empty canned food, a busted table, and an all consuming smell of feces.

"Place smells like shit," whispered Eddie.

Justin inched towards the stair case. He peered up it. It appeared to be unoccupied.

"C'mon," he said.

He led the slow walk up the stairs. He felt his body shake.

"This is fucking terrifying," he thought, not daring to look down at Eddie, who had never expressed as much as an inkling of fear over their chosen profession. He suddenly doubted himself, doubted his ability to successfully perform the duties of his job. Each step up the stairs was a reminder of the risk he faced every day he walked the streets. He saw Sarah's face. He couldn't die here. He needed to see her again.

He reached the top step. He held Sarah in his arms. He slowly peeked his head down the hallway. She rested her head on his shoulder. He cautiously moved his feet, gun pointed forward, keeping his back against the hallway wall and approaching the closed bedroom door. She turned her head up towards him. He reached the door. She kissed him and he savored the feel of her lips on his.

"Fucking do it," said Eddie calmly. Justin nodded.

He kicked down the door.

"Police!" screamed Justin.

Eddie and Justin immediately and nearly simultaneously brought their non gun holding arms to their noses, an absolute necessity to block out the noxious smell. The room contained no bed. Its sole decoration was a series of scattered heroin needles. In the center of the floor lay what appeared to be a woman, slowly stirring, covered in shit and blood.

Eddie spotted a gun about a foot from her. He ran over and kicked it to the other side of the room.

"Ma'am," said Eddie.

The blood was pouring out of her stomach. He hands were covered in her own excrement. She held them to her head and cried.

"Just let me die," she stuggled to get out.

"Fuck," said Justin, shaking as he brought his radio to his mouth. "We need an ambulance."

• • •

At five AM, Sarah would hear the door and breathe a sigh of relief.

At first she had stayed up unintentionally on the nights when Justin worked the late shift. She would lose control of her thoughts until they took over, spinning around until the foundation of her energy left her more awake than hours before when she had collapsed on her pillow. Anxious that something might happen to her houseguest in the late hours in the most dangerous part of the city. Fighting with herself over the true nature of her concern. "He's become a good friend," she would tell herself. "I'm just concerned about my friend." She might have convinced herself if it wasn't for those pesky fantasies she kept having of him coming home with some sort of wound, harmful, but far from fatal, and her tending to him as Jimmy slept. She was not sure which was more disturbing to her. The implication of her desire for Justin or the implication of sadistic kinkiness that came with the inclusion in her fantasy of an injury to him whom she was fantasizing about.

After a few weeks her insomnia became intentional. She'd sneak a glass of red bull before bed, concerned that her unfiltered thoughts might let her down some evening. That she would fall asleep not knowing if Justin had safely returned home. She would turn her body over, listening to the silence of the day's earliest hours and look at Jimmy. He always slept so peacefully. And every time she looked at him she would be racked with guilt. Nervous that he might wake up and see her awake and that she would spill the whole thing. The reason she kept falling asleep in the daytime. The reason she had been extra irritant as of late at work and upon returning home from work.

She kept telling herself not to jump to any conclusions. Emotions could be very misleading. But the more she fought against these frustrating new feelings, the more of a stronghold they built. There was becoming no doubt about it. She was falling in love with Justin.

The children had been particularly horrendous as of late at school. As if the entire school year was a slow process of finding their teacher's tipping point and then resting awkwardly on top of it until she finally toppled over. She couldn't get through a math lesson without two boys calling each other derogatory names for homosexuals. She couldn't get through a reading lesson without finding a child out of their seat, even though she swore she never actually saw anyone get up. She couldn't even take attendance without the whole class breaking out in impenetrable chatter. There were a couple of nice kids. She always felt bad for quiet Brianna Williams and nerdy Donovan Leeds, patiently listening to her lessons, who were equal victims of her furious screaming reprimand of the whole class. They were also probably the only ones actually affected or hurt as the rest of the class quickly devolved back into their apocalyptic personalities following a quiet of no more than three minutes.

In the brief seconds here and there, shaking like a leaf as the babble overwhelmed her, she filtered out the din thinking about Justin, running over events of the past few months again and again and trying to decode exactly where it was her feelings evolved. She certainly thought he was attractive when they had first met, but that didn't translate to anything beyond simple observation. A classification of his features, filed away with age, race, height, and so on. The level of excitement she felt when she asked Justin to move in was perhaps somewhat oddly high, but that was as much based around the person Jimmy seemed to become around his friend as it was on the likeability of the friend himself.

But then something happened. She started overhearing snippets of conversations between the two men she was living with. She probably eavesdropped more than might have been particularly proper, but if confronted she figured she'd use the excuse of thin walls. A tinge of guilt did pop up here and there but she just couldn't manage to turn away. At first, Sarah realized, she was curious as to whether Jimmy would let his guard down around his old friend. It had not previously occurred to her until she had a resource other than herself to communicate with her boyfriend, but she still felt a bit isolated from Jimmy. That he was always hiding some deeper side of himself. And subconsciously she had formed the hope that Justin's presence might be the key to that still locked door.

The eavesdropping, however, had a different result than she had expected. Jimmy was essentially the same around Justin. Maybe minutely more macho. A smidgen more juvenile. But overall the same warm, intelligent, sporadically witty, and not overly talkative or self revealing person she had come to love. The minor amount she learned about Jimmy during her sessions listening at door cracks was in complete parallel to how much she learned about Justin, who was ostensibly bursting at the seams from held in emotions finally getting a long delayed breath of fresh air above their buried surface. He would speak of the inner torture of still somehow loving his brother and missing him terribly while objectively reasoning that his sibling had been making the world a worse place. Of a pervading restlessness he could not shake. Of the life he had led the past few years, immersed in unfulfilling indulgences and desperate to find something worth caring about. Of how grateful he felt for his current situation, living with Sarah and Jimmy, and how frustrated he was that he would still at times feel unsatisfied with existence. Of how he was wary that his work as a policeman would make no difference to the horrible state of the world and how he was angry that he didn't always care, concerned more with his own personal pleasure. Jimmy had always been a good listener. But, it currently occurred to Sarah, that this was partially because he didn't full engage the speaker. He didn't offer back his own passions, hopes, and fears. He gave the speaker the spotlight, which she supposed was what they really wanted since this line of thinking had never occurred to her when she herself was rambling on and he was listening calmly. But there was something separate and wonderful about two people bearing their soul to each other, even if they were only waiting for their own turn to speak.

That's when she started to feel tenderness each time she looked at her houseguest. And when her ability to fall asleep at night began to fail her. And when she would find herself in the middle of a daydream where her and Justin cried together and the tears evolved into an emotional kiss. "Who cries in their own fantasies?" she thought, deeply disturbed by the content of her fixation. Her old craving for romance was acting up again, and threatening to harm the quite healthy relationship she was only just realizing might not be all she wanted. Each time the craving flared she took a self induced dosage of the memory of that magical night when Jimmy had first mentioned his friend. When she had been won over by his meaningful thoughts on life. But how long was one memory expected to sustain as the basis for an entire relationship? Doubt was now present and it was causing an ache that was making it difficult to get through the day.

• • •

Justin stood out in front of Lashaun's house. He hadn't seen the boy in several days and wondered whether he was inside.

He briefly considered knocking. But he realized his affection for the boy could be taken entirely the wrong way and, not particularly wanting to lose his job as a police officer over unwarranted child molestation charges, he moved on to the filthy streets he was coming more and more to hate.

He was beginning to worry that he was making no difference at all. He felt like the third grade hall monitor, anxiously stuttering to class cutting bullies that they could not pass, only to be trampled over with barely a flicker of recognition. The thought passed through his mind that maybe the world would be better without policeman or hall monitors. That these guards trying to protect the people and maintain the status quo only gave the rebellious a game to play. A figure of opposition who made their actions worthwhile. That it would be better to remove the guards and let the world descend into anarchy. That maybe then the filth would wash itself out, leaving only those who wanted to live reasonably and peacefully. Although, he supposed that at one point that filth would have included himself.

He spotted Eddie.

"Fucking dry today huh?" his partner said.

"Yeah, I guess."

They stood together quietly.

"I'm gonna go check out over there," said Justin, indicating no spot in particular.

He moved on. He was feeling restless. Like he almost wanted some sort of violent action to occur. To bring some excitement to the day. He was fully aware of the enormous contradiction between this and his previous thought pattern of wishing for a complete cease in all criminal activity and this made him even more restless. What would he even do with himself if he wasn't a police officer? Becoming a cop had saved him. Had given some purpose to his existence. If he hadn't made it through the academy or decided that this was what he wanted to do, he couldn't even think of what he would be doing. The memory of the life he had lived so shortly before was a haunting one.

He kept moving. He thought about Sarah. He always thought about Sarah. He'd be shocked if thirty seconds passed before he imagined holding her again. He was now shaking every time he returned home, wondering if she was standing just behind the door. He was staring way too long at her soft skin, wishing he could brush up against it. He was also glancing down at her crotch far more than was safe. When he walked the streets he always vaguely imagined that she was holding his hand. Though he tried not to sink too deep into the fantasy, lest someone spot him lost in a daydream, curling up his fingers and smiling.

A giant crack sounded. Justin fell threw himself against the wall. It was almost certainly a gunshot.

Justin peeled himself off the bricks, pulled out his firearm, and ran in the direction from which the shot appeared to sound. His heart beat.

Ahead he saw Eddie running. Chasing. He followed. Tried to make his legs move faster.

Out of the corner of his eye he saw a gathering crowd. And a puddle of blood. He heard moaning. Faster.

Eddie jumped over a fence. The criminal was trying to escape behind Almond St. Justin sprinted right. He would cut them off.

He ran around the block. Faster. His breath was running out. He pushed his legs.

He reached his destination. Watched the last house on the block. Waited.

He heard a noise. A man holding a gun jumped over the fence.

Justin raised his gun. "Police! Freeze!"

The man hesitated for a moment. Then snapped his gun-holding hand in the air.

Justin shot him the chest.

A moment later Eddie jumped over the fence. He looked at the criminal, lying on the ground. He looked at Justin, frozen, still holding his gun in the air. He took out his walkie.

Justin had known that your teeth could chatter. He had never known that your whole body could.

• • •

The light of the fridge hurt his still adjusting eyes and Justin searched anxiously for something to eat, not the least bit hungry but desperately needing some activity to reduce his shakes.

He pulled out a can of soda. He left the refrigerator door open and rummaged through the cupboard. He pulled out a box of chocolate chip cookies, nudged the fridge door on the path to closing and sat down in the dark at the table. He ripped open the sealed bag and grabbed aimlessly at several cookies. He stuffed them in his mouth.

"Hungry?"

He looked up. Sarah stood in the doorway. She switched on the light.

"Actually no. I just can't sleep."

"I know what that's all about," she said.

She flinched. Like she was about to sit down but didn't follow through.

"Do want a cookie?" Justin asked.

"Are you offering me my own cookies?"

She smiled.

"I suppose I am."

"Alright then. I accept."

She sat down next to him. He swore he could feel her warmth. He looked at her face. She'd been crying.

"Are you okay?" he asked.

"I'm fine. Just can't sleep."

"Oh."

"Are you okay?" she asked, noticing his unsteady hand.

"Yeah I'm—"

He stopped. He didn't want to lie to her.

"I'm a little shaken up."

"What happened?"

"I shot somebody today."

"Oh my god."

"This idiot gets into an argument and shoots his friend in the middle of the sidewalk. In the middle of the day. With two fucking cops right down the street. I just don't get it."

Sarah listened closely.

"So we chased him down and he pulled his gun out at me. And I shot him. I didn't even think about it. It was a defensive thing. I shot him before I'd even realized I had. He died Sarah. I killed him. Stupid fucker."

He stuffed a cookie in his mouth.

She leaned over and hugged him. A real hug. She held him tight. He put his hands on her back. He held her.

"I don't know that I can do my job anymore," she said.

"Why?"

"The kids. They're just so horrendous. They don't want to

learn. They have no use for learning. They don't even give me the respect of treating me badly. They treat me like I'm not even there. So what am I supposed to do? Just yell constantly? Act like I'm a prison guard trying to keep the inmates in line? Ignore the idea of teaching all together? It's just so defeating."

"I'm sorry Sarah. You deserve better than that. You deserve kids that want to be taught."

"Thanks." She held him tighter.

"I really did want to make a difference out there," he said. "But actually being on the streets, I feel helpless. Like there's never gonna be anything I can do to stop the world from just getting worse and worse. I don't know what to do Sarah. There's only a couple things that are even keeping me going."

"You're a good person," she replied.

They held each other quietly for a moment, then each felt it was appropriate to separate.

Halfway through the separation they paused, still holding each other's arms.

They looked at each other, neither speaking.

They didn't blink.

"Thanks for talking," he said, finally pulling his arm away.

"You too," she responded, doing the same.

"I guess we should go to sleep."

"Yeah."

"Goodnight."

"Goodnight."

• • •

Justin pounded on the door. No one answered.

"Police! Open the door!"

He pounded harder.

"Open the fucking door!"

He heard movement. The door cracked open. A woman peeked her head out.

"What?" she said.

"Are you Lashaun's mother?"

"What he do?"

"Where is he?"

"I don't know."

"Is he home?"

"The boy does what he wants. Doesn't listen to me."

"When's the last time you saw him?"

"I don't know."

"Ma'am. Do you know where your son is?"

"No. I don't," she said, exasperated at having to continue speaking.

Justin stood still.

"Is there a problem or can I go back in my house?" she asked.

He wanted to kick the door in and break the woman's nose. She closed it before he had the chance.

Justin retreated into the streets. He ached at the thought that something might have happened to that nice kid. And he thought of Sarah.

Had he seen some sort of affection in her eyes the night before? Had he sensed that she didn't want to let go of him either?

The notion was almost too torturous to consider. What if Sarah did feel something for him? There wasn't anything he could do about it. He could never betray Jimmy. Not after he had been forgiven so kindly. Not after he had offered up his home so graciously. Not after all the kindnesses he had received.

But how long would he be able to resist temptation if it was hung out in front of him? He had never had a very strong resolve. The safest thing to do would probably be just to move out. But where would he go? How could he survive on his own? He supposed that he could make due on his new income but emotional strains worried him just as much as financial ones. He couldn't bear to live alone again. The idea terrified him. Solitude ate at his stomach, made his chest feel like it was caving in on itself.

Laughter sounded from the nearest corner.

He looked over at the three teenagers occupying the sidewalk. He had seen them before. Or maybe not. It hardly mattered. The youths throwing away their lives were all interchangeable. And constantly replaceable. Eddie had been right of course. There was nothing they could do to stop these sons of bitches.

"Get the fuck off the corner."

The teens stopped their laughing. They looked at each other, seemingly trying to recall if they had done anything.

"Am I speaking a foreign language? Get. The. Fuck. Off. The. Corner."

Uncomfortably the teens waited.

"What'd we do?"

Justin smiled. Then attacked. He lunged forward, pushed the teen who had the gall to question him to the ground. He grabbed his legs and dragged him down the sidewalk away from the corner. The teen struggled to get loose, screamed, but Justin held a tight grip. His friends watched, shocked. They didn't dare move. A policeman trying to do his job was one level of threat. A policeman acting completely on his own accord was entirely another.

"What are you doing?"

Justin looked over. Eddie was standing next to him. The tough chain smoking self declared bastard looked almost scared.

Justin let go of the teen. He sprinted away.

"What just happened?" asked Eddie.

"I don't know."

"You better watch it man. I got your back but you can't just flip out for no reason."

"Yeah. You're right."

◆ ◆ ◆

Justin entered the unexpectedly quiet apartment. The lights were out and the only sound was that of muffled crying.

Jimmy sat on the couch, his face buried in his hands. He looked up. There was a brief flicker of expectation. He saw Justin and it was immediately extinguished.

"Sarah left," he was just able to get out.

Justin ran over to the couch and sat down next to him.

"What happened?" he asked.

Through tears Jimmy answered. "I don't know. She just— she was crying. And I asked her what was wrong and she wouldn't tell me. She asked me to guess but I couldn't guess. She insisted so I guessed that her grandmother died, which really set her off. I don't know, it was— it was a stupid thing to say, really stupid. I didn't know what to say, she kept yelling at me to guess. She said I should know. That she didn't expect me to know but that I should know. She said she was leaving. She said she didn't know when she'd be back. If she'd be back. She took a bunch of stuff with her. I pleaded with her. What happened? Please tell me what's wrong. She said she knew she was awful. That she hated herself. But that she needed to leave. I said please don't go. Please. I said you're not awful. You're great. I told her I loved her. And she just looked at me. I asked, are you breaking up with me? And she just said I don't know. And then she left. I tried calling her about ten times but she won't answer her phone. I don't know what to do. I don't know what happened."

Justin pulled his friend in. Hugged him tight.

"Fuck her," he said. "She's crazy to leave you. She'll never find a better guy."

"I love her," said Jimmy.

For the next few hours Justin sat with Jimmy. Tried to comfort him. Told him everything would be okay. He used any of the classics of the consolation rule book that he didn't actually believe in the hope that his words might improve the well being of his friend. Eventually he convinced Jimmy to go to sleep. He told him that he needed some rest. And he promised he would be there for him the next day.

Justin stood in the living room alone, finally having changed into his street clothes. He knew Jimmy would not actually be falling asleep anytime soon. He could still hear the distant sound of crying coming from his room. He had never even seen Jimmy sad, let alone distraught. Emotional breakdowns were not in his character. He's not supposed to be fucking fragile like me, he thought. It infuriated him that he had to watch amiable stability incinerated in such a way.

"I'm never going to see her again," Justin said aloud, the painful realization finally making its way into words.

He grabbed a vase sitting on a side table and threw it as hard as he could against the wall. It smashed into a thousand pieces.

"Fuck!" he screamed at the top of his lungs, sure that Jimmy had used up too much of his strength crying to exit his room and investigate the particular nature of Justin's outburst.

He went into the closet and took out Jimmy's baseball bat. He took his gun from the pile of clothes where he had thrown his uniform and tucked it in the back of pants. He grabbed his keys and left the apartment, slamming the door behind him.

• • •

"Who the fuck is it?" screamed Lashaun's mother through the closed door.

Justin kicked the door in and her with it. She collapsed to the carpet.

He gripped his baseball bat, looking primed to swing it should even a word be not to his liking.

"Where is your son?"

Footsteps thundered down the stairs. A large man wearing only boxers emerged from the stairway. He was holding a knife.

"I suggest you get the fuck out of the house."

Justin turned towards the man. He swung his bat as hard as he could at the man's hand, knocking the knife from his grip. He swung it again at the man's side, knocking him to the ground. The man screamed in pain, clutching his ribs.

"Is this your boyfriend?" Justin asked Lashaun's mother. She didn't answer. "I'm going to ask you again where your son is. And every time you don't answer, I'm going to hit your boyfriend. I'll start at the bottom and work my way up. Now, where is your son?"

"Fuck if I know. He just left."

"Not good enough." He swung his bat at the man's calves.

"Please mister, she don't know," the man said through the pain.

"I don't fucking know!" she screamed. "Ask Jameel! I bet he knows."

"Who's Jameel?" asked Justin.

"Boy's friend. He spends every fucking minute with him. Gonna get himself killed if you ask me and I don't give a shit. Let him fucking die."

Justin's fury grew. He almost swung his bat directly at the woman's head but he held off.

"Where's Jameel?"

"He lives a few houses over but you ain't gonna find him home any more than you find my son home. He's probably at Douglas Park hanging with all his fucking low life criminal friends. The boy doesn't listen to me! The boy doesn't listen to nobody! Now would you get the fuck out of my house!"

• • •

Justin walked through the empty streets, holding the baseball bat by his side.

He made his way to Douglas Park. He marched in past the junkies asleep on the benches.

He made his way to a circle of thirteen year old drug peddlers, standing together, riffing about who they were going to "fuck up." He walked right through the social circle's outer edges, silencing the conversation. He turned, looking each one of the defiantly confused children in the eyes.

"Where's Jameel?" he said, not so much asking as demanding.

"I'm Jameel," responded one of the boys. "What's it to you?"

"I'm looking for Lashaun."

"Lashaun? What do you want with Lashaun?"

"I want to know where he is. And I want to know that he's okay."

They laughed. All except Jameel. Something in Justin's expression told him that the man who questioned him would not be holding a weapon unless he intended to use it.

"He's with Drew. Drew watches over the new kids. They don't

get their own spot yet."

"Jameel, what the fuck you telling him for?" shouted one of the other kids.

"This motherfucker wants to deal with Drew, let him deal with Drew," said Jameel.

"Where can I find Drew?" asked Justin.

He found Drew at 12th and Thornton. He was impossible to miss. He wore an extra large hoodie that was still too small for his massive exterior. The hood only covered the back end of his head. He was the atypical overweight man who looked like he kept on his weight just for the fun of it. But that his extra pounds would not hinder him the least in a confrontation. Rather, they would only act as an added weapon he didn't have to bother holding in his hands, easily accessible for the occasional necessary smothering.

Barely visible behind him was the petite frame of Lashaun.

Lashaun was being trained to be a drug dealer. And the confirming evidence broke Justin's heart. It almost hurt him more than it would have had he found what he originally suspected. That something had happened to the boy. That he would find him dead in some alley, a victim of the violent world he was raised in. But instead of being a victim the boy was becoming a perpetrator. Just another nameless soul sucked in to a world of greed and death. His interactions with Lashaun had been minimal. But he had hoped that maybe the boy was the one person in whose life he could make a difference. That he could help nudge him along a proper path. He had failed.

He gripped his baseball bat tight.

He felt so much anger. Towards Lashaun for giving in so easily to becoming part of the criminal world. Towards society for existing such that lives of children like Lashaun were routinely wasted.

And towards Sarah. For leaving. And for the fact that he would never get to love her the way he wanted to.

He thought about Adam. Maybe his late brother did have the right idea after all. Care about nothing and no one and rather than fight a world built on destruction, become in sync with the destruction.

He walked up to Drew and Lashaun.

"What can I do you for?" said Drew, spotting what he imagined was a potential customer.

Justin drew his gun.

"Lashaun, you're coming with me," he said.

"Who the fuck are you?" said Lashaun.

"Stay back boy," said Drew, completely calm, not in the least bit phased by the firearm pointed at his face. "Do you have any idea who it is you're fucking with?"

"It doesn't matter."

"It's not too late. Put the gun away and turn around. And if I never see your face again no harm will come to you."

"The kid's coming with me."

"Fuck you," spouted a heated Lashaun. "Let me pop a cap in this motherfucker."

"You've been watching too many movies boy," said Drew, staring down Justin, completely calm. "Do you see how nonchalant I am right now?"

"Nonchalant?"

Justin was suddenly overcome with the odd feeling of displacement. Like he had called a wrong number and mistaken the person on the other line for the person he was trying to reach for a full conversation.

"Yeah, nonchalant," said Drew. "It means to have an air of

unconcern."

"I know what it means."

"Funny thing about the word nonchalant. You never hear about anyone being chalant, right? I don't even think that's a word. But how can you be nonchalant if you can't be chalant?"

It was absurd. Here Justin stood, on the brink of a complete mental collapse, preparing himself for the possibility of murdering someone in cold blood in order to win back a child who he was honestly not sure whether he would rather hug or beat, and the vicious drug dealer who stood in his path was discussing linguistics.

Somewhere in his lungs a laugh was born. It expanded, ricocheted up his throat, and jutted out of his mouth like a deranged hiccough. He heard the laugh as the others did, as if someone else had produced it. But he knew it had come from his own body.

There was a long silence. The three looked at each other, all unsure of how to resume the proceedings after the interrupting guffaw.

"Well," said Justin finally, "I suppose it was either that or start crying."

And with that Justin lowered his gun and walked away.

• • •

Justin inserted his key and opened the door, surprised to find the light on.

Jimmy was awake. He was sitting on the couch. Sarah was with him.

The two were holding each other. Their eyes were dry but their faces were both stained with the tears they had clearly been crying shortly before.

They turned to look at Justin.

Jimmy smiled, kindly offering the reassurance of his own renewed contentment that he imagined his friend desired to see.

Sarah's expression was harder to read. It was not quite happy. It was not quite sad. It was not quite apologetic. It was not quite resolved.

And yet somehow her indiscernible look told Justin everything he needed to know.

He took a moment to take in the sight of his friends, then turned around and closed the door behind him.

BOOK III

THE FIGHTER

I.

In the rarest of moments, Jake Porter would find himself all alone, in a position to inflict injury upon himself, a chance to test the resolve of his apparent condition. He prepared stories of running from a rabid dog, tripping and falling off a ledge while trying to retrieve a fifty dollar bill serendipitously hanging off a rain gutter, and being hit head on by a drunk driver of a small vehicle, to explain his future broken ankle, dislocated shoulder, and head contusion. He always failed to go through with it. Either in order to avoid the triviality of procedures the doctors would dictate as required for a malady he could not even feel, or in intelligent anticipation of the incarceration steps his mother might take to guard him should he suffer even an unnoticed paper cut.

Each day in school he watched, jealous, as some victim of an athletic mishap wandered in wearing a cast of mild constriction. He witnessed these sufferers of brief ailments attract large circles of supposedly worried onlookers, delighting in the chance to comfort the supposed invalid and mark the temporary addition to the person's body with their namesake. The signers felt boosted for showing such concern. The victims rejoiced in the fortuitousness of suffering such an attention grabbing injury. Jake cursed the contradiction of his own condition. He was unable to feel pain and therefore not allowed to engage in any potentially harmful physical activity. He understood the reasoning well. Were he to suffer major damage to his body, particularly of the internal variety, he would likely never know it, lacking the natural alert system. And simple damage that could have easily been amended could turn destructive or even fatal. Yet he also felt there was an inherent benefit in not feeling pain that he was never allowed to take advantage of. While others suffered he could feel physically peaceful. The reality of his body's damage seemed very unimportant in the face of such a perceptual advantage.

Jake was a marked man. His mother, Melanie, was a constant bag of nerves. In situations of even the smallest possibility of danger to her son, her body convulsively shook, starting with the finger tips, extended out as if she was halting traffic or about to sing "Stop In the Name of Love," and then moving rapidly through her arms and into her slinky-like torso. What was odd to Jake was that she had the same physiological response when he was in the path of a furiously peddling biker as when he started daydreaming at the dinner table. At moments when he was smiling and laughing, or even frowning or yelling, she remained calm and still. But the instant an expression disappeared from his face, she behaved as if he had been possessed by the devil. She refused to explain her reactions to Jake. She would only respond that she loved him. She loved him so much that she insisted each one of the schools he attended send out a letter at the beginning of each year, warning all the other students of his presence and the ailment he was diagnosed with. The intention was his protection. Physically, this was a great success. Even the worst of the school's bullies would not dare breach this contract, perhaps more because they saw it as pointless to harm the innards of someone who could not feel the pain they were inflicting than because they were scared of the legal repercussions. And certainly not because they had any moral reservations in doing so. But as far as verbal abuse went, the letters were a red cloth, just taunting the bulls of school yard not to plow their sharp horned words right through his chest.

Once a week, as Jake sat on the sidelines in gym class, barred from participation during even the bowling unit, he was met with a tirade of "wussy" chants in the locker room. In his older years "wussy" turned to "pussy," but the abuse remained the same. Any time he spoke to a girl, he was stared at with exaggerated pity eyes from a group of hyena males hovering at the back of class or peeking their eyes out of the air slits in the lockers, seemingly included in the design just for the preparation of a nerd's encasing, but also used for concealment when bullies took extreme measures to torment another or avoid going to class. And God forbid he ever trip in the hallway. For he would be met with such a barrage of mock concern and over analysis of his medical features that he would be unable to make it on time to his next period.

He had become a specimen. Nothing more than a human petri dish, laughed at for his strangeness, barred permanently outside the boundaries of normalcy. He hated it. He watched the others, sharing the delight of making youth a living hell for those around them and desperately wished he could be a part of them. He knew he should really want only to be better than the scum that they were, but he didn't. He wanted to be one of them. He felt so terribly alone in those school halls. He did know some fellow students who could only be called his friends but they barely entered his thoughts. He was focused on those who had somehow obtained a position of superiority over him in the social fabric. Who ridiculed him and made him have to deal with the intolerable pain of insecurity. It was an obsession. He often felt disconnected from himself. He felt so deeply that if he only did not suffer from his condition he would have been popular and beloved and the leader of a pack of fellow teens instead of a sideshow act, left in the dust.

He blamed his mother. And there were times when he found himself loving her less. He was overcome with shame when this happened. He tried to counter it with positive thoughts about her but he was incapable of forcing them. And so whenever his mind went down such a path, he turned to an old method that he recalled using in the distant memories of his long gone father's abuse. He thought of nothing. And felt whole again.

Jake had a crush on Gladys Schowenholtz. A girl who was easily excused for her arcane name because of the extremity of her good looks. Lots of people fell for Gladys Schowenholtz. That didn't stop Jake from joining them. In fact, it was likely why he did. It was hard to ignore his longing to beat others at their own game. But she also fit perfectly into the mold of Jake's desires. Gladys was not overly kind. Lots of girls were. Some of equal attractiveness to Gladys. They would watch the swinging doors as Jake passed through them, ensuring the door knobs didn't puncture his fragile skin. Would defend him against his persecutors, unintentionally fanning the flame towards greater taunting as they hilariously insisted his condition was "really serious." He had no use for anyone who acknowledged his condition any more than they would have a spec of dust on his shirt sleeves, under the assumption that movement would brush it off soon enough. He did not wish to be comforted about his ailment. He wanted to be ignored about it. Gladys never gave any indication she was aware of him having a weakness. She picked him to help him carry a heavy box of books a teacher had asked her to move to the third floor. She could have just as well kissed him on the lips.

Jake longed for Gladys. He constantly imagined walking hand in hand with her in the hallway, sneering at his tormenters, besting them in the game of winning over she who was such a persistently valued prize. He went to sleep thinking about her face and woke up thinking about her body. He saw her image in every girl he passed, hoping he had somehow come across her in a shopping mall, or a supermarket, or whatever out of school location he might find himself in. He even thought he saw her name in his alphabet soup, then questioned his mother as to why they were eating alphabet soup for dinner when other families were having real meals. She didn't take kindly to the comment. They got into a fight but Jake was only half paying attention as he was still busy thinking about Gladys.

And for her part Gladys was not discouraging his pursuit. Each time she caught Jake staring at her across the room, she smiled back, inviting further invasions of her privacy. Each time he chatted her up in the hallway she playfully leaned up against his arm. And when he finally got up the courage to ask her on a date she readily accepted, casually insinuating that it had taken him a long time, while smiling enough to eradicate any fears that she had lost interest. Jake was an attractive boy, many of Gladys's friends were surprised to realize when she instructed them to actually take notice of his features. His image had been tainted by perceived characteristics of weakness and frailty. Communal knowledge can often displace literal perception.

Jake fell in love with Gladys the moment she asked him whether his condition would make it dangerous for him to have sex. He responded that he didn't think so but was hopeful no pain would be involved even if he could feel it. He decided she was the only girl for him when they kissed after an extended dialogue about the particular ways in which each of Jake's harassers would fail at life. He wanted to be with her every moment. Sure, his biggest thrill was always parading her around in public, voraciously consuming the jealousy of others like a starving man would food. But he also came to love private moments with her in a way he had honestly never realized he would. He brought her to dinner with his mother. She was charming, polite, perfect. As he lay with her afterwards elation surged through his veins. It was paralyzing happiness.

• • •

Jake had never been more enthusiastic about life. Melanie had never been less. The dinner was a breaking point. Gladys seemed to be indeed all the things Jake had described her as. She was a sweet, attractive girl. Maybe not as smart as her son but smart enough for him. And she seemed to be genuinely fond of him. But Melanie still found herself wailing after dinner in the bathroom, water running just in case Jake and his girlfriend could hear through three floors, a hallway, and two locked doors. She had never been as close as she would have liked with her son. The thought was hard to admit to herself even though it occupied her mind throughout every second. She had devoted her whole life to him but still saw him as nothing more than a foreign being. She spent her days protecting him to ensure a negation of horror, not to enable moments of joy. And as she sat with him and a girl who was displacing her in a spot of all important prominence, she fell into despair. She felt jealous about losing the only thing she had. Her relationship with a boy that she was fond of but felt no passion for. A boy she had devoted her life to anyway. And she decided that she missed her husband. Her drunken, abusive, asshole bastard of a husband.

A week later Jake returned home with Gladys after a date at the movies in which they saw what they thought was a good comedy but was actually a bad drama. Jake sensed a particularly strong fondness in the air and thought it a prime opportunity to move to second base. He took Gladys to his room and briefly observed the obscure entrance angles of her rather modern top before turning out the lights as she herself requested. He had just figured out how to get to her bare skin with his hand (through the side, surprisingly) when he was interrupted by the unmistakable sound of smashing glass. Much to his embarrassment, Gladys jumped on top of him, a protective reaction programmed into her by the constant talk of Jake's weakness. He tossed her aside, annoyed at failing to be the protector and at being halted in feeling her up, then ran downstairs.

"Hello son."

There in the kitchen, impressively having only dropped one of the six beers he held in his arms, stood his father. A man he had not seen in a decade but who was unmistakable. More from the stench of alcohol than anything else. It was a feat that he was even still alive.

"What the fuck are you doing here?"

"I'm here with your mother. She said she wanted to try starting things up again."

Gladys entered the room. She was still adjusting her shirt back into place. The modern design made it far more difficult than it needed to be.

"Who's this?" said Howard.

"I'm Gladys," she answered for herself.

"My little boy's all grown up."

"Who is this?" Gladys questioned Jake.

"I'm the boy's father. You can thank my semen for his semen."

"Jesus Christ," said Jake.

"Anyway, we can catch up later. Go. Dry hump or something. Don't let me stop you."

"I think I should go," said Gladys.

• • •

"I've never stopped loving your father," said Melanie the next morning when Jake confronted her.

"Well what are you waiting for?"

Jake found the state of his newly reinstated family to be end-lessly annoying. While it remained true that Howard's continued alcoholism had not led to abuse ("I'm a reformed drunk," Howard would say) Jake was getting pestered by the inevitability tapping him on the shoulder. He could still sense a seething anger hiding under his father's every action, shaking when he couldn't open the applesauce jar and reciting a version of the serenity prayer Jake could not believe was accurate.

"God give me the power to know everything," Howard would say.

Jake desperately tried to convince his mother she was wan-dering down a dark path.

"It's not a dark path. It's just the path less traveled by."

Jake groaned. He had been studying "Two Roads" in English. "I don't really think that applies here."

"It always applies. Smart man that Robert Frosty," she said.

"Robert Frost. You're thinking of Frosty the snowman."

"He's got some wisdom too."

Jake tried very hard to maintain respect for his mother. Con-versations such as this made it difficult.

Faced with unhappiness at home, Jake put all his energy into his relationship with Gladys. But something seemed off about her after that interaction with Jake's father. At first Gladys seemed distant. Then she seemed bored. Jake upped his romantic efforts, kissing her seductively, praising her at every available opportu-nity, but these actions only seemed to make her want to spend less time with him. There was no mistaking that whatever spark had been lit within her had seemed to go out just as quickly as it had been ignited. But Jake mistook it anyway. He had to, for the sake of his sanity.

• • •

Jake spotted Gladys making out with Ryan Friedkin under the bleachers while he was sitting out a kickball game in gym class. As with most activities of any interest, he had been forced to stay on the sidelines because experts feared for his physical well being. He was already lost in a meditation of frustration from the events of the day. In the morning his father had criticized his lack of breakfast. He found the lecture rather hypocritical coming from someone who broke the fast with an English muffin and a Corona. And he told him so.

"I'd smack you in the face if you could feel it," said Howard.

Jake was the bigger man. He walked away. He walked right on past the bus stop and on the road to school by foot. He thought some exertion of energy might erase his anger. It did. But as soon as his temper cooled it was replaced with a gnawing hopelessness. He had managed to walk away this morning. To be the bigger man. But how often would he be able to garner this resolve? Sooner or later he would lash back. And this would help nothing, because Howard was apparently sticking around, and the more tension he responded to the more tension he could look forward to being faced with. He tried to calm himself with the assurance that soon enough he would be off to college but at the moment the notion of being cast into such a lonely fresh start was hardly a comfort.

He arrived late to school. As it turned out, a ten minute bus ride could be quite a long walk. He was lectured at the door by the school security guard who had no authority to punish him and lectured further by his homeroom teacher who did. He was given detention after school. He had to endure a whole day of nonsensical bullying about whether his body would be able to withstand the trauma of sitting in a chair for an extra hour after school. He arrived in gym class desperate to take out his frustration through the release of endorphins while kicking or throwing one kind of ball or another. He was told he had to sit out and his energy was given no release.

He had but one peaceful place his mind could go to. Thoughts of Gladys. And he was able to nap in the warm cove of love musings for only a moment, because it was then he spotted Gladys under the bench with a boy whose facial hair could not be seen from any farther than nine inches away. He realized he should not have been surprised. Her behavior had been a clear indication of drifting even though he had intentionally been in denial about it. And she did have the reputation of a girl who jumped fairly quickly from guy to guy, a fact he had ignored from the beginning. But seeing her with another still hurt. Even if he had been able to feel physical pain, this hurt more than any blow to his body ever could have.

If there was a chance to sit still upon spotting Gladys and Ryan he wasn't aware of it. He was marching over to the bleachers before he made the decision to do so. He was leaping onto a boy twice his size before he had made the effort to jump, and he was wailing away punches before he got the chance to hear his mother's ever present voice screaming in his ear about the dangers of engaging in such a violent physical activity.

Gladys seemed more excited than upset as she watched the somewhat one sided battle for her love. Jake, in his first fight, threw unplanned punches that were repeatedly blocked and were countered by shots to his stomach, chest, and head, that theoretically should have knocked him out regardless of the fact that he could not feel them. But Jake remained tall, his perception, or lack of it, a decided advantage. He had no way of knowing when to go down. All he knew was he was still standing and still angry. And he would not stop throwing punches until the pain stopped or the pain began.

• • •

Jake was suspended from school for a week. His family was required to pay for Ryan Friedkin's dental bill. Jake had knocked his tooth out, plunging the hardest part of his forehead into Ryan's offensive mouth, which had been tasting his girlfriend's saliva. Jake felt new appreciation for his condition and the three days spent in the close supervision of doctors, ensuring he had not progressed past some point of no return did nothing to change that. He was without fear. Ryan Friedkin's tooth could have been lodged in his head and he would not have known the difference.

After a period of disconnected concern in which Melanie focused on nothing but ensuring Jake's health, she took some personal time to be angry. Furious that the one thing she had worked towards for the past eleven years, her sole purpose in life, the protection of her son against his obscure medical condition, had been violated. Not by some outside perpetrator. But by her son himself, who had flagrantly ignored the extensive database of warning knowledge beaten into his head.

Howard demanded that she reprimand him.

"By what? Yelling? Beating? What the hell am I supposed to do Howard? None of it's going to do any good. It's just going to encourage him to injure himself more!"

Jake's action was a broken contract. She had given him care and support and occasional motherly affection in exchange for the promise that she would never again have to witness the freak-show of his abnormality. When he had come from school, bloody and bruised, the calm of his physical demeanor nearly put her into apoplectic shock.

"The fucking boy needs to learn his fucking lesson."

"No!"

Melanie screamed and dragged on her foul former and current husband as he made his way up the stairway. She did not even fully understand her actions. Never had confusion been so pervading. Her mixed feelings about her son. The societal dictation about how she should feel versus her own established conception versus how she was actually reacting versus the complete instinctual protection she was now showing. And the nagging question of whether she was doing what she was more for herself or more for her son left her almost mentally catatonic, performing actions while hardly thinking about them.

Howard also had no need for thinking. He was a carnivore who had sniffed out his prey and once thrusted on the path of destruction could not even feel the creature, known as his wife, gripped to his side.

Jake was reliving his fight, delivering an intense beat down to his back up pillow, when Howard burst in the room.

He did not run from the beast. He had nothing to fear. He stood, smiling, spitefully ready to receive the blow when he became fully aware of the state of his mother. The sight of her tears. Her pleas that Howard not hurt him. It got to him. He didn't wish to hurt her. He prepared to step aside but before he could Melanie jumped in front of him.

"I won't let you hurt my boy."

"Fine."

For a moment getting beaten up by her husband was nostalgic. Then the pain set in.

Jake tried desperately to intervene, but Melanie, in a display of unknown strength, held him off, even while taking a tremendous beating.

• • •

The déjà vu finally ended when the police arrived and took Howard away. Jake figured his arrest was about thirteen or fourteen years too late. The damage had been done, had been imprinted, had undergone withdrawl, had a major relapse, and finally had a near fatal overdose. Jake watched his mother quiver into a protective shell. He imagined it would be a permanent hibernation. And he felt such an overwhelming swelling of sorrow for her that he thought he would collapse. He felt for her. He also needed her. He fed on her protection. Just as he fed on his desire to be included at school as a member of the cult of normal human injury and remedy. He was tired of this dependency. He was sickened by the fear he was facing now that his mother resided in an emotional coma.

That night Jake sat alone in his room. And alone in his house. His mother was in the hospital, having her injuries checked out. Surely, she was shaking, silent, her voice in the middle of a losing debate with her mind as to whether it should ever speak again.

He thought about Gladys. The thrill of pounding Ryan Friedkin had settled and the boost of fearlessness that it provided. He remembered the bliss he had felt during those brief moments he had been granted with her, lying on the couch, looked at with such affection. And the loss hit him in the pit of the stomach. He could hardly imagine finding such happiness again. His life had been a succession of unpleasantness and the thought that having gotten to experience joy only exacerbated the pain, because now he had the added stress of having to recall all that he had lost, was almost more than he could stand for.

"Fuck you," he thought, directed at no one in particular. He was angry. Angry that everyone else around him seemed to have it so good. His fellow students at school lived the lives they wanted. They had normal families and loving parents and the admiration of friends. At the moment he was in no mood to acknowledge the probable truth of complication in the lives of others. They at least had control over their own lives. They didn't have their entire story written in advance because of a goddamned obscure condition. They all have it better, he thought.

"Fuck you," he thought directed at Gladys. She had caused him such pain. She just did what she wanted, without a care in the world, and never experienced the revolting vulnerability he was suffering from. He hated having no power over his emotions. He hated the way a jolt of anguish could take over him and there was absolutely nothing he could do about it. He was not in command of himself and it was infuriating.

He thought of how easy it was not to feel physical pain. He had never known it. Had no concept of what it was like. If only he registered emotional pain with the same emptiness.

He felt a small glimmer of hope. Was it possible? Could he get rid of that which ailed him?

Jake turned on one small light, just to keep from falling asleep, closed his eyes and contemplated the erasure of feeling. He allowed disturbing images to pop into his head at a steady pace, and struggled to prevent the fear or hate or suffering that generally came linked to each successive thought. It was difficult. And with each failed battle against such an ingrained biological response the struggle became greater. As if his mind was becoming angry with him for his attempts to deconstruct it.

He had too much experience with mental anguish. He didn't

need to stop it as it arrived. He needed to unlearn the very process of it.

He continued his attempts the next day in school. He was noticed by his English professor, Mr. Thurber. A young man with an excellent beard and an encouraging outlook on life, which he tried to spread to his students. Mr. Thurber called him to his desk after class.

"Is something wrong?" Jake inquired.

"Well. You spent my entire class either daydreaming or meditating. And either way you weren't paying attention to my lesson."

"That's not true."

"What was I talking about then?"

"I'm going to go with language and symbolism."

"Good answer. You're smart. Smart enough that you should really be paying attention."

"I'm sorry."

"Listen. I've heard you've had some troubles at home recently and I just wanted to say that if you need someone to talk to, I'm always here."

"Thanks Mr. Thurber. I'll be alright though. I'm just going to stop feeling pain. That's what I was working on in class today."

"I beg your pardon?"

"Yeah. The way I see it there's so much out there that's upsetting or disturbing and it's just starting to waste my energy to feel bad all the time. I don't really see the point. But I guess it's not that easy to just not be affected. Anyway, I'm working on it."

Mr. Thurber paused for a moment. Jake could see his teacher's wheels turning.

"Jake, do you have some time after school today?"

"Yeah, I think so."

"Why don't you stop by? I'd like to talk to you a little more about this."

When Jake returned later that day he found Mr. Thurber's room reorganized. The desks had been cleared into an open circle. The circle contained piles of books and a throw rug that looked uncomfortably thin, but felt like sitting on pillows. Jake discovered its surprising texture after he was beckoned to sit down by Mr. Thurber who was already on it, his legs folded in an impossible contortion.

"Mr. Thurber, what is all this?"

"It's not often that you come across a high school student with such lofty spiritual ambitions. Most are concerned only about the sensual pleasures of this or that night or how to acquire enough money to buy the latest innovation or why the remote is on top of the television when they're already lying down on the couch. I know. I was one such student."

"You forgot the remote?"

"No. I thought there was a remote. To life. And I could just press play or stop or fast forward or get or need and that would answer all my problems. But there's no remote control to life. It has to be viewed differently."

"Mr. Thurber, I have absolutely no idea what you're talking about."

"Suffering. I'm talking about suffering. You don't want to suffer anymore."

"Yeah, that's right."

"Right, and neither do I. And there's a way to get past it. I can't say I've mastered it. But it's the best that I or anyone else has come up with throughout modern civilization. Jake. I want you to meet Siddhartha Gautama. Also known as the Buddha."

Mr. Thurber handed Jake a book titled "The Four Noble Truths."

"I want you to read this," he continued. "It's short. And I want you to come back tomorrow and talk about what it means to you."

That night Jake opened the book. This is what he found.

Truth number one. Life means suffering. Jake was surprised by the perceived pessimism. He had always been under the impression that the far eastern religions thought everything was peace and love and spent their days sitting on flowers beds telling everyone so in poetic words that did not actually make any sense.

"The flower is the eye of the mind of the soul." These are the sorts of things he expected to be reading. Instead what he found was, "Life is filled with inevitable suffering, both physical and mental." Followed by a page long description of the various sicknesses, maladies, traumas, depressions, and frustrations the average person will face over the course of his life. "Real encouraging stuff Mr. Thurber", thought Jake facetiously. "But honest." He read on.

Truth number two. The origin of suffering is attachment. Everything in life is subject to impermanence. All the people and things and ideas and states of health we strive for will unavoidably pass away or change and when we attempt to cling to what we will lose we suffer. This includes clinging to a conception of ourselves. An identity. A self that is just as much an illusion as any other impermanent concept.

Jake took a moment to think about this. It made sense to him. Any time he had suffered it was because he desired *something* or because some state he had been in had disappeared and he could not return to it. He read on.

Truth number three. The cessation of suffering is attainable. Let go of attachment. Let go of passion. Let go of desire. Accept impermanence. And in removing the causes of suffering you will remove suffering.

It was so simple. If he was not attached to anything or anyone he would not feel any pain if anything happened to it or him or her. If he did not allow himself to be concerned of some sense of his own identity or how he was viewed by others or how others viewed him he would have nothing to suffer about. He envisioned himself in a world populated by no one. Wandering abandoned streets and quiet forests. He felt peaceful.

The fourth truth dictated a complicated eightfold path of action, speech, mindfulness, and various other steps of enlightenment. He just briefly skimmed through these stages that were supposed to lead to the lack of attachment referred to in step two. He found this fourth truth unnecessary and didn't bother reading its full description. As far as he was concerned he had found his answer. And he was ready to start living it.

Jake returned the next day to Mr. Thurber's circle of pillows.

"This makes sense," he said.

"I'm glad you found it helpful," responded his teacher.

"People just end up hurting you. It's just stupid to hold onto attachments. If you think you need someone else or something else to make you okay, you can never be okay, because you'll always be waiting for something that never comes or never stays."

"To an extent, yes."

"This is the answer. I just need to be like this. I just need to be one of these people who doesn't need anything. Especially not people. I don't need people and I don't need to care what people think."

"Uh...yes. Although I wouldn't say that it's encouraging complete isolation."

"Well yeah, I mean I'm not going to go live in a cave or anything. I feel like that would just be running from the fear of suffering anyway. No, if I'm going to do this right I'm going to need to be around people so I can look them in the eye and know that I don't care about them. That they can't hurt me. Because I don't need them."

Jake noticed a look of concern appear on his instructor's face.

"What is it?" he asked.

"I just think you need to be careful."

"About what?"

"Don't get me wrong. I'm glad that these ideas have really spoken to you so quickly. And in some ways they are very simple. But in other ways they can take a lifetime to understand. My suggestion to you would be to just keep the following in mind. That there is a gigantic difference between seeing yourself as one who is unattached, making that your identity, and actually being unattached."

"I see what you mean. But anyway thanks so much Mr. Thurber. This is the answer I was looking for. And I plan to live by it."

• • •

Jake went away to school. Far away. To a state no one he knew had ever been to, in a town that no one he knew had ever heard of. He left everyone and everything he knew behind. He left his things at home. His books, his video games, his DVDs. He brought only as many clothes as he needed. Only material items that might be necessities, ready to cast them aside should they prove unnecessary. He took all pieces of memorabilia from his childhood, school projects, drawings from his toddler days, photographs of himself with family and supposed friends, and put them in a big trash bag which he promptly disposed of. He said goodbye to his mother, gave her no contact information and left with a clear mind. He got a job in a department store in the town his campus resided in, in order to help pay for his tuition and the loans he had personally gone to his new bank and applied for.

Whether it was the new people, or the new circumstances, or his new attitude towards existence, people now seemed to find him very appealing to be around. He was invited to parties where he conversed with anyone he actually cared to listen to and stayed away from the needless consumption of alcoholic beverages and excessive amounts of chips from improperly opened bags. He left the parties when he found them too loud, stayed when he found the company satisfying. Though many people now wanted to be his friend he felt no need to align himself with any particular individuals or group. He did not understand the difference between a good or bad or fun or unpleasant evening or day. He went to sleep with same impression of the day that had come before him, regardless of how its content had turned out. That it was gone.

The new people he met certainly found his condition unusual but they met the abnormality with fascination rather than ridicule. The few who did react with fright or who indicated some sense of superiority because they had not been born with such a flaw, were barely a penny dropped in the thought well of his brain. A slight ripple passed through only on the basis that he couldn't help to perceive them. But whether he was interacting with a professor praising his sentence construction or an attractive female student turning up her flirting dial or an academic competitor smirking as Jake was derided in a lecture for asking a stupid question or being an individual of general sadism who wished nothing but harm to everyone he passed, all he perceived was an outside entity.

• • •

Even with the sixteen plus hours he spent working each weekend at the department store Jake was running out of money. The cost of tuition and school books and food was momentarily to pass the level of funds that were coming in. He had already cut out any expense which was not a necessity. Not because of financial constraints but because of the philosophy of life he had acquired. Nevertheless the fact remained. Jake needed more money.

A spontaneous walk along Main Street to take in the air and clear his muddled mind proved fortuitous to this dilemma. Outside of a record store belonging to another era, on a telephone pole plastered with various notices of guitar lessons, and garage sales, and reasons not to vote for certain candidates for state representative, was a call for amateur boxers to try out for time in the ring. Jake had not been in a fight since his tooth rearranging session with Ryan Friedkin, but his skin remembered the tingling sensation that engaging in combat gave him. His heart raced with the remembrance of thrusting himself into a high octane situation and feeling no fear. He could fight. And he could win.

The gym was owned by a man named Creed Hulcon, who looked as much like a special operative from an action film as his name made him sound, but whose demeanor was more that of a cartoon bunny concerned that he had displaced his carrots. He held his tryouts with a steady conviction of warning, fearing for each contestant's well being while thrusting any unqualified auditioner who ignored his words of caution into a thorough pummeling at the hands of someone with arms made of steel.

Jake waited his turn, not out of shape but a bit girth deficient compared to some of the man beasts entering the ring. Not that Jake was engaging in the game of compare and contrast. He knew his chances at failure just as well as his chances for success. Whatever the result, he would walk out of that gym at the end of the day, the gears of his life still turning.

Finally, he was called into the ring to face a man named Henry Buckner. He was not the largest of that day's boxers, but he may have been the most rowdy. He was performing a half dance of anticipation, each of his toes likely wiggling inside of his boots. Jake was the picture of calm. Creed Hulcon began the obligatory warning he gave to those who might suffer bodily harm. From a distance Jake looked like a peaceful worm about to be fed to an anxious eel. He stopped halfway through. Jake was staring right back at him. He was definitively listening. And yet he was masterfully, almost frighteningly calm and disconnected. Hulcon realized his hands were shaking. He considered turning around and giving his trademark warning to Henry Buckner instead but in the end just fled the ring, feeling like he had just been speaking to someone he had only known in a dream, whose personality had to be dictated by his own thoughts in order to be a complete individual. He signaled for the fight to begin.

True to his appearance Henry Buckner began the fight like a caged tiger released upon a juicy steak left conveniently on a plate just outside his holding cell. He wailed away without much direction. He likely missed contact on nine out of ten of punches, but his arms moved so rapidly that it was impossible for Jake to issue a blow of his own. Jake seemed less than bothered. He made a few half hearted attempts at blocking but mostly just stood there, receiving the punches Buckner did manage to land, completely unaffected by their rather forceful impact and waiting patiently as his opponent tired himself out. Creed Hulcon and the rest of the observers watched the fight with open mouths, vaguely fearful for reasons they did not completely understand. There was just something incredibly off putting about the whole display. Perhaps they realized that if the steak was left out for the tiger to pounce on, some creature of much greater capacity had left it there, and would without doubt complete some plan he was working towards.

The fight continued on round after round. Jake's face was bloody and battered but no one bothered to stop the fight because there was no indication he was the least bit concerned by any of it. He just stood calm, blocking more and more as time went on and Buckner's rapid fire punches slowed down. He waited for the right moment. Finally in the sixth round, it happened. Buckner threw a wide circular punch that Jake easily ducked under. The effort took his breath away. And for period of about five seconds he stood with his hands at his side as he tried to regain some semblance of breath, not even able to cover his face on the chance that Jake might respond. Everyone in the crowd saw it coming. A rock solid bullet train of a punch. Jake hit Buckner with a direct shot to the forehead and knocked him out with a single saved up blow.

Creed Hulcon and his fellow observers watched silently. What they had just witnessed was not a boxing match. It was the slow destruction of a man's spirit.

II.

There was a time when there were few activities Jake looked forward to more than dreaming. As a child, every night, as his body grew more tired from the grind of the day, a subtle anticipation grew within him, his physical being weakened but his mental state became ever more clear and thrilled at what was imminent. The thing that he loved so much about those mysterious nighttime moments when your mind took over, placing you in some bizarre twist on reality, tweaking real life, displacing one person for another to no apparent notice, and fully convincing your consciousness of their veracity, was that it was the only time you could ever really live a life that wasn't yours. In waking moments you could daydream and fantasize, but there was always the annoying recognition of actuality hiding behind each wish that your life was a little bit different. But in dreams, you did live a different life, if only briefly. It may have been a life strangely similar to your own, and it may be that it didn't make any sense on further analysis, and it may have sometimes been entirely unpleasant, but it was at least different. For a brief period of time Jake could escape from the existence he had come to know.

All of that seemed like a long time ago now. For lately, Jake was finding dreams to be nothing more than an intolerable nuisance. During his waking hours he managed to keep his feet grounded solidly in the present and his mind soundly separated from the grips of yearning and desire. He was in control. But when he went to sleep, Jake was completely powerless to stop the intense emotions bombarding his dream imagery. He would dream of falling in love and longing desperately. He would dream of his old high school tormentors, unable to escape the breadth of their torture. And he would dream of complete isolation, stranded in a desert or an open plain, desperately searching for what seemed like an eternity for some sort of companionship he was never able to find. He would wake up sweating, agitated, and would have to spend a good part of the morning erasing the residue of uncomfortable feeling the dream left in him, impatient to return to a place of peace.

Sometimes though, the effect of the dream would linger, and it would come to affect Jake's thoughts. He started to feel that he might be bored. That the powerful relief he had found in separating himself from any attachment had somehow lessened. He started to imagine running into people he used to know, deeply satisfied by the idea of being able to tell them how successfully unattached he had become. He became irritated by the fact no one knew the tremendous extent of his accomplishment in taking control of his own being. Other times, after a powerful dream, he would see a couple strolling down the streets hand in hand or a young family with their freshly born children and feel a strange pang. He could not quite identify it as desire to be in their position, perhaps because he simply refused to, but he felt spiteful of those he saw anyway. At some point, in the aftermath of any dream, he managed to regain his composure, reestablish his control, and at no point was he set back so far as to feel pain. But then sometimes something even more frustrating would happen. He would miss the dream. He would mourn the loss of the frustration he felt throughout the morning. And that was the most frustrating of all.

As a likely result of it all, certain questions about the future now repeatedly appeared in Jake's mind. The question of career, as far as he was concerned, could be left to the side. He would be a fighter for as long as his body held out. The position he was forging himself in the amateur leagues was lucrative enough to keep him alive and he thought of the physical action of the fight as a peaceful experience. Not knowing the damage being dealt, the connection forged with another human being on the simplest physical level seemed right out of nature. The question of how to treat his personal life did not dissipate as easily. He contemplated the issue one match as an opponent with an angry dragon tattoo on his face became exasperated with the failed results of his punches. Angry dragon man punched him in the ear. He considered life alone. The idea was not distasteful. Just blank. Angry dragon man punched him in the stomach. He thought that similar to throwing himself into physical bouts to emphasize the lack of physical pain that made him who he was, perhaps throwing himself into precarious social situations would test his resolve at limiting emotional and mental pain. It was easy to just avoid anything that might cause suffering. It was quite another step to leap into the fire and stay cool. Angry dragon man put everything he had into a jab at Jake's unblocked shoulder. His arms dropped to his side from exhaustion and Jake lashed out with a vicious uppercut. There was no reason he ought to bar himself completely from dating and relationships, he thought. As long as he remained at his most basic level, unattached. He had to promise himself though that he would keep looking out through the same eyes regardless of who he found and whether or not anyone was romantically present in his life at any particular moment.

So Jake opened up the door to the dating world and found a waiting room of females, most complaining that it was taking so long for them to be let back. Since his entire goal was to keep his emotions locked in place it mattered little to him who it was he asked to share a meal. He had no particular thing he was looking for and thus didn't spend a whole lot of time looking. He asked out whoever passed in front of him. He was in shape from his years of boxing and attractive enough that his calm audacity reeled in a bulk of dates. He went on one date, two dates, dated for a month. He held true to forming no attachments and sometimes didn't even realize when he had stopped seeing someone. He never cut off the dating. It mattered little to him that he did not develop any feelings. In fact, the occurrence of feelings would have made him run. Each time a woman failed to return his call or told him that she was feeling no connection he was not in the least bit hurt. He shrugged his brain's metaphorical shoulders and moved on.

One of his companions, a woman named Nick ("Short for Nicole?" he asked. "No," she replied), kept the awkward unconnected, unemotional dating going for six months. A weekly or bi-weekly meal followed by time spent at one or the other's apartment quietly watching TV, followed eventually by routine sex that satisfied nobody. Instead of ending the proceedings like the rest of Jake's women, she seemed to revel in the stability. Jake occasionally speculated that some horror must have befallen in her past. He never bothered to ask what it was. He never even learned her parent's names. Or whether they were still alive. After a period of time he noticed that she had started to shake. And become angry with him over slight non-actions like an incorrect movement of his fork. Her annoyance evolved and she became a yeller. Yelling at him for reasons he didn't bother to pay any attention to. He was hardly fazed by it. Finally, she put an end to things in an explosion of insults and screaming. She slammed his door and broke a hat rack that had been hanging on it. He didn't mind. He never wore any hats.

Throughout it all, Jake remained unattached, just as he promised himself he would. The physical contact he shared with the women gave his body the most base form of pleasure but he corked up his nerve system so that the sensation never spread upwards to his mind. He found that his dreams bothered him less. He felt more confident by sharing his time with these women who were so insecure, so incomplete, and so determined to search for something to fulfill them that they would likely never find.

Occasionally he thought of Gladys Showenholtz. Of the thunderstorm of nerves he had felt whenever she had so much as passed his sightline. The horrible tumult of heart beats and shaking fingers that was disabling and that would have been horrible in a different situation but in the context had been a source of the most ecstatic pleasure imaginable. She had been a drug. Pleasure and pain all mixed in to one but always the most intensely satisfying feeling of feeling a person could ask for. Her very presence had induced smiles and reminded him he was even there.

These days though, he made sure to think of Gladys in only the most detached way. As if he was recalling an algebra problem. Jake had trained himself not to experience memories like the common man. He recalled the images, the contexts, some background noises, but the recollection never translated to his nervous system. There was no sensation of the past. Only a distant awareness that something had occurred. He had cured nostalgia. The continued calm of his heart was reason enough to continue along the path he was on. He kept dating, no chance of any of the relationships lasting, no chance he would change himself in the slightest. At peace. And incredibly satisfied with the peace he had managed to achieve.

And then he met Lizzie.

• • •

Lizzie Nelson could often be heard proudly referring to herself as a people person. Every test she had ever taken to indicate personality or career choices had always drawn a solid arrow pointing in the direction of working with others. Of extreme extroversion. Of a compassionate helpful nature on the positive side and on the negative, a sometimes damaging need for contact and investigation into other people's personal lives. Nothing gave her a greater thrill than issuing comfort. Than peering into a friend's head and helping them through a problem. Sometimes she worried that she didn't know how to deal with the status quo. That she was only truly happy on occasions that gave her opportunity to access her skills.

Her closest friend Sandy was a perpetual fuck up. This was Sandy's term, not hers. She spent the bulk of her late teens and early twenties falling somewhat intentionally into abusive relationships and covering her bruises, mostly emotional, sometimes physical, with band aids of pill popping and excessive complaining. But every time Sandy dug herself into a ditch that was seemingly too deep to climb out of, Lizzie was right there to pull her out, clean her up, comfort her, embrace her with love both tough and soft, and be the only person in her life who could truly be counted on. Sandy used to joke that she didn't know if they had remained friends more because she always needed help or because Lizzie always needed someone to help. Lizzie would laugh but in truth she wasn't sure of the answer.

Lizzie's love life, to underestimate the issue, had been a dismal failure. Doubly frustrating when viewed in the light of her usual social success. Her need to help and give to others converted to an attraction to unhappy, unsatisfied, and often unpleasant characters who were more in need of a psychologist than a lover. She wanted to be turned on to intelligent figures waxing philosophically at college lectures. Instead she was inexorably drawn to the man stumbling out of the bar, flailing punches into the air, powered by anger towards who knows what.

She generally boiled her romantic history down to a progression of five men.

In high school there was Gregory Kischlewski, who took double duty as class clown and starting shortstop on the baseball team. Lizzie never blamed Gregory for his faults, but pointed the finger at his parents who had apparently viewed parenting as an optional add on to having a child. Gregory threw tantrums. Actual fist-banging-against-table tantrums that were ignited when he struck out in a baseball game or his restaurant order was wrong or he was told he had spelled a word incorrectly. She left him when her sexual desires became confused after feeling more like his mother than his girlfriend.

In college there was a succession of three. First Reggie Spector, who had the most attractive voice she had ever heard. Unfortunately he had almost nothing interesting to say with his golden tool but it mattered little to Lizzie who could spend hours listening to the music of his vocal tones saying any inane uninteresting facts he wished to share. That is, until the primal instinct of her ear drums gave way unto the reality of the context. And she discovered that prejudice sounds awful regardless of the particular sound that conveys it.

Next, Dan Moupoponos. A wonderful cook. A seemingly sensitive listener. A probable sufferer of bi-polar disorder who didn't believe in taking medicine. Another lost cause.

Third, was Kevin Jeanes, whose name was Jeanes and who liked to wear jeans and who liked to talk about that he wore jeans when his name was Jeanes. Kevin may have been borderline developmentally disabled, which, Lizzie was ashamed to admit later, was probably why she was drawn to him, in lieu of all the help he needed simply to function like a normal human being. Lizzie always thought Kevin was a good person but realized she had to end the relationship when she realized that kissing him embarrassed her.

Finally and most notably, up until very recently Lizzie had been with Eric Lieber, who she had met at an internship the summer after college graduation. Eric was a dick. There was simply no better way to describe him. His friends said he was a dick. His parents said he was a dick. He was unappreciative of all those who surrounded him, incredibly selfish, and unsurprisingly quite needy. And Lizzie fell head over heels for him. Every time she saw him she felt such an eruption of passion within her nervous system that she could barely keep herself still. She thought about him every moment of the day. Even with the qualities which made him fit obviously into Lizzie's normal mold of attraction, she had no way of explaining just why it was she fell so in love with someone who was so callous. It was exasperating how fiercely her emotions had a life of their own, which no rationality could penetrate. She began to watch romantic comedies and feel sympathetic to the poorly drawn female characters who always bafflingly started the films dating someone entirely unlikable until the hero came along to win them away. She now understood why they were with the villain in the first place. They simply couldn't help themselves. They had fallen in love and there was nothing they could do about it. Her passion for Eric never actually ceased. The relationship only ended because she found obnoxiously inarguable evidence that he had cheated on her multiple times. And even then she was ready to accept his half hearted apologies because her feelings were so strong, but Sandy, in a courageous role reversal, barricaded Lizzie in her apartment, hid her phone, and saved her from continuing on down a path that could only lead to misery.

• • •

When Lizzie met Jake, entering a relationship seemed about as pleasant as sticking her hand into a tub of rats. She was always fond of the term "incurable optimist." She felt it correctly implied the need for optimism to be cured. She met Jake only a few months after the end of her relationship with Eric. She was determined to remain single but for her determination was always a fragile state, that easily melted away in a moment of possibility. She was a sucker for hope even if the moment of hope was consistently more satisfying than the moment of fulfillment.

They met under extraordinarily ordinary circumstances. They were at a coffee shop. He was buying a muffin. She was buying coffee. She relied on it. He never touched the stuff. She commented that the muffin he had bought was very tasty. He said that it was impossible she could have eaten it because he was still holding it in his hand. She laughed. He asked her out because he had the inclination to. She accepted because she found him attractive and even with her current desire to be alone, could not bare to regret a missed opportunity.

They went on several initial dates. She found him to be an incredible mystery. He was an amateur boxer, he had told her. And yet the behavior of rage had no place in his personality. He was devoid of anger. He was never even peeved. Not when a driver dangerously made a left turn in front of him as he was going straight through an intersection. Not when his soup was brought out with a piece of unidentifiable filth in it. He calmly sent the soup back to be replaced. He never even mentioned the driver.

"What are your pet peeves?" she asked, on their third date.

"I've never had a pet." He smiled, to make clear he was not stupid, just not answering her question.

He was not particularly flirtatious. He smiled at her often, but it was more the smile one gives when a butterfly passes by your eyes. She made gestures of physical affection. She put her hand on his at the restaurant table. She put her arm around his as they walked down the street. He was always responsive but never made any indication he needed any of it. That life would have gone on exactly the same had she never touched him. And probably if she hadn't even been there at all.

He was clearly intelligent. He did not flaunt it very often but when asked a direct question about political or philosophical issues he would respond concisely, dictating a deep understanding of the discussion at hand, without ever truly revealing an opinion. Awareness without concern. That was how she thought of his manner. Even without the concern his choice of profession was odd. Strange that he should choose to flex his physical muscles when he could have been using his mental ones.

"Why do you want to be a boxer?"

"I don't want to be. I just am."

Sometimes it was like talking to a fortune cookie.

She had no expectation that their dates would turn into an actual relationship. Early on she figured it was only a matter of time before something brought about the end. She still thought about Eric quite a lot, but the less she was alone, the less her thoughts seemed to wander.

Jake was strikingly different from any other man she had ever gone out with. For one, he did not need. He seemed to take pride in being completely self sufficient and never asking for help. For another, he was rather quiet. He kept his feelings to himself. A stark contrast to the string of motor mouths she spent her time with before.

And yet, as time went on, she realized that she had developed feelings for him. They made little sense as he had not so far proven to be much more than a first impression. But they were there. It wasn't his personality. It wasn't his looks, though they didn't hurt matters. It was his demeanor. His aura, she thought, using a word she never thought she would have used. Here was a man, who for the sake of all appearances, seemed to be completely at peace. Not peaceful in the way of many pacifist types she had met throughout her life. Advocating love and the end of violence. He was a boxer after all. But at peace. Completely content with his existence and all that flowed from it.

Lizzie was also a bit of a contrast for Jake. Most of the women he had been spending his time with had possessed a rather abrasive demeanor. He had honestly not found it very likeable, but he had no intention of falling for the women he saw. His satisfaction, rather, came through comparison and the illumination that his own peace underwent when it was put side by side with a person filled with tumultuousness. Not only were these women not at peace, they did not want peace. Their goals involved money and marriage and other irrational notions Jake did not even bother to investigate. Lizzie was different. She was kinder. Gentler. And she actually seemed to care about him as he was, attracted to the attitude and lack of attachment he worked to maintain, rather than threatened by it. He still felt disconnected from her as he would have anyone, but he did think that she was entirely pleasant.

So the relationship continued. Because she fell in love with his peacefulness and he found peacefulness in her love.

• • •

Jake and Lizzie had been together for just over six months when they began renting an apartment in the city. She hadn't worked up the courage to say I love you yet. But she had run out of enough money to suggest the move as a financially viable option. Jake, always looking to lessen his reliance on thin strips of paper with designated worth realized when she asked that he was more than happy to comply.

She had spent the previous two years living with an intolerable opera singer who was completely polite about never singing when Lizzie was home, but never once cleaned the bathroom. He had spent the previous three living in an apartment that looked like it might have literally been constructed out of a cardboard box. Jake was fine with his living situation but was in favor of a change that might cut down on the already small cost.

Jake stayed away from doctors. He fully expected purported medical experts to tell him that he had sustained years of internal injuries. He was a near comatose victim, broken down inside, and only functioning physically because he was unaware of the hurt he had undergone. He felt fine. Perhaps there were aches that might have bothered him were he able to feel pain. But thus far nothing had impeded his ability to function perfectly normally.

He had slowly risen in the ranks of amateur boxing. Beating one surprised opponent after another. Shocking the spectators with the ration of what he took to what he gave out and how he managed to survive the match at all, let alone win. He was now in a position of prominence, having gained some renown on the circuit.

Lizzie was concerned about his health. She had mentioned her concerns only once, when they had first started dating. Right after he had told her about his condition. And the fact that he thrust his body into violence for a living. And the fact that his primary strategy was to stand still and take punishment until the other man had thoroughly worn himself out. She suggested that perhaps he move on to something else. He did. He moved on to another conversation topic.

Smacking her voice back into her head didn't silence it. It made it ricochet from wall to wall of her inner skull, ping ponging and searching for an escape. On the day that they moved into their new apartment, her voice echoed so loudly from ear to ear she had to find some door by which to release it in order to even formulate a thought. Her mouth was the easiest accessible exit.

It was their first dinner in their new apartment. They ate take out Chinese food on a table made from an upside down cardboard box and a sat on chairs made from piled up couch cushions. Jake smiled. A rarity. His usual expression was not a frown, it was just blank. The same look most wear when they sleep. She loved his smile and hated the statement that was prying itself through her teeth. She was well aware that it was an inopportune time to bring it up. The biggest match of his career was taking place in two days time, and though Jake denied that he cared whether he won, she could sense an obscure excitement in him whenever he brought it up. Some sort of pride that came with the idea of showing others he was the best.

"Jake."

"Yeah?"

"I think you should stop fighting."

He smiled. "You know how I'm going to respond to that."

"It's dangerous. And it's violent. And you could be doing better things with your life."

"It's not about doing things. It's about being. I'm good at boxing. It lets me just be. It's okay I don't expect you to understand that. I just expect you to let me be."

"But I want to understand it. I want to understand you. And I don't."

"Why does it matter if you understand?"

"Because we're a couple. I want to feel completely connected to you. I want you to be the one person in the world who I can speak to and feel like I really know. And I don't."

Jake took in her statement. He was surprised by the gravity of it. "Do you really believe that's possible?" he asked.

She was becoming upset. He could hear the tears slinking through the cracking walls of her composure. "Do you really think there's anything about you that is so important? No, not important. So fragile, that you'll be immediately shattered if you just open yourself up for once? I want to know you Jake! And sometimes I feel like I have no idea who you are. I know there's someone inside there you won't let me see. And I don't know why."

"Well," he said as he took notice of the loud beats of his normally quiet heart, "I didn't mean me exactly. I meant that I don't necessarily believe you can ever really know anybody."

Lizzie's faucet was now completely turned on. "I just wanted to ask you to stop fighting. Because I ... Because I worry about you. I didn't even mean to say what I just said. I didn't even know that I ... We just moved in together."

Her speech ended there. Jake took a moment to let the conversation naturally evaporate before responding.

"I'm glad we moved in together," he said, out of character, surprised to hear himself saying it. He had not even realized he was glad but as it came out of his mouth there was no denying it was true.

"I am too," she said.

• • •

The morning of the big fight Jake felt restless. His normal peacefulness was hidden under the shadow of anticipation, something he was normally able to avoid. He woke up at five in the morning. Lizzie was still sleeping. She looked adorable. He began to wish she was awake. He almost shook her. He wanted to talk to her. He wanted her to encourage him to win. He slipped out of bed, shaken by his uncommon neediness.

Jake stared out of the window and took several deep breaths. His heart was pounding and he wished to calm himself down.

"Was it a dream?" he asked himself, wondering if an anxious experience had overcome him while he was asleep, victim once again to the nighttime emotions he could not control. But he could not seem to recall what it was he dreamt about.

"Was it the conversation with Lizzie?" They rarely fought. It was the evenness that appealed to them both. Occasionally she would initiate a touchy topic, trying to get a rise out of him. He was perceptive enough to see the part of Lizzie still attracted to the allure of drama. In the past he had been able to observe this detached, almost amused by her humanness. Attracted to it, really. But he knew that last night she had broken through. She had annoyed him. He wasn't quite angry. Just peeved. And enough so that he wanted to win his title match as a childish sort of revenge towards her. An I told you so.

I'm in love with her, he realized with a jolt.

"Shit," he said aloud.

Jake went for a walk. Perhaps fresh air would cure the powerful evolution of his fondness. Take it back down a couple notches. He picked the bank about a mile away as a destination just to have one. He had a check he had needed to cash anyway.

It was a Saturday morning and the bank was crowded. Jake watched his fellow city dwellers take advantage of their day off, making themselves feel better about the excessive number of hours they worked during the week by counting the material result of their hard work. Men and women enjoying the ability to wear shorts even though it wasn't that warm out because they were never allowed to show their thighs on days that weren't brought to you by the letter "S." He got in line behind a particularly bad smelling man and tried not to think less of him as a person because of his stench. He kept thinking about Lizzie.

Jake had the sudden urge to run home, grab Lizzie and kiss her all over her body. He abruptly realized that lately he had become more and more gripped by sexual passion. His physical desires infuriated him because he knew they were one aspect of himself he could never completely control. But at least with the girls who came before Lizzie and with Lizzie at the beginning of their relationship, he had been able to simply experience the physical pleasures, briefly silencing the maddening cravings, without emotions working their way unnecessarily into the proceedings. When it was only physical desire that he had to contend with, Jake had felt that he could maintain a certain amount of power over when he would fall victim to his wants and when he would deny them to remain his own master. But now that love had become involved he was thinking about sex all the time, imagining the feel of Lizzie's body when he was nowhere near her and had no reason to be tempted. It wasn't just sex though. He wanted to just hold Lizzie. To lay quietly with her for hours just so he could be close to her. All that he had been feeling for the past couple of months in small doses came pouring out along with the revelation of his love. He felt like a fool for not being aware of what had overcome him sooner. And it made him angry. He had worked so long and hard to maintain a grip on his feelings. To dictate his mind set without any outside interference.

"Everyone on the fucking floor!"

Jake turned around to see three men holding guns and laundry bags. Either he was in the midst of Dog Day Afternoon or he was being confronted by men who held a passionate hate for dirty clothes.

Screams. The crowd of customers were good direction followers when confronted with deadly weapons. They did as they were told and dropped to the ground, mostly face down. One man in shorts and a blazer laid down on his back. Jake followed suit and slowly lowered himself. It was the sensible thing to do. But he could also feel his heart rate increasing, his stomach starting to hurt. He was scared. And that made him angrier than the fact that he was being robbed.

He caught a closer glimpse of his oppressors. The two men holding the laundry bags were large, bulky, wearing matching brown suits that were just too small. They held a small revolver. The third man was short, wearing a black suit, and holding a shotgun that his arms were barely long enough to wield. He was apparently the leader. Jake gathered this from the fact that he was issuing the orders, but having watched cartoons as a child may have done just as well in deducing his status in the comically decorated trio.

The leader took one of the giants into the back as the second hulking mass watched over the customers and the tellers who had also been forced to the ground. They returned after several minutes, the laundry bag overflowing with bills.

"Okay. I want you to all take out your wallets and my associate here is going to go around and collect them. I don't want any fucking trouble. Anyone moves I shoot em. Anyone talks. I shoot em. Anyone looks at me wrong. I shoot em. Got it?"

Everyone's eye balls rolled around towards each other, not

sure if the shotgun toting maniac actually wanted an answer. Several opened their mouths to speak but no noise came out. Each person's unsteady hands shook their way into their pockets or purses and pulled out whatever device they used from convenient money hoarding. Jake took out his own wallet. It contained the checks for his last three fights. He had far from a love for money but recognized the loss would cause a serious dent if his employers refused to rewrite the payment. Even so, it was not the imminent loss of money that was making his brain itch. As hard as he tried to remain completely unattached from the situation, it bothered him that he was being robbed. It was a silly thought to have, he knew most people would think. That there was nothing more infuriating than being robbed. Most would wish countless levels of harm to befall on their oppressors and spend at least two and half weeks simply sitting around being angry about these men who had entered their past and taken their material goods.

It wasn't the loss of goods that bothered him. Or even the fear of a threat made on his life. It was the lack of control. For years he had felt a near complete command over his existence. This morning his stronghold was falling apart. Lizzie had penetrated the lock on his feelings of love and now these sons of bitches had penetrated the lock on his feelings of hate. He felt disgustingly vulnerable.

Jake stood up. It was an action completely of his own volition. No person or circumstance dictated it. He stood because he decided to stand and no outside source could prevent him from doing so. It was defiance.

"What the fuck?"

The expletive was accompanied by a gunshot. It was the last sound he heard.

• • •

Jake woke up to the sound of an ice cream truck. It attracted children with a twinkling chime version of Beethoven's Fur Elise. Jake thought the tune held a far too ominous connotation to be representative of ice cream sandwiches and Mickey Mouse ice pops. He found himself craving a Choco Taco. He sat up, prepared to run the truck down. Or rather he planned to sit up. Until he realized he was fastened to a hospital bed and connected to about a thousand wires.

"Jake!"

Lizzie spotted his open eyes. She rushed over to his bed and gave him a no contact hug, her arms carefully remaining about two inches from his carefully guarded body.

"Oh, thank god." She was crying.

Lizzie had been watching him for hours, waiting anxiously for him to wake up since the first possible moment they allowed her into the room.

"I love you so much," she said.

She had realized it was true the instant she heard what had happened to him. It amazed her the speed with which an enormous amount of thoughts had entered her mind in that frozen moment, as if she had been ruminating over them for several hours. Thoughts of the confused dynamic of longing and fulfillment she felt around Jake. Insight into the fact that although she had previously thought Jake was different than every man she had ever fallen for, needing no comfort, he might actually be the most reassurance deprived of them all, having buried his ever present needs so deeply they were only rarely unearthed through no conscious intention. And more than anything, there was the frightening but wonderful realization that she had fallen in love with him. All running through her head before she even had a chance to hang up the telephone.

Jake observed Lizzie. Then he fell back to sleep.

On his second wake she was calmer.

"Hi there," she said.

"Hi."

"How are you feeling?"

"Like I've been shot."

"Don't scare me like that again okay?"

"Okay."

"Why did you do it Jake?"

"Do what?"

"Why'd you stand up like that?"

"What do you mean?"

"The other customers at the bank. They said that the burglars told everyone to get on the floor. Said they would shoot them if anybody moved. Why'd you move?"

Jake thought about his answer. Anything he said he knew she would not understand.

"Because I chose to. And they couldn't take my choice away."

"What does that mean? You're life was at stake!"

"Do we have to get into this right now?"

She paused. Took a deep breath. Calmed herself down.

"No. We don't."

She leaned over and kissed him on the forehead. "You're okay. That's what matters," she said.

"Did they get the bastards?"

"No. They got away just before the police arrived. They're searching for them though. It's all over the news. These kinds of bank robberies don't really happen anymore so everyone's curious. They mentioned you. Said one man had been shot."

"Lucky me."

• • •

It took two weeks for the hospital to discharge Jake. The attendant insisted on wheeling him to the door even though he felt perfectly strong enough to walk. He was lucky to have been shot in the stomach. It was able to withstand a lot of bleeding and he was rushed to the hospital quick enough that all of his physical faculties would return. But despite all the good news, given value solely on the basis of the situation's direness, Jake's action was not able to avoid an equal and opposite reaction. He was not allowed to fight. Not ever again according to the doctor. Ironically in a sport where concussions and brain damage rule the long term physical injury chart, it was the less exciting stomach shots that children rarely acted out when pretending to box their friends, which were forcing him into early retirement.

Back at home, Lizzie was wonderful. Objectively anyway. She wore a continuous smile for about two weeks before she put it into a quick laundry load and threw it right back on, clean and fresh. She cooked delicious meals, and was ready to cater to Jake's every need should he only express one. Unfortunately doing unto others is an action that generally requires acknowledgement or recognition or at the very least observance for it to become anything at all. And Jake could hardly be said to have been interacting.

Jake was restless. He spent most of his time contemplating. He had not realized just how reliant he was on his profession for his well being and the loss he felt at being told he could never fight again aggravated him. He could not think of what he was going to do with his life and he had a sudden thirst for violence that came from the fighting withdrawal. He considered ignoring the doctors orders completely but he imagined that by now all of his prospective employers would have heard his story and been alerted by the irritatingly thorough medical staff of the hospital and his even more irritatingly thorough girlfriend, who was determined to ensure that he stay out of harm's way for the rest of his days. He couldn't decide if it bothered him more that Lizzie insisted on telling him what to do or that he didn't want to go against what she said because of a fear of losing her.

Lizzie repeatedly tried to engage him in conversation but he mostly kept quiet, annoyed with her for being so appealing. To her credit though, she did not become discouraged. She did not give up. And occasionally, she would break him down.

"What are you thinking about?" she asked one night, as Jake stared out the window.

"Overpopulation," he said.

She chuckled. "What about it?

"The fact that it's probably going to be the end of us."

"How's that?"

"We've survived too well. Us humans. There's just going to be more and more of us and less and less resources and eventually we'll all die, either because we won't have enough to survive or because we'll all kill each other trying to get what's left."

"You seem like you're in a positive mood."

"I'm serious Lizzie."

"I know you are." She walked up close to him and put her hand on his lower back. "Look, I know this has all been very hard on you, but you're going to get through this. *We're* going to get through this."

He looked at her. She was staring at him tenderly.

"I just need to get back to how I was. To what made me feel

good."

"And what was that?"

"It's not important."

"Jake, you can talk to me. Tell me. I'd like to hear about it."

He breathed deeply.

"Being unattached. Not letting my emotions bother me. Letting nothing and no one affect me."

"You can't always control your emotions. You're entitled to be upset sometimes."

"I'm not talking about being upset."

"Then what are you talking about?"

"I'm talking about being unattached! Not being afraid of losing anything because I never let myself get too attached to anything in the first place."

"But Jake, that's not how we are. Us people. We get attached whether we like it or not and sometimes that leads to a lot of pain but sometimes it leads to a lot of happiness."

"Maybe it's how you are. It's not how I am. Trust me. I'm better off when I can stay unattached."

"It sounds to me like you expect too much from yourself."

"I know what I need."

"Okay," she said. She leaned her head on his shoulder.

He wanted to push her away. But he just watched her.

•••

Jake didn't feel like sleeping. He stayed awake in the living room watching a late night film about a man who wins the lottery and blows his millions of winnings on a soul sucking prostitute (the film's words, not his). It was disgusting fluff. He realized he was watching it as an exercise of restraint. If he could watch such a poorly written, poorly acted, morally bankrupt, visually grimy shit bag of a film and not kick the glass of the TV in, remaining still in his chair, he would at least have a minor grip on his old peacefulness.

A breaking news story interrupted the prostitute's murder and made Jake sit up from the intense imprint his restraint had made in the old couch. There had been another robbery. Police suspected the same perpetrators. This one had not gone so smoothly. Three people were killed.

For a moment Jake was angry. But then he paused. He made an effort to pay attention to his emotions.

Then he was still angry but he was watching his anger.

Then he was a complete spectator, watching someone else be angry.

Then he was no longer angry. It was empirically bad news, but the news meant nothing to him personally. It meant nothing to his still body. Jake was still a fighter. Just not of an external nature. There were practical considerations that overrode emotional ones.

Practicality. It was just the thing he was looking for.

"I'm going out today," he told Lizzie the next morning during breakfast.

"That's great! Where to?"

"I'm not sure exactly. Into the city. I want to wander a bit."

"You're feeling better than yesterday then?"

"Yes. I'd say that's true."

"That's great Jake." She moved over to him. She kissed him. "I love you."

It was the second time she had said it. The first in the heat of the passion of fright at the hospital. She did not expect a response. But she hoped for one.

He said nothing.

• • •

He parked his car in the warehouse district. It seemed a nice balance of shady suspicious alleys with enough of a tinge of graffiti to attract riff raff, but not too much to cause the higher forms of criminals to run from cracked out street thugs. He really had no knowledge of where to begin. How does one track down a criminal who conducts his crimes with flash and ado and who nonetheless, the police themselves had yet to find the slightest trace of? This task is likely impossible, he thought. He had no knowledge of how to act as a bounty hunter or an assassin other than what he witnessed secondhand in fictional movies and television programs.

A man stood outside the door of a warehouse that looked otherwise abandoned. He was smoking a cigarette. He was dressed far too nicely to be standing in the eyesore of a location in which he was located. Jake approached him.

"Hello."

The man shook from instinctual fright. Every part of his body convulsed for a split second except for his cigarette holding hand which remained steady as a rock.

"Where the fuck did you come from?"

"The suburbs. Originally."

"A fucking wiseguy."

"I was just taking a walk. I didn't know anyone actually worked in this area."

"Just fucking pimps and crack hos and dock workers and your occasional businessman."

"So you'd be a crack ho then?"

"Fucking comedian, huh?"

"What sort of business are you in?"

"Kid."

"Yeah?"

"I think it's best if you stop asking questions."

"Fair enough. I'm looking for somebody. Maybe you can help me."

"Kid."

"That wasn't a question."

The left half of his mouth smiled. Only the left half. As if the two sides of his face were sewn together by only the finest string.

"Fair enough. Who is this lucky object of your quest?"

"Have you watched the news recently?"

"I'm more of a newspaper man."

"Fair enough. Then you're probably even more informed."

"I do enjoy information on occasion."

"I'm looking for one of the men who've been in the news lately. One of the men involved in those couple of large bank robberies. One of the men they've been unable to find."

"Do I look like a detective to you?"

"You look like a man who knows people."

The man with the cigarette burst out laughing. And coughing. Coughing caused by laughing and laughter extended by coughs.

"Kid. If this is really what you're trying to do. Track down these 'bad guys'," he said, his hands making the quote symbols, "then you need a better tactic then coming off as a character from a good forties movie or a bad seventies TV show. Asking questions so obvious that everyone would think you were a cop if everyone didn't know that cops are never stupid enough to be that direct. I should shove you into a puddle and send you on your way but it's not raining and I think you're attempt at being a vigilante is kinda adorable so I'm going to give you a small hint. But if you're smart you'll fucking run from it because if my tip's any good it might get you killed."

Jake took a moment to feel inferior. To notice that he was being treated as such and that any spectator would watch this conversation and see him as a pathetic poser, playing a role he didn't belong in and being shit some information purely out of pity. It was an adjustment to be the lesser in an interaction. By separating himself he usually maintained an air of superiority. People always admired those who paid them no mind, he had learned. Here he wanted something. He wanted something he did not have direct knowledge of how to get. He was placing himself in a position to be ridiculed. And if he was not absolutely determined to stay separate from any aspect of himself that might be attached to superiority he may have given up then and there. He stepped out of the moment of inferiority. He smiled. Fully. Showing the man with the cigarette that both sides of his face were capable.

"What've you got?"

• • •

He was directed to a small antique shop on the southside of town. Mildred's Antiques. Hidden in between two ultra modernized furniture outlets and scrunched beneath four heavy levels of concrete apartments, Mildred's Antiques was black and white enough to be an actual photograph. Jake was, however, able to walk in, proving its three dimensionality.

"I'm looking for Frank," he said dictating the name he was supposed to repeat.

"Who's asking?" answered Mildred, who was four foot nine

and whose face was hidden behind a lamp from the nineteen tens.

"I'd give you my name but I'd have to take it right back." The man with the cigarette had told him to use that line. Made it seem like a sort of code word. The disgusted look on Mildred's face told him he had only made him speak such corniness for his own enjoyment.

"No seriously who the fuck are you?"

"I'm someone looking for the people who've been on the news lately, robbing banks. I was at the first robbery. I received a bullet in my stomach for trying to cash my check."

"I'm sorry to hear that."

"Do you know where I can find Frank? I was told he could help me out."

"Sure. Just a minute."

The lady disappeared behind a mahogany desk. Jake turned around for just a moment, distracted by a marble statue of Buddha, and when his face turned back he was blindsided by the minute hand of a grandfather clock. Then. All was black.

• • •

Jake woke up in a cold wet basement tied to an old rocking chair. The more he shook, the more he rocked. His body was oddly soothed by the gentle rocking even as the obvious concern about where he was and what was being done to him seeped into his brain. He corked up the seepage. This was no more or less unpleasant than sitting on the couch waiting for a commercial to end. Or so he told himself. And so he believed. He waited what he imagined might have been anywhere between twenty minutes and three hours when he finally saw a figure enter the room.

"Well hello there."

He looked up. He saw a familiar face. One of the bulbous buffoons from the bank. Jake said nothing.

"How you feeling?"

He did not respond.

"I guess you can't answer. After all, you're a little tied up at the moment." The bulbous man laughed a disgusting fragmented laugh. Pieces of food flew out as the chuckles increased. When he was finally done humor regurgitating he hit Jake as hard he could in the front of his face, instantly shattering his nose.

"I hear you've been asking for someone you shouldn't be asking for. Why don't you leave the policework to the police?"

"Why all the mystery?" Jake replied. "I just want to have a conversation with the man who thought he knew me well enough to shoot his gun off into me."

Bulbous scrunched his face. Likely trying to figure out whether or not the sentence was meant as sexual innuendo. He gauged how angry he should be.

"Little guys like you need to stop asking questions." He lit a match. He threw it at Jake. It hit his shirt and immediately went out.

"Well done."

"Shut the fuck up." He re-punched the already broken nose. As usual, when it came to being the victim of physical aggression, Jake was unaffected. He yawned to show his aggressor just how little impression the whole to-do was making.

"Mind if I take a nap while you do your business?"

"I said shut up!" Bulbous pushed Jake, intending to knock him over. Instead, the rocking chair held its ground, rocking rapidly but staying steady. Jake hummed rock-a-bye baby softly just to piss Bulbous off. He thrusted again. This time Jake did fall over. But didn't stop humming the children's tune.

Bulbous ripped Jake from the chair and dragged him across the basement to a deep corner, home to an old fashioned coal heater. The heater was slaving away at its job. The heat could be felt from a few feet away, exuding from every inch of its surface.

"You wanna get cute," said Bulbous. "Be my guest."

He grabbed Jake's left hand and forced it with little resistance against the scalding surface of the heater. Jake stared back without blinking, bored and unimpressed. He took his right hand from the shocked criminal and placed it next to its counterpart. He smiled.

"Surely you can do better than that?" he said.

• • •

Jake was blindfolded and retied. He put up no resistance but did formulate a phony cough so that he could freely imagine the saliva particles hitting bulbous in the face. He was thrown in the back of a van and driven without much precaution to a place some fifteen minutes or so away. He slid back and forth on the van's smooth surface, slamming into the walls. He enjoyed it. Without the pain it was like a water slide.

They reached their destination and Jake was dragged from the van into a cold mucky building. He was then thrown down two flights of stairs. All the while he maintained on his face the most satisfied, most chipper of smiles. Daring Bulbous to question him about finding the experience as even a slight bother.

He was locked in a closet. He could feel several unwrapped packets of toilet paper with his fingers. He was left there for what he imagined to be several hours. He spent the time acquainting himself with several variations of the smell of mold.

Much later, the door was slammed open (an interesting contrast but a possible one nonetheless) and Jake was dragged to yet another central location. This time his blindfold came off.

He was surrounded by seven men with scorched fuming faces. Each held a variety of weapons and torturous contraptions. At the head of the pack stood Bulbous and his compatriot from the robbery who Jake fondly referred to as Bulbous Two.

Each man waited patiently in line for an opportunity to torture the stubborn investigator. Each man's exasperation was filled to the point of unacceptability as hammering his fingers or setting his leg hairs on fire or sticking pliers up a single nostril of his nose only made him smile. And not a smile of defiance. This they might have been able to accept. It would have been some indication that their actions were getting to him. But instead it was a smile of complete indifference. The slightest incline of his lips, to show how unaffected he was. They blindfolded him. Apparently under the impression that pain disconnected from the visualization of its source might be able to frighten him. He laughed out loud. Blocking his vision took away any chance they could intimidate him.

• • •

Things went quiet once more. He waited. Patiently.

Lizzie popped into his mind. She might be worried about him. Likely would. He enjoyed thinking about it. About her peering out the window, thinking she might catch a glimpse of him returning home even from the awkward canted angle their apartment had of the street. Calling his cell phone number and receiving no answer. Wondering if another terrible tragedy had blindsided him. If he was back in the hospital. If he had wandered off, finally making due on his philosophical promise of no attachments at all.

They might kill me, he thought. He wasn't sure whether he cared.

"So you're the fucker who's been asking for me?"

The blindfold came off. He kept his eyes closed. He thought about the fact that your eyes are never really closed, just covered by a flap of skin so close, it provides the illusion of darkness.

Then he raised the flaps and allowed himself to see the short bastard who'd felt the need to shoot him in the stomach.

"That's me," he replied.

"Well. Here I am. What would you like?"

"To fight you."

He heard several forced laughs and one genuine. Murmurs of "Did you bring your boxing gloves?" and "Fucking guy wants to fucking fight you," and the surprisingly culturally astute, "Guy thinks he's Butch Cassidy," managed to cut and paste their way into his ear.

"What kind of fight?"

"Hand to hand. No weapons. No rules beyond that."

"I'd say yes but my boys might be jealous. Might want to join in."

"I'll fight them too."

"Now even I'm not that cruel."

"Maybe not. Or maybe you're just a coward."

Frank grabbed hold of Jake's already tattered shirt.

"What makes you think I won't slit your throat right now?"

"Well for one you're not holding a knife."

Frank slid a knife out from his sleeve. Jake thought about how dangerous it was to carry around a sharp object so close to one's wrists, then responded.

"And I also think you don't seem like the kind of person who backs down from a direct challenge," he said.

Frank shifted his eyes around but didn't break contact. Jake knew he had a check mate.

"Untie the fucker."

• • •

Jake felt good to be back in the ring, even though the ring was a hard stone slab floor littered with occasional shards of glass and the ropes were criminals waiting for a taste of his blood.

Across from him stood Frank, who he had four inches on, but who he was far from foolish enough to believe did not pose a serious threat. One of his cronies bellowed to indicate the first and continuous round's beginning bell and Frank launched himself onto his opponent. As expected he was a feisty mosquito of an adversary. Quick punches. Less forceful but with a sort of landing pinch between the fingers because there were no gloves. Repeated kicks to the shin as there were no limits on lower body shots or use of the legs. Incredibly predictable, thought Jake, who employed his usual strategy of casual waiting.

Jake spotted Frank's underlings noticing the peculiarity and uneasiness of his strategy before Frank did. They were confused and wary. Jake was engaged in the same deeply disturbing distance as when he had been tortured and they seemed prepared that some recourse, some punishment was on its way. Jake felt it. He experienced an entirely new sensation. Power. And its imminent release.

Frank remained focused. His quickly tiring arms noticed the concerning oddity before he did.

Jake struck just as the Bulbouses led the rest of the weapon wielders into the ring of the fight. He unleashed two or three forceful shots before ducking the stampede he was prepared for. He swooped down low, picking a gun hanging from a stray boot, firing it in the exact locations he could imagine before any of the beasts could trample him, hitting heads with unknown accuracy, provided for purely by confidence. He left only a terrified curled up Frank, watching everyone associated with him killed as they were unable to even land a shot on the man with no fear.

Jake dropped the gun. Impressed with how quickly thought could become reality if all strings of doubt or apprehension were cut loose. He picked up a knife. He stood above the trembling burglar.

"As far as I can tell," he said, "life is a privilege that not everyone deserves. It's simple practicality."

He dropped the knife into Frank's face.

III.

Ten years of time had little effect on the old house on Fernrock street. The mailbox was still silver. And still crooked. There was still an unfixed hole in the chainlink fence that surrounded the backyard and part of the side. The front door was new. Uglier. Maybe to warn visitors of the bastard who lived inside, thought Jake.

Jake's mother had killed herself. He had gotten the news a month ago. He didn't attend the funeral. He had no desire to hear her oversimplified eulogies. The news didn't make him sad. It seemed natural. And he had taught himself far too well to become upset by a piece of information that made perfect sense.

Nevertheless, a month after the phone call he booked a flight home. He decided to return for the first time since he had fled. He would briefly recognize that he had a past. Nostalgia was no factor. Not even a consideration. Nowhere on the agenda. But he did have unfinished business that he thought needed to be attended to.

No one recognized him as he walked down the street. No one had any reason to. His face had not been shown nor his appearance described on any of the recent news stories about him. No one had learned what he looked like. They speculated he must be a spectacularly large, muscle covered, beast of a man, with gorilla hands equipped to wrestle weapons from even the quickest of shooters, but with thin arms and rapid reflexes that allowed him to dodge any shot from any weapon that might be fired towards him. The big handed thin armed speculation sounded to him a bit like a description of Mickey Mouse.

He had received quite the press coverage for the incident in the warehouse. After he had crawled from the bloody scene he had called the police, leaving them an anonymous tip of where to find the felon who had been staging the theatrical bank robberies. He didn't mention that he was no longer alive. He thought it would be a nice surprise for the police officers who came to retrieve him.

He had left every detail exactly in place except for the guns. He had taken all of the guns.

The story was already all over the news by the time he returned home to Lizzie who spotted his bruises and hugged him like he had already died. She had the television on in the background as she kissed him all over, believing her lips held some sort of magical healing power. He didn't stop her to remind her that he didn't feel any effects of the damage he had received. And she didn't question him when he refused to tell her exactly what had happened, failing to put two and two together while the awed anchors on the television spoke of a real life super hero who apparently took down an entire crime syndicate.

She continued not to question him two days later when he said he had to take a flight for a few days to a place he could not reveal. Although this time, in the settling of her passions, she was disheartened by his concealment.

"If it was something I was hiding from you, I would lie about it rather than just not tell you. It's just something personal I have to take care of."

His explanation was sensible enough but it made her feel no better.

He knocked on the door of his childhood house. After a long moment, his father answered.

They stared at each other for about a minute. Neither of them was ever a huge proponent of language. "Well, come on in," Howard said.

Jake looked around. The inside was as unchanged as the outside, except for the smell. The place had taken on the most unpleasant scent of body odor and air freshener. The air freshener was apparently meant to disguise the body odor, but it somehow made it more pronounced. Like placing a beautiful object next to a pile of garbage.

"Would you like a beer?"

"Sure."

For the first time in his life, Jake sat down casually on his old couch, and shared a beer with his father. It was a humorous snapshot. If a complete stranger had walked in he might have thought he was witnessing the end point of a close father son relationship. A poignant moment of bonding with no speech necessary. Life, when placed out of context, can completely lose its thread, thought Jake. For a brief second he even considered putting his beer down and walking far away, forgetting what he had come for altogether. He even thought that it was the right thing to do. The true nature of the unattachment he had been searching for. If not forgiveness then at least forgetting. But his father's next words erased the memory of these thoughts from his mind.

"You killed your mother, you know."

Jake remained silent.

"Second you left she started dying. You were the only thing that held the poor bitch together. I tried to comfort her. Tell her you were nothing but a no good bastard. That she should try to pretend you'd never come from either of us. That she'd given birth to a child who couldn't feel. And that nobody should have to go through such a thing."

Howard waited for a response. He smirked.

"Fuck. I can't even get a rise out of you anymore. I guess you've changed. The truth is, I have too. The real truth is—"

Howard didn't finish his statement. He was interrupted by Jake's fist, which had made its way across his face, knocking him to the ground.

"Fuck kid."

Those were the last words he spoke. He didn't manage to form any more intelligible sounds as his only child used his curled up fingers as bettering rams, draining all the blood out of his face at intervals both fast and slow, engaging in both the hitting and observing the receiving, using nature's original weapons to drain every last breath his father had.

Once he was dead he poured the rest of his father's unfinished beer bottle down his still open mouth.

• • •

They called him the "Bullet Man." It was an uncreative and mildly confusing way to refer to him. He didn't even shoot all of his victims. It was coined by a local newscaster in upstate New York who claimed, upon learning the full details, that he said it because the lone man struck as quick as a bullet. People seemed to buy that and the newscaster went on reveling in the free meals and national attention he got for being someone with a face that could be shown in lieu of any image of the mysterious hero. A few weeks later no one believed the anchor. He was turned away from restaurants for the gall of such a claim. Bullet Man was what he had always been called. No one had originated it. It was stamped on his birth certificate. Whoever he was.

The burglar bloodbath at the warehouse had been followed by the deaths of a series of child molesters, rapists, murderers, drug pushers, and just all around morally bad people. Culprits of recent crimes, who posed immediate threats. Many of them were recently released ex-convicts, who had just finished serving their time for their second or third horrible felony. Bullet Man was doing his research.

The police force supposedly had devoted an entire task force to capturing what was technically a serial killer, though one who children were pretending to be during recess. No one had seen where this task force was centralized or had identified any of its particular members. Faint chuckles could be heard in the background every time the chief of police insisted on how hard they were working to stop this "Bullet Man." Truth was, he was making their lives easier. Sure they had to clean up the crime scenes, but there were low level men to do that work, and if someone had to be dying, it might as well be the criminals.

One month after it all started teenagers were spotted in malls wearing Bullet Man t-shirts. He was the new Che Guevara. The man, unseen in real life, was depicted wearing a typical super hero costume, sans cape. A red suit with black vertical lines extending down from the shoulders to the legs. The image spread. People started to take it seriously. And as criminals continued to die, they kept their eye out for the one in the black and red suit. All the real bullet man ever put on was a ski mask.

• • •

Jake was having strange convulsions at unpredictable times. He would be brushing his teeth and his fingers would start to shake, vertically and horizontally, flinging the tooth brush across the room, his palm heavy and solid as a rock while its extensions lost complete control for about two minutes. Walking down the street his head would swing wildly back and forth, attracting stares from those who pitied him and those who saw him as a lesser form of man. Going for a run in the park he could feel his belly button trying to escape from his body, thrusting him forward from the most inopportune of pinpoints. He didn't dare see a doctor. Filed in the back of his mind was the irrational fear that an examination might reveal he had been dead for months. But mostly he feared some medical examiner might put together the clues and deduce his identity.

As he shook, the knowledge that he had done irreparable damage to his body was the musical rhythm that accompanied his uncontrollable dance.

It was almost a point of pride. He was taking his body to a limit that few had ever known. Living without pain had become like driving a car without a gas gauge. He kept driving, fully aware he was running out of gas, but never stopping because as far as he knew, he had enough left to keep going.

But the real problem was Lizzie. Keeping late nights of crime fighting and the seizures they caused from his girlfriend was becoming increasingly difficult.

She stopped asking questions almost as soon as he stopped answering them.

"Are you having an affair?"

"Absolutely not."

She must have believed him. Otherwise she would have left.

He withdrew from her. He walked right past her crying and said nothing. In truth he didn't care and was relieved about it. The largest jolt of fear he had experienced in recent times was the fear that he might have fallen in love. The inevitable end of the joys that would come with it was a prospect he did not wish to have to face. His "crime fighting" as the news men called it, had filled any emotional need he had.

He found her occasionally going through his things, but

made no issue. If searching for answers appeased her in some way he was happy to let her do it.

That's why, when he left the house one evening, in search of a murderer just released from prison, he did not turn around or provide any acknowledgement when he realized Lizzie was following him.

Jake had been spending most of his time doing research, as he liked to call it. He ventured into the slums. He listened for talk of abusive husbands, drug pushers, and the like. He went mostly unnoticed. Some taunted profanities at him, trying to assert their toughness by frightening a presumed stranger, but they backed off as soon as they saw the look in his eyes.

Today, not because Lizzie was following but because it had originally been his plan, he was going after a white collar criminal. He had momentarily abandoned the abandoned lots and relocated to halls of records. Perpetrators of insurance fraud hardly got under his skin. He had no attachment to money and thus, paid them no mind. But he had been running low on the lowest of the low, who were apparently hiding in their houses until "Bullet Man" blew over or moved to another city. He certainly wouldn't have been persuaded by any argument saying that Lawrence Bilford, his victim of choice, deserved to die anymore than the average American who had committed no crime. But he wouldn't have been convinced by any argument saying he deserved to live either.

Lizzie followed at an obvious pace and he allowed her to keep up. He paused briefly after rounding each corner, making sure she had plenty of time to spot his next destination. He swung the door of the building he was breaking into wide open to ensure she would have plenty of time to sneak in before it clicked back into its locked position. He took the stairs rather than the numberless elevator to ensure easier observation of the floor which he got off. He paused in the hallway in clear sight. He donned his ski mask and took out his guns so that she could see with her own eyes the shocking truth she was looking for. He kicked open the door instead of performing his usual polite knock to give her a bit of a show and left the door off its hinges so she could easily peek inside.

He shot the man seventeen times instead of his usual twice. He thought she would appreciate it. And when he walked into the hall to see the look of complete horror on her face, he couldn't help but laugh as he said, "As you've probably gathered, I'm the Bullet Man."

"Jake," she barely got out, whispering, "Why are you doing this?"

"Well," he said, "I suppose it's my own personal fight against overpopulation."

He allowed Lizzie several hours of head start time before he returned to the apartment. When he returned she was gone. She had not taken her time in packing. Clothes and items were strewn everywhere and she had forgotten some things she would probably later wish she had, but certainly would not return for. For the next few days, he waited around, wondering if the police would come to call. They did not. He couldn't be certain that she had not told them his identity. They may have ignored it because of the ways in which he made their life easier. But he guessed that she said nothing.

When she was gone, he was surprised by how quiet his living space suddenly became. And by the forceful presence silence managed to maintain.

• • •

Jake wasn't sure when exactly the transition happened. When he stopped caring who it was he was killing. When he ceased pretending that his murders were beneficial in any way. When having someone else's blood on his hands became little more than an uncontrollable addiction and the only thing that drove him. When the police slowly realized they had let a mad man run loose and refine his craft, so that by the time he ended the lives of the innocent he knew how to avoid being caught.

Before the papers had called him a hero. Now they called him a serial killer. The name calling didn't bother him much. He was too far gone to let any opinion affect him.

As he sat in the stillness for days on end, feeling his convulsions increase, steadying himself just long enough to venture out and kill some poor bastard who didn't deserve it, wondering if the damage to his nerve system affected his sanity, reading about public burnings of t-shirts containing his image, and sifting his thoughts through an increasingly dense fog, one notion became increasingly clear, absolutely refusing to stay out of his mind.

Without pain, there could be no such thing as pleasure.

BOOK IV

THE PROPHET

I.

Sitting by the light of his newly purchased, wonderfully comforting desk lamp, Michael Bailey drifted away from his studies and became caught up in one of his favorite thought patterns. He traced back, memory by memory, the endless seemingly insignificant events of the past that all added up and led to the exact moment that he currently found himself in. Events that, if the slightest variation had occurred, might have led to a radically different outcome.

He thought of sitting with his father as a child, butchering pumpkins that they unsuccessfully strove to turn into jack-o-lanterns. He thought of stubbing his toe at summer camp on a jagged piece of wood as he tried to impress his fellow campers with his acute sense of balance. He thought of making fun of a female classmate in eighth grade because of the particularly bizarre way in which she walked and feeling horrible about himself when he realized she had overheard. He thought of breaking out his Lego collection one lazy Saturday afternoon after it had sat in the closet for nearly five years and using his older sensibility to build a castle any observer would have been impressed with. He thought of cafeteria lunches eating horrendous food and not caring. He thought of a hiking trip with his father just before he left for college when they stared in silence at beautiful waterfalls and he felt closer to him not talking than he ever had conversing. He thought of coming across a classical symphony on a television channel he had never heard of and listening to it in its entirety. He thought of applying to colleges and molding his essays into words that the applications offices were sure to want to hear, justifying disingenuousness in view of his ultimate goal of knowledge expansion.

Michael just let his mind go. Let one image flow to the next taking any intention completely out of the equation. He loved to do this. It left him feeling peaceful and there was nothing quite as thrilling as that moment when he realized he was still there. Michael had never had a drink. He had never taken any drugs. He felt no need to take outside substances to influence a mind that could slip into such wonderment almost entirely on its own. He was always surprised by how fascinating a topic of conversation all his fellow students at college found his lack of indulgence in the world of mind altering substances. They seemed as shocked as if he had just told them he had murdered his parents.

His roommate Dan was one such individual. Their very first night in the dorm, after they had each had their obligatory good-bye dinners with their respective families, Dan popped out a bottle of Captain Morgan and invited his new roommate to partake in a toast to the upcoming four years. Michael thanked him politely, but informed him that he didn't drink.

"No fucking way." said Dan. "How come?"

"I've just never had any desire to."

"So you've *never* had a drink?"

"Nope."

"Can we make this your first?"

"I don't think so."

"What's holding you back?"

A number of reasons always floated through Michael's head whenever someone he interacted with asked this inevitable question. There was the lack of necessity in influencing the mind's natural wonderment and the uncomfortable sensation that came with the idea of not having full control over his actions. There was the opposition to taking a substance which could lead to all sorts of violent accidents merely because society told him to.

There was the fact that not drinking saved him money. There was precaution, in not knowing whether he had an addictive temperament and being aware that the best way to stop an addiction is to never start it. Each of these possible responses came from a core of truth, but whenever he rattled through what to actually tell the shocked person who questioned him, he couldn't help but feel that it was his decision that came first and the reasons which came second. He would think up the reasons to explain an action that he somehow felt immediately was the right one to take without thinking about it at all.

"I've just never had any desire to," Michael repeated, settling on the fact that it was the most honest answer he could give.

"I bet I can get you to drink by the end of this year," Dan said, downing his own beverage and setting himself on a peer pressure mission.

"We'll see," said Michael. It was one of his best qualities that he could disagree with someone trying to bring him over to their own line of thinking without becoming annoyed by them. He had been refining this technique of calmly listening to another's attempts to assert superiority without issuing a rebuttal for years with his father. There was not a single activity Michael could engage in that Bill Bailey did not have a better method of doing. Whether it was driving or cooking or taking out the garbage or flossing, Bill had helpful advice to offer. Occasionally his suggestions would be rational and Michael would give them a shot. Other times, he felt sure that he was already going about his activity the correct way and he simply continued, feeling no need to justify himself, and not at all shaken when his father rediscovered the supposed flaws in his performance and used the same words with a higher decibel level to insist once more the proper way of doing things. Michael could recall a time when his temper rose.

When an opinionated assault riled him up and he felt the need to argue back, as if he was doing a disservice to his own thoughts by keeping quiet. But somewhere along the line, through no particular influence that he could pin-point, he had come to the realization that responding usually did nothing but create derision and inspire each side to lock themselves further into their convictions. At which point the argument would no longer be about the subject that was being argued over and would subtly take on the meaning of general worth of the individuals arguing. Michael no longer felt any use for these primal competitions. Life was far too exhilarating to get caught up in useless battles over nothing.

"I'm going to get you to drink," repeated Dan.

"Ok," said Michael, smiling.

Dan held true to his word. Like clockwork he offered Michael a drink every single time he had one of his own, which was quite often. And any time they attended a party together Dan made a point of spreading the word of Michael's non-drinking to all of the party's attendees, ensuring that each one of them also try to convince Michael to drink. A lesser person would have become exasperated or at least would have stopped hanging out with Dan but Michael was not bothered. He understood people. The games they played. The societal rules they all agreed upon without realizing they were doing so. And the silly way everyone's feathers were ruffled whenever one in their midst failed to follow the rules. His fellow students were only behaving the way they had learned to behave. And Dan was far too enthusiastic an individual to stop spending time with.

If there was one human quality Michael valued above all else it was enthusiasm. He cherished those who, like himself, had an intense spirit for living. Who embraced existence in all its mysteries and complexity and above all, who loved life itself. Michael often told people that he wanted to survive until at least age 120. There was so much to see, so much to read, so much to partake in, that the longer he could prolong his time on earth the better. It was not as if Michael did not have dissatisfactions. He did. First and foremost was the fact that he had never had a girlfriend. At his core was a loud desire to fall in love and there were moments when he stood alone in the hand-holding overrun campus walkways when he would identify a strange ache most people called loneliness. But Michael never stayed down long. Even not having found a companion became a source of enthusiasm when he thought about the exhilaration of facing the unknown. Optimism came to Michael without any effort. It was his natural state. He had a great instinctive grasp of human nature and understood what brought other people down even if it was impossible for him to actually feel what they did.

The only human action that he could never manage to comprehend was suicide. Shortly after arriving at the university he had heard of a suicide attempt in his dorm that had occurred just three floors below him. Likely while he was in his room. A new freshman had tried to hang himself but was discovered by his roommate in the process, and was cut down before he died. The incident disturbed Michael. Perhaps more because he could not grasp an understanding of it than because it had even happened in the first place. He knew he had lived a comfortable, easy life and he knew many did not have it so good, but it was still impossible for him to conceive of any situation where someone would just give up on existence. His main concerns were not having enough time to gain all the knowledge he wished to have, to visit all of the places he wished to go, to converse with all of the fascinating people out there just waiting for someone to talk to. It was hard for him to imagine someone thinking they were facing too much time rather than too little. He attributed it mainly to chemical imbalances. He was hopeful that advances in modern medicine could put anyone in the right perspective.

Michael's first year at college had only amplified his passion for existence. Socially he felt satisfied enough. There were abundant opportunities to spend time with new people. Dorm life certainly provided for its fair share of random chatting. If he didn't have a particularly strong connection to any particular individual he was unconcerned. If the constant talk of sex sometimes made him a bit shy about sharing his virginity it didn't do too much to lower his self esteem, as he reminded himself that he had no desire for random hook ups and would eventually share the experience with the right person. He liked being constantly surrounded by people even when he didn't speak to them. Knowing he was part of some larger social being created by all of its specific individual parts. But it was the academics which really inspired him. He loved searching the course catalogue and reading up on the various ultra specific obscure courses with vague intriguing names like "The World of Everything" and "Investigations into the Interlocking Networks of Communication in the Pre-Ancient Civilizations." In his first twelve years of schooling the reach of his lessons remained isolated to a select few subjects deemed as important by society and resulting in reserves of information shared by all who took the time to learn it. In college a wealth of new areas of study became available. He could learn about specialized histories of tribal populations who refused to assimilate to the outside world and the development and practice of logic and the philosophical ideas of the German Idealists and how those ideas spread to world today. More than anything he could study through intricate science, meticulous experimentation, and thousands of years of archeological research the true nature of reality, continuing his personal exploration of learning about his fellow humans and newly exploring the greater universe that lie behind them. Michael had chosen the dual majors of Psychology and Religious Studies. Some people found this to be an odd combination but to Michael it made perfect sense. What more natural a pairing than the modern search for reasons and the ancient ones? Michael was the ultimate optimist but he far from felt he had all the answers. The more he learned, the closer he hoped to get to that ultimate truth we all seek. What would he do when he got there? Well, that was another question entirely.

Michael looked up and caught the light of his lamp. He loved light. No artificial creation matched the breathtaking energy that came any day the sun shone down directly upon him, but man's production of light was still thrilling in its intentional ingenuity and in the giddy sensation he got resting his face, eyes closed, directly under a bulb.

The brightness awoke him from his memory meditation. He felt energized by the descent into his own head. He wanted to exercise. Do something with the bliss he was feeling. He stood up.

He stopped. Something felt strange. He looked down. His feet were floating a few inches off the floor.

Michael looked at his lamp. He must have been staring at it for too long. The light must have affected his eyes. He wasn't seeing correctly. Or perhaps he had slipped into an actual meditation without knowing it and had not taken the proper time to exit, causing hallucinations. He took a deep breath and looked back down.

There were his feet, right on the floor as they should be. He felt himself unclench. His imaginary levitation had sent a jolt of tension through his body.

He sat back down. He still did have a good deal of school

work that needed to be done before the night was through. He tried to forget the strange incident and resumed the task at hand.

• • •

Michael entered the dining hall. He took in the daily smell of just made food no longer fresh seconds after it is cooked, the sight of stumbling students who haven't bothered to take off their pajamas, shaking off their hangovers with coffee, the sound of chatting cliques sharing the latest gossip while the hung-over pajama wearers shush them because the noise hurts their brains, and the feel of the hall's year round frigid temperature. He took a tray and walked to the food station so that he could take in the taste of the incredibly mediocre food that he had nonetheless grown quite the affection for over the course of his freshman year.

At the grill station he picked up a plate of scrambled eggs and sausage and at a nearby table he sat down to eat his breakfast.

He reached for the ketchup then noticed it was already in his hand.

"That's strange," he thought.

As he squeezed the ketchup from the bottle he glanced up. Diagonally across from him sat a male student he had never seen before. The student was staring directly at him. His mouth was hanging open. His fork, latched onto a piece of egg remained held in the air, frozen midway in its journey to his mouth.

Michael gave him a polite nod of recognition then returned to his meal. He ate a few bites and hoped that the staring student had looked away. He looked back up. The student did not appear to have even moved.

Michael braced himself. He would eat while being watched and he would not let his observer bother him. Some people were a little quirky. There was no need to judge beyond that. He ate his eggs.

"How did you do that?"

Michael looked up. The student had spoken.

"Do what?"

"Make that ketchup bottle come into your hand without touching it."

"What are you talking about?"

The student's voice was shaking. "You sort of turned your hand and the ketchup bottle just went flying into it."

"I think you might be confused."

"I saw it. I know I saw it," he said less than fully confident, clearly terrified that he was losing his mind.

Following one of the most awkward pauses he had ever experienced, Michael said, "I think I should go eat over there."

He took his plate and moved to a table across the meal hall. He sat facing in the opposite direction that he had been. He ate for a minute then turned his head. The student had stopped staring at him. Now he was staring at the ketchup bottle. He held it in his hand, investigating it for any trickery that might be hidden in its construction.

Michael tried to forget the incident. Hardly anything had occurred and he wasn't typically fazed even by what most would classify as stressful situations. Something was lingering though. What was it?

How did that ketchup get in my hand? he thought.

• • •

As Michael walked to class he got the strange feeling that he was being followed. He turned his head.

The student from the meal hall saw he had been spotted and jumped behind a mail box that covered maybe a third of his body. He shifted a few times in an attempt to disguise himself more but only made his presence more obvious.

Michael thought about what to do. Part of him wanted to just label the student as a crazy person and run away. But with his hallucination the night before and his complete inability to recall how the condiment had actually made it into his hand, he was somewhat beginning to doubt his own sanity. In his current position, who was he to judge the mental state of someone he had just met?

He approached the student.

"Hi."

"Oh, hey," the student said, coming out from behind the mail box and pretending their meeting was pure coincidence.

"I'm Michael."

"Aaron."

"You're following me Aaron."

"Yeah, sorry about that."

"Well?"

"I just...I just need you to tell me that there was some trick or something you were practicing with the ketchup back there."

"I wasn't practicing a trick."

"I know I saw something. If I didn't see something then there's something wrong with me."

"The truth is that I'm not sure how the ketchup got into my hand. I sort of just looked down, and there it was. I actually thought it was kind of strange but I figured it was just some odd lapse in short term memory."

"So it's possible that it flew into your hand?"

"I suppose it's possible."

"I knew it."

"I'm not saying it happened. I'm just saying it's possible."

"I saw it. It happened."

"There's something else actually."

"What?"

"I don't know why I'm telling you this. But last night I stood up from my desk and for a second I thought that I was…floating off the floor."

"You levitated?"

"It seemed like I was. That's not the same as it happening."

"Maybe you're some sort of illusionist and you just didn't know it."

"Or maybe we're both just losing our minds."

"Do you think you could make other stuff happen?"

"I didn't make this stuff happen."

"Here." Aaron reached into his backpack and pulled out a pen. "Try to take this from my hand."

Michael sarcastically reached over and grabbed the pen with his hand.

"You know that's not what I meant," said Aaron, taking it back.

Michael looked around to see if anyone was watching. He tried to figure how one goes about trying to perform telekinesis. He stuck out his hand, more embarrassed than he liked to feel and he tried to mentally summon the pen. He shook his fingers, thinking that perhaps the dramatic flare might help. Aaron watched enraptured but after about thirty seconds it became clear that nothing was going to happen.

"This is silly," said Michael.

"Maybe you just need more practice."

"Look, I don't know what happened over the last couple days

but I'm not going to spend my life worrying about it. Life is filled with mysteries. This is just another to add to the pile."

"You don't want to explore the fact that you might have some strange powers?"

"Not particularly. No. And I really have to get to class."

"Well at least do me a favor," said Aaron, tearing out a piece of paper from a notebook and jotting something down. "Take my phone number. If anything else happens, give me a call."

Michael took the paper. "Fine," he said, surprised at his own defensiveness. But I'm sure nothing else is going to happen."

• • •

Michael laid in bed. He had woken up several times through-out the night from strange dreams whose content he could not recall upon waking. He was feeling jolts of fear, present before he remembered why it was he was feeling them. The questions would form into words. Was I levitating? How did that ketchup get in my hands? Then he would remember the content the words were referring to and the fear would amplify. Partly because of how bizarre the questions were and partly because he didn't have good answers for them. It was one of those nights that felt like an eternity while trying to get through but he knew would feel like nothing once he reached morning. He had been shaken up by these peculiar incidents. He hated feeling apprehensive or unconfident. He avoided these emotions at all costs. They made him feel like a different person. But he just had to work his way through the night. All of this oddness would pass like an aver-age dream. He might remember it at first, but as he slipped into his usual reality it would vanish from his consciousness and he would forget any of it ever happened. He thought about forgetting. In his half asleep state he wondered what it would be like to forget everything. His family. His friends. His knowledge of himself. His memories. His life. Maybe it was the fact that it was the middle of the night and he was deprived of sleep but the idea of total forgetting pleased him. He tried it. He visualized everything he knew just dissolving away, leaving him as nothing in particular.

He stayed in that state for quite a while. He was not sure how long. Time lost all meaning on erratically slept nights. After a bit he noticed that he had to go to the bathroom and sat up. He opened his eyes. It was too dark to see anything.

"Where's the lightswitch?" he thought.

The lights turned on. He hadn't moved.

"What the fuck?" Dan spurted out, pulling his blanket over his eyes and shifting his body towards the wall.

"Sorry," said Michael. He thought about turning the lights back off. They seemed to hear him. The room became dark.

• • •

The next morning Michael called Aaron.

"You turned the lights on and off with your mind?"

"Either that or there was a very coincidentally timed electrical malfunction."

"We need to meet somewhere."

Aaron signed them up for a two hour slot in a room in Penrose Hall, the college's student center. Rooms were available for private club meetings and study groups. This was likely the first time one had ever been rented out for super power testing.

Aaron was already in the room when Michael arrived. He had pushed all of the desks to the side walls, leaving a vast open space to experiment. He had brought with him several plastic bags worth of unidentified goods.

"Oh good, you're here," said Aaron. "We shouldn't waste any time getting started."

"What exactly do you have planned?" asked Michael.

"Well eventually we have to figure out exactly what kind of powers you have. Your abilities kind of seem to be all over the map. There must be some area of focus. Something around which they're centralized. But before we get to that I need you to tell me if there's anything unusual that happened recently. Anything which might have caused the strange appearance of these powers?"

"No. Nothing I can think of."

"You didn't come into contact with any radiation? You weren't bitten by any mysterious animals or didn't eat any experimental plant leaves?"

"I can't say that I did."

"There must be something. In the stories there's always something that triggers it."

"What stories?"

"You know, the super hero stories. The comic books."

"Oh. Of course," Michael said, with a hint of disdain. "You're a comic book geek. That's why you're interested in me."

"I mean, yeah, I love comics but—"

"You feel like you can live your fantasies in real life through me don't you?"

"No. I just— "

"This isn't a comic book Aaron! This is my life! And I don't know what the hell is going on!"

Aaron shrunk away. Michael wasn't sure where his anger had come from. It took him completely by surprise. He had not yelled in over six years.

"If you don't want my help I'll just go away," said Aaron, some-what hurt, but also scared of what Michael might be capable of in a state of fury. He walked to the corner of the room and started to gather his bags.

"No. Wait."

Aaron turned his head and managed to look Michael in the eye.

Michael was terrified. And he was taking out the frustra-tion of being terrified on possibly the only person he could talk to about what was happening. He had lost track of himself once again. He needed to focus on preventing that from occurring. And besides, who else would believe him?

"I'm sorry," he said. "I'm just scared. I want your help."

"Well alright," said Aaron. "Then let's get started."

For the next two hours Aaron subjected Michael to a series of intriguing tests in an attempt to lure his apparently shy pow-ers out of their hiding place. He lined up a row of near weightless items such as coins, paper clips, and feathers and had Michael do his best to move them from the one side of the room to the other. No luck. He took out an ice cube and asked Michael to melt it and took out a bottle of water and asked Michael to freeze it. The water remained unchanged. The ice cube eventually melted but Michael was fairly sure he had not assisted in the process. He held out a plank of wood and asked Michael to punch through it but he only marred his fingers. Aaron tried to convince Michael to let himself fall face first off of a pile of tables and see if he would instinctually levitate off the ground before he smashed into it but Michael declined.

"Our time in the room is up," said Michael, noticing the clock.

"Damn," said Aaron, who had not yet even descended into his

final bag of goodies. "I could try to see if we could rent the room longer if no one else booked it."

"That's okay," said Michael, who felt that it was more than enough for the day. "Why don't we get some lunch?"

On this visit to the meal hall, Michael grabbed the ketchup with his hands. Aaron was clearly disappointed.

"We'll try again tomorrow?" suggested Michael, wanting to raise his new companion's lowered spirits after their first attempt's failure.

"That sounds good," said Aaron, straightening up his back, excited to hear that he would be given another shot.

"This is so bizarre," said Michael. "It does feel like I'm suddenly living inside some sort of science fiction story or some weird dream and yet at the same time it feels so real, because it is, and regardless of what your beliefs are, when something is right in front of yours eyes you can't help but sort of accept it, even if hallucinations might be involved, and this dichotomy between the commonplace and the absolute obscurity is such a strange mix. It leaves me not knowing exactly how to feel."

"That was a mouthful," said Aaron.

Michael smiled. "I've always liked thinking about philosophical stuff. And this opens up all sorts of questions."

"Are you religious?"

"No. Are you?"

"Not really. I always liked the stories. But I never really thought they were real."

"You know, I haven't asked anything about you?" said Michael. "I'm sorry, I've just been so caught up in myself and all of this craziness. Tell me about yourself."

"What do you want to know?"

"I don't know. What's your major?"

"English."

"Oh yeah? What are you looking to do?"

"I don't know."

Michael noticed that Aaron seemed a bit uncomfortable with being questioned. It didn't seem like he wanted to hide anything. More like he was afraid of how little he had to share. He decided he wouldn't ask anything more.

"Why, what do you want to do after college?" Aaron asked.

"I guess I don't know either."

•••

Michael and Aaron returned to their room in the student center every day for the next two weeks. At first Aaron continued to create new tests. Running around the room to see if he could reach abnormal speeds. Lifting a cinderblock to see if had abnormal strength. Expanding and contracting a classic slinky to see if he had an abnormal control over metal. All failed. He also instituted new methods of initiation. Yoga and Meditation became prerequisites to attempts at punching through the plank of wood, in the hope that a more relaxed state of mind would assist Michael into a condition to use his powers. Eventually Aaron ran out of ideas and the sessions just became a grind of determination.

For all the creativity Michael possessed, he didn't bother to suggest any means of his own. He enjoyed being a part of Aaron's mental flow. For one, it fascinated him to descend completely into another's mind set and with it a world of intriguing solutions to a completely unique problem. But in some way, it also provided a great deal of freedom to let another shoulder the problem. If Aaron was frustrated over the strange occurrences and their subsequent disappearance, he didn't have to be. By the end of the two weeks, Michael's abilities had made no indication they would resurface and his stress level had slowly dwindled away to nothing.

Michael went into their eleventh testing session feeling like his old self. Optimistic about the future, free of fear, simultaneously calm and enthusiastic, having cleared a major hump. Walking into the room he noticed that Aaron had bags under his eyes.

"Hey Aaron."

Aaron merely nodded. He was skimming through notebooks he had been jotting in religiously during the testing even though there had at no point been anything new to report.

Michael looked at him and saw nothing but overwhelming defeat. He felt pity for his new friend. Where the implications of the events that spurred the whole to-do had terrified him, they had been a source of life-affirming excitement to Aaron. Michael had learned a great deal about Aaron through the little bits and pieces of conversation they shared during their mostly focused time together. Maybe not the specifics of his story but important indications of his character. He had learned that Aaron found life to be a bit of a struggle. He wasn't quite depressed, just bored with day to day existence. And he learned that the primary way he kept himself up was by retreating into fantasy. He loved comic books, yes, but he also loved movies and novels. By imagining his life as part of some greater tale, he found some purpose. Unfortunately, most of the time there was nothing story-like about his life and the boredom only increased. Michael had been a gift. A mythical figure, born straight from the stories and dropped into his lap. He needed Michael's powers to be real. He needed these insane, impossible to believe, circumstances to continue on. And he wanted desperately to be an integral part of them. He wanted his determination to be the reason that the world was saved. (Michael had no doubt Aaron was thinking big.)

Michael did not want to be the cause of someone else falling apart. He decided that at the end of that day's session he would tell Aaron they were done. It would sting at first. But in the end Aaron would be better for it. It would prevent him from descending in an all out obsession. It was necessary for Aaron to figure out how to be okay apart from crazy fantasies of what life should be.

"Let's get started," said Michael enthusiastically. After today this abnormal and uncomfortable patch of his life would be over. He felt free.

"Try to pick up that battery," said Aaron without much emotion, pointing to the end battery on a line of eight that he had just arranged.

"Sure," said Michael. Free. Free of all cares.

He reached his hand out and the battery flew into it.

Aaron's face lit up. He was about to explode in excitement but Michael put his hand up to halt him.

"Wait," he said. Michael closed his eyes. There was no time to think. No time to waste. Free, he said to himself.

He reached out his hand. The other seven batteries came flying towards him.

"Yes!" Aaron screamed, leaping into the air, throwing fist pumps every which way.

Michael ignored Aaron for the moment. He thought about how good he had just felt, thinking he was done with these unexpected abilities. He thought that he should be gripped with a new wave of fear now that they had returned. But he wasn't. Something was altered. It was control. He had control. And that made all the difference.

"Line them back up," he said.

Aaron didn't have to be told twice.

◆ ◆

Michael descended into the midst of his peers, hiding a tremendous secret from the rest of the world. It was an incredibly surreal thing, walking around campus, watching the other students living in their assumed versions of reality while his view of all that was possible had been expanded to near infinite.

After the flying battery, the sessions with Aaron had been moving incredibly smoothly. He now felt comfortable moving any small to medium sized object in any direction he chose. He had also successfully repeated his trick of turning the lights on and off. (He now had a running joke going of switching them off whenever Aaron spoke too excitedly, which Aaron had quickly grown tired of and Michael couldn't imagine ever not being funny). He had not yet managed to recreate his moment of levitation but he had unexpectedly melted a penny and on a whim heated up a container of leftover macaroni and cheese that Aaron was about to go find a microwave for. It was hard to know what it was they should be trying and even when there was a specific aim, such as the levitation, it was hard to know how to go about attempting it. The importance of Michael's new confidence could not be understated. Acting with his abilities rather than experiencing them act on their own changed his frame of mind completely. Instead of wanting to escape from the powers he wanted to learn as much as he could about them. He wanted to be an archeologist of himself, digging until he uncovered each and every thing he could do. As for Aaron, he was in a constant state of rapture, watching every other worldly phenomenon with glee as he savored the sweetness of sodas through straws and opened up his blinds each morning glad to be alive.

And though they were spending a significant amount of time together and were daily powered more and more by each other's mutual enthusiasm, neither Aaron nor Michael ever spoke out loud the question that was constantly on both their minds. How? How was this happening? Or sometimes the even more intangible – why? Neither of them wanted to spoil the ecstatic mood by grappling with the implications of the question, even though they already were on their own. Speaking it out loud might spoil the mood.

In completely private moments Michael had started speaking to God, though he still did not think he believed in him. Michael had never been a fan of the Occam's Razor argument – that the simplest explanation was the correct one. He thought that it made more sense if the complex and inconceivable had complex and inconceivable reasoning behind it. Not that he didn't hope to find the reasons anyway. And not that the existence of God would be the simplest answer, since all other sorts of questions would be raised if he did. In any case, what had been happening was undeniably miraculous and he thought it was best not to rule any possibilities out. So he quietly spoke to God and waited to see if he would hear anything back.

Meanwhile, as he walked through campus, he tried to make eye contact with those he passed. He tried to see into their personalities and figure out how each individual might react if they learned of what he could do. If they would scream "apocalypse" and want to burn him at the stake like the supposedly false witches of Salem (he was newly reconsidering the possibility of any previously impossible tale of the fantastic throughout history) or if they might fall to his feet in worship and expect him to be some sort of savior. He mulled over whether he had any moral responsibility to use his abilities to help the world and considered the specifics of what he could do if he did. And he kept stumbling out of his own mind, suddenly feeling like he had been thinking someone else's thoughts. Those of a character in a movie perhaps. Or those of himself in a dream. These questions could not possibly be those of his waking actual life. But in the end he always determined that they were. That the impossible actually was happening. And that he now had practical matters to take into account.

Michael stopped at an open bench and sat down to think. He would be late to class but it hardly mattered. With his mind as active as it was he wouldn't retain any of the lecture anyway.

He and Aaron had not explicitly discussed keeping everything quiet but doing so was a presumed agreement. He was sure that in the back of Aaron's mind there was always the assumption that eventually the larger world would learn about Michael and about the tests they had been conducting. How else could he be given his due for the major part he played in this saga and bask in the glory of being a vital supporting player? It was just a matter of perfecting the powers and then putting them on display for all humanity to marvel at. As good as he felt, Michael was more apprehensive about revealing himself.

He watched a petite female student with her head in a book pass by. She looked up, caught him staring, and timidly directed her eyes back to her book. How would someone like her react? Most likely with fear. It was hard for him to optimistically expect that if he showed people what he could do they would respond only with intrigued delight. The consequences would be more far reaching. He knew that much. It might just be safer to never let the secret out.

But just then, the decision was taken out of his hands.

Across the lawn students screamed. Michael turned his head, to see what was causing the commotion.

When he looked up, the suicidal student was already falling through the air. She had jumped off the school's tallest building. She was seconds from hitting the ground.

Everyone was watching, about to witness the last moments in a young girl's life.

And then she just stopped.

In mid air.

Maybe twelve feet off the ground.

This extraordinary sight induced more screams than that of her imminent death.

Michael made his way through the crowd of staring statues holding out his hands. He concentrated. He had never moved something so big and he did not wish to drop her. Stopping her in mid air had been a desperation effort and he was incredibly relieved it had been successful.

He moved directly below and lowered her slowly. At first the students only saw her descending. They stared directly above. Her body just covered the sun and beams shone down on every side of her. It was heavenly.

Then a few started to notice the boy beneath her with his hands in the air.

"Is her lowering her?" they asked in whispers, tapping their neighbors on the shoulder to point out the mysterious male on the ground.

He turned his hand. Her body shifted to a vertical position. Everyone gasped.

He continued to lower her until her feet were only about six inches off the ground. Her eyes were closed. He directed her into his arms, afraid that she would not stand on her own if he lowered all the way. He held her.

Everyone watched. Campus had frozen. But Michael didn't notice any of them. He was completely focused on the girl he was holding. She was apparently unconscious.

And she was beautiful.

II.

When Aaron arrived the scene was already swarming with news trucks. Representatives of every major local station interviewed hundreds of students who had bared witness to the afternoon's events. And they each told the same impossible story. The girl, one Zooey Shelanski, had jumped from the Jenkins Building and just before she had reached the bottom she had stopped in mid air. She was then, for all appearances, lowered down slowly through some sort of telekinesis by a student that someone had identified as Michael Bailey.

As Aaron pushed his way through the crowd he caught drift of what happened through the conversations and tried to hear if anyone knew of Michael's current whereabouts. He had come when he had received a mysterious text message from Michael.

"Come to Jenkins right away. They know."

He thought that perhaps Michael could have phrased his summoning a little less ominously. He pictured Michael being thrown in a cage by an army of uniformly dressed dystopian literature style guards, now poking and prodding him with needles in order to extract his powers. And even though the word choice led to a bit of apprehensiveness about the state of his friend, Aaron couldn't help but bask in the dramatic glow of what surrounded him. He watched the shocked and amazed individuals attempting to figure out what they had seen and thought, here I am, right at the center of this crazy story, with the answers that everyone wants. He walked forward with his head held high.

• • •

Michael was not speaking. He had vocalized exactly one

sentence since he had been led away by campus administrators through the silent crowd, none of whom moved a single inch, and brought to a professor's office for safekeeping.

"Is the girl okay?" That was his sentence.

He was told that she was. He wanted to add a second question and ask where she was but he decided to keep silent.

The administrators asked him repeatedly what happened but he did not respond and eventually they gave up for the time being, leaving him to stare out the window at the news cameras.

As he observed the confused chaos he thought about what to do. Should he pretend that nothing out of the ordinary had happened? That he had somehow caught the girl leaping to her death and everyone who saw him lowering her were just seeing things? Should he say that he knew her and that they were magicians practicing some new illusion? Thus, putting him in trouble for disturbing the peace but in the clear from more intrusive questions? Or should he just take the ultimate leap into a new life and reveal himself completely?

He needed to talk to Aaron. He remembered that he had sent him a text message in the immediate moments of the event, as he held the girl in his arms and felt frozen as to how to proceed. He sent him another message.

"I'm in Professor Hardy's office in Martin Hall. Tell them I'll only talk to you."

When Aaron finally did arrive he noticed the administrators observing him with a rather strange mix of apprehension and disdain. He imagined they had been waiting anxiously for his arrival, expecting him to be some striking guru that was the key to the entire strange situation. They were shocked by his meekness but still too wary to look down on his scrawny self in the usual way, so instead they graced their best expression of defensive threat, which was entirely inapplicable to anyone involved. Aaron took advantage of the rare opportunity to be in control and smiled a polite hello they were entirely unprepared for. He introduced himself and one of the administrators hidden behind an enormous chair coughed out Michael's direction. Aaron thanked them and proceeded on his way.

He found Michael at the window.

"Quite the sight," said Aaron.

"Thanks for coming."

"Of course."

Aaron waited for Michael to continue speaking but he seemed too busy staring out the window.

"You did it, Michael. You saved that girl's life. If it wasn't for all the practice we'd done you wouldn't have been able to do that."

"What should I tell them?"

"Tell them the truth."

"What if they don't believe me?"

"They'll believe you. You have the best proof in the world. You can show them."

"And then what?"

"Then... I don't know, does it matter?"

"Does it matter? Maybe it doesn't matter to you. You're not the one who's going to be poked and prodded and tested to see how you can do what you can do! You're not the one who people are going to expect miracles from! You're not the one who won't ever be able to do the things you enjoy again because everybody's going to be looking at you from now on, wanting to use you for god knows what end! Don't you get it, Aaron! My life is over! Things won't ever be the same after this!"

Aaron took a moment to compose himself following this berating.

"This is bigger than you. Somehow, whether by God or some other source we don't understand, you've been blessed with the ability to do some pretty incredible things. And you have a responsibility now. No, your life isn't going to be the same. It's going to be better! People are going to love you! You saved that girl's life, Michael."

A reasonable argument, Michael thought, disconnected from his own screams even as they had still been coming out of his mouth. It seemed the proper way to respond. As if the script had been written months before and he was too afraid to start improvising. Really, he was only thinking of the girl.

"What's her name?"

"Zooey."

"Why was she trying to kill herself?"

"I don't know."

Michael watched the people outside. Some students were still trying to get a glimpse of the news trucks who were still trying to get a glimpse of the students. But most were just going about their days. Mystical events held only enough sway to rupture the fabric of their routine for a short while. Around an hour and forty five minutes by his count.

"I don't feel like myself," he said, turning to Aaron. "I'm sorry you never knew me before all of this. I was really pretty agreeable."

"I still think you're pretty agreeable."

"Thanks Aaron."

Michael looked out the window. He could feel the pressure of what he was about to do closing in on him. Tension pressed up against his cheekbones and clogged his ears. A reality saran wrap that would hopefully manage to preserve him. But what if he flew away?

What if he just opened the window and flew away?

"Well," he said after a long moment, "Let's show them what I can do."

Michael walked determinedly past Aaron into the room of waiting university stiffs. With a couple waves of the hand he ruined hours of carefully sorted filing in the creation of the thickest of paper fogs. He watched jaws literally drop and eyes attempt narrow escapes from their sockets. The theatricality was probably unnecessary but it gave him a laugh.

"Here I am," he said.

• • •

The story unfurled itself quickly from the local to the progressively larger national media until primetime where it replaced two weeks of coverage on a real life superhero turned supervillain calling himself Bullet Man in the coveted news slot of unending curiosity.

Michael, tied up in an all day grilling session with every figure of authority from within thirty miles had not even had a chance to call his parents.

"Michael. You're on the news. They say you have super powers. Your father's thinking of buying a sports car. Call me back. It's your mother." That was one of the thirty-seven voice mails he received when he finally had a chance to check his phone.

"Hey mom," he said, sneaking in a moment to call her back.

"Michael! What's going on?"

"Oh not much, you?" he said out of habit, before he remembered why she was calling.

"Why are they talking about you on the news?"

"Well, mom, it's kind of strange to describe, but I've discovered recently that I have the ability to do some pretty crazy things."

"Like what?"

"Telekinesis seems to be the one I have the best grasp on. But I've been able to turn lights on and off, change temperature, uh, I can melt things –"

"I don't understand. When did this happen? How could this happen? What's happening to my life!"

Michael's mother started to cry.

"So," he said, "Dad's buying a sports car?"

If Michael had thought his life had become odd before when he was engaging in his experimental sessions with Aaron, he was completely unprepared for the circus it would now turn into.

Phone calls from magazines and newspapers and television profiling programs, all wishing to be the first to unveil the full story or the first to expose the inevitable scam that was being perpetrated. Money hungry skepticism reverberated from every one of his suitor's voices. Visits from military officers, presumably looking to determine the particular benefit Michael's powers could offer the United States in battling the forces of terrorists, who thankfully were turned away by the college administration, itself selfishly prying for the benefit Michael could bring the university. Perhaps increased tuition for the possibility that attendance to their school gave you the ability to move things with your mind. Proposals from the school's biology and physics professors to conduct personal study sessions to get to the bottom of what was happening in Michael's physical system, their mouth's watering at the new frontier that sat before them in the form of a college freshman. Not to mention thousands of Facebook friend requests, most from people he had never even met, and hundreds of messages from those he'd lost (or never really been in) touch with who had apparently been meaning to check in with him for some time.

And this was all the first day.

When he finally convinced the administrators to let him go to his dorm, well after the sun had set, he returned his mother's call, gave a brief recap of the day's proceedings to Aaron that he promised to expand upon later, and shuffled quickly through the campus's darkest pathways hoping to get home without being recognized for his sudden newfound fame.

He raced up the stairs of his building, threw open the door of his room, slammed it behind him, and breathed a sigh of relief.

"There you are."

Dan. He had forgotten about Dan.

His roommate clicked off the television he had been watching only while he waited for Michael to return home.

"Hey," said Michael, lying down in bed and naively hoping that he could somehow avoid further conversation.

"You've been all over the news."

"So I hear."

"Did you really lower that girl to the ground?"

"Yeah."

"That's incredible."

"I suppose it would meet the definition, yes."

"How did you do it?"

"I really don't know."

Dan paced around. He looked thoughtful. Michael laughed to himself. Dan and thought were two things he did not usually associate with each other.

"Michael this is a miracle. You've been chosen by God."

"What?"

"I admit I've had doubts over the years. But this is proof. God exists."

Michael stared at Dan. Was this really the same person who a few weeks before went on a weekend long Jello shot diet?

"I don't know."

"How else could this be happening?"

"I mean I've considered the possibility."

"Michael you've been chosen. You have something you need to do. You're supposed to lead people. You're a prophet."

"Well if it is God, he hasn't said anything to me. So that might be helpful."

"Be patient. He will."

"I don't know Dan. I appreciate the opinion but I really need to get some sleep. Please, if anyone tries to see me, just send them away. It's been a long day."

"Okay Michael."

To his credit, Dan did just as his roommate asked. There were quite a few knocks on the door over the next several hours and Dan loyally sent each of the visitors away. Michael pretended to be asleep but was unable to actually be so, the day's events too busy swimming through his head. At around 1:30 there was a knock just like any other. He listened as Dan opened the door and told the female visitor to come back another time.

"Can you give him a message for me?" she asked.

"Sure," said Dan.

"Can you tell him Zooey Shelanski was here?"

"No problem."

Dan shut the door. Michael sprang out of bed. He ran into the hallway past his bewildered roommate.

"Zooey," he said, catching her attention just before she entered the stairwell.

She looked over at him. She was so beautiful.

"Hi," she said, a bit shy now that she was actually interacting with who she came to see.

He walked over to her.

"I was asking about you all day. They wouldn't tell me anything."

"They didn't want to let me go. I guess they thought I'd try it again."

He paused. He wanted to phrase all his words very carefully, terrified that the girl he'd spent his entire day thinking about might run off and leave him alone again.

"How are you?" he said.

"I'm okay. A little confused."

"Yeah me too."

"Is it—" she said "Is what they're saying true?"

"What exactly? They had me locked up in a room all day. They're probably saying any number of things by now."

"That you caught me. In the air. I can't remember. It all went blank after I... Until I woke up in the health facility, people looking at me like I was a ghost."

Michael looked at her for a moment. He smiled.

"Come with me," he said.

Michael took her hand before he even realized what he was doing. By the time he became aware of his actions he had already led her half way down the hall and she had made no effort to pull away.

He led her down the dormitory stairway to the basement where he remembered once coming across a lounge on his way to do laundry. He peeked inside and let out a deep exhale upon finding it empty. They went inside.

"I want to show you something."

"Okay."

He walked over to the pool table and pointed his fingers towards the racked balls that lie on top of it. One by one he levitated the balls into the air.

Zooey let out a gasp but didn't move an inch as Michael made the balls rotate around each other in a spherical pattern. He was impressed with himself. He had never lifted so many objects at once and he had definitely never added any artistry into the process. But here he was, desperately wanting to impress a pretty suicidal girl he knew nothing about, creatively juggling pool balls in the air in increasingly more complicated patterns without so much as touching them. At a certain point he figured he better give it a rest or else risk seeming arrogant and lowered the balls down onto the felt.

He looked at her. She was crying.

She ran up to him and hugged him tight. He hugged her back.

"I have to go," she said.

She let go and went to the door.

"Wait," he said.

"Yeah?"

"Can I see you again?"

He wasn't sure but he thought he spotted the slightest roots of a smile on her face.

"Okay."

• • •

"So you're telling me that if my food is cold, I don't have to bother sticking it in the microwave? You can heat it up right here for me and I don't even have to get up?"

"Uh, yeah Dad, I guess that's one repercussion."

Michael had gone home for the weekend and was having

dinner with his parents. He told the anxiously impatient media, military, and scientists that no decision would be made as to his immediate plans until he had a chance to talk with those who loved him.

"My potatoes are actually getting a bit cold."

"Okay Dad."

Michael warmed up his father's potatoes.

"Amazing," said Bill Bailey, boiling down everything that had happened to a way for him to no longer have to get up in the middle of a meal.

"Michael, the news people keep coming and knocking on our door," said Martha Bailey.

"Yeah, I know mom, you don't have to answer any questions though."

"I tell them all how good of a boy you are."

"Thanks mom."

"And I say we just need to find a nice girl for you."

"Mom!"

"It's true Michael. You have so much to offer. You should have a girlfriend. Just look at how much these reporters want to talk to you."

"Michael could you get me the salt?" said Bill.

"Sure," said Michael, mindlessly standing up and walking to the pantry.

"What are you doing?"

"I'm getting you the salt. You just asked for it, remember?"

"I never said you had to get up."

"Ugh," said Michael, thinking that his father's laziness was so tremendous, it wasn't even satisfied until it spread to others around him. He picked up the salt with his hands and defiantly placed it on the table.

"See, this is just like you Michael. You have all this built in ability and you just don't take full advantage of it. There's so much more you could be doing with this."

"I don't know why you see my discovery of super powers as merely an excuse for me to never get any exercise."

"I wouldn't consider getting up for the salt exercise."

"Neither would I."

"So we're on the same page."

"Listen. It's great to see you guys, obviously, but I really came home because I need some advice."

"We're your parents Michael," said Bill. "We're always here to help."

"We love you Michael," said Martha.

"Thanks," said Michael, his heart a bit warmed. "I just don't know where to go from here. Now that I've discovered I have these abilities everybody seems to want me to come over to their personal needs. The military wants me to help destroy, presumably, the university science professors want to study me, the media wants me to just be some sort of celebrity, displaying my powers for everybody to see. And I don't really want to do any of it. But I'm not sure what to do instead. It doesn't seem like I'm going to be able to just go back to being a normal college student. And that sucks! Because I was really enjoying college."

Michael started to cry. He hadn't seen it coming but in the quickest of moments he became all too aware of just how sad he was that his previous life was gone. He suddenly remembered how he defined himself. He was happy. It was happiness which made him who he thought he was. And yet he hadn't felt happy for weeks. He'd felt stressed, confused, discouraged, and in a couple of brief moments, elated, but elated in a way that only led to more sadness when the elation passed. If he wasn't happy, he wasn't himself. Then who was he? He thought of Zooey. Her image was the only thing that brought comfort.

"Oh Michael, I think you should do whatever you want to do," said his mother, kindly, but unhelpfully.

"I'll tell you what I think," said his father. "I say screw all those other people. Go into business with this for yourself. There's a lot of money to be made on these powers. A lot of people who'd pay good money to have their food heated up, if you know what I'm saying. I'm proud of you Michael. And you can show them. Show them you're better than all of them."

It hit Michael that his father must be deeply unsatisfied with the life he had led. That he was bitter towards all those around him who he thought had it better. And that his parents would be completely unhelpful in giving him any answers.

Michael saw a large group of his high school friends while he was in town. He had put out a feeler that he would be home for a couple days if anyone was going to be around the area, even though several of those he contacted were attending colleges a great distance away. Each and every person he contacted made the journey home. He was excited to see them, hopeful that they might be more helpful than his mother and father in offering advice on what path to take with his sudden new life. But instead he felt awkward. They didn't look at him the same way they always had. He was not their friend but a wonder to behold. He no longer felt close to them. Watching them watch him, waiting for some sort of explosion of ecstatic supernatural joy, he felt so deeply alone. He told them he wasn't feeling very well and went home early, much to their disappointment. He was glad they felt disappointed. He was angry that they wanted to see his powers instead of him.

When he got home he called Aaron. He now understood the

situation. His life had been divided into two the moment when that ketchup bottle had made its way into his hands. The people he had known before hand were part of his past life. Aaron was the only person he really felt he could talk to because he was the only true member of this brand new life he was living.

He had to give up any attachment he had to the time that was gone. That life wasn't coming back.

"There you are," said Aaron.

"Here I am," said Michael.

"How's home?"

"Doesn't feel like home."

"I'm sorry to hear that."

"Thanks. How've you been?"

"Me? I'm fine."

"Good."

"I'm just waiting to find out what the plan is."

"The plan?"

"Yeah, what's the next step for you?"

"You're really here for me, aren't you Aaron?"

"Yeah. Of course I am."

"Well then what do you think?"

"Me?"

"Yeah. Should I be a media puppet? Government weapon? Scientist guinea pig? Or should I just run off somewhere? I'm in your hands. Tell me what you think I should do and I'll do it."

Aaron decided on scientist guinea pig.

He argued that the professors would be the least likely to exploit him in complete selfishness, theoretically less interested in money or power than an unquenchable thirst for knowledge. And hopefully in the process they could learn something about the specifics of Michael's condition for themselves. Maybe there was some genius lurking around the corner with his head stuck in a microscope who could solve the ultimate mystery of what the hell was going on with him in the first place.

The answer seemed obvious once Aaron illuminated it. Michael thought that in the past he would have come to the conclusion himself, but in the haze of all that he had been experiencing his thoughts had been filled with a fog that was difficult to see through. He was immensely grateful to Aaron for seeing things clearly. This way he would be able to remain at the university. He would inevitably grab the attention of strangers whenever he walked around but it would be better than the constant media exposure some of the other choices would dictate. He made a deal with the scientists that they could perform any testing they desired, if the university made an effort to keep the studies secretive until a time where some publishable conclusions were discovered. They agreed.

In just an astonishingly short period of time following the initial incident, with no new remarkable circumstances to report, the media moved on. At which point most people, Michael was sure, forgot about him. Sure, the story had been extraordinary. But life altering stories are reported all the time and rarely do they alter anyone's lives. When someone sees a report on the news of some massive tragedy their heart might ache for a few moments, they might feel affected for a day or two, but then their life returns to normal and they forget that anything ever happened. It was the same with positive or enlightening news. The effect never lasted unless the development somehow affected you personally.

Nothing ever lasted.

• • •

The night the clocks were sprung forward Michael walked home from the labs and basked in the newly extended sunlight.

It amazed him the massive fluctuation in feelings that could occur over just a few short weeks. It had been a rough transition. The roughest Michael had ever known. He was now able to separate himself from the circumstances and objectively analyze how his optimism had been tested. He knew it was a silly inaccurate metaphor but he liked thinking to himself that he had survived a war and come out on top. He was back to being his old self. Just with the addition of a few spectacular super powers.

As it turned out he was becoming very close with his scientist colleagues. They treated him as an equal. He was both the one being experimented on and the experimenter himself. He was working with a core group of three men and two women who had a passion for discovery. They had thus far been unable to locate any primary cause of Michael's condition. The DNA testing results had come back displaying nothing out of the ordinary. The MRI and Cat Scans were common place. But they had made some fascinating progress in terms of learning what Michael was capable of.

He had grown a seed just planted in the dirt into a fully matured plant in a matter of minutes.

He had changed the colors of the walls with a snap of his fingers.

Feeling a bit high on himself one afternoon, he had completely healed a gash on one of the scientists arms, which she had sustained in an awkward bicycle fall the day before.

And perhaps most amazingly, he had, on a microscopic level, changed the physical structure of certain bacteria which had been brought into the lab.

The more optimistic Michael felt, the easier he found it.

The lack of definitive answers was not a discouragement to the crew but rather an inspiration to push harder. There was such spirit, such enthusiasm within those laboratories. Michael thrived on it.

Besides, they had not been able to determine why Michael could do what he could do, but they believed they had gotten to the crux of *what* he could do.

"Michael," said Dr. Hauser, the team's leader, "it seems to me that at the very center of all of your abilities is one central ability – the ability to manipulate matter."

Michael was learning. He was learning more than he ever had in his life. Both from the scientists and from continued research in his own time. He was finding out what makes up matter and the strange way matter acts on the smallest of levels.

He didn't understand all of it. But he tried to explain it to Zooey anyway.

"It seems like when you get down to a certain quantum level, particles behave both like particles and like waves. Which is crazy! And what's even crazier is that what all the experiments confirm, is that which state the particle appears in is completely dependent on the observer and what it is they're trying to measure and how. It's like if I were both me and an elephant at the same time, but every time you looked at me you only saw one or the other, depending on whether you wanted to see me or the elephant."

She laughed. "I bet you'd be a really handsome elephant."

"Well thank you. But really, I mean it's crazy this stuff. It's like reality behaves completely different when you get to this certain small level. Like it's not anything fixed at all and it doesn't become fixed until we look for it. So we're an essential part of reality that makes it what it is. It's mind blowing. And that's just the tip of the iceberg."

"I like it when you talk about science to me."

She kissed him.

"Well I'll have to do it more often then."

He was spending a lot of time with Zooey. He had fallen for her completely. And in what he considered the most amazing of all the bits of amazingness that had occurred, she seemed to be falling for him too.

The second time he had seen her they had ended up talking for over four hours. They discussed all sorts of things. Medieval European literature. Early nineteen-nineties Saturday morning cartoons. Classic rock bands. Different procedures for shoe tying. She was extremely shy at first but Michael went the extra mile to make her feel comfortable. To let her know that she would not be judged and he would not broach any subject she did not want broached. Even though questions about her attempted suicide were eating away at him. And she returned the favor, not mentioning his super powers once. Considering the circumstances of their meeting, it was an extremely normal first date.

From there on he saw her nearly every night. They spent most of the time in her dorm, because she had her own room where they wouldn't have to be burdened by Dan and the way he looked at Michael as if he was constantly about to turn water into wine or ascend to heaven.

Mostly they just laid around and talked. He had wrestled with a full body earthquake of anxiety on the third night and kissed her. She had kissed him back.

"Are you my girlfriend?" he had asked a week later.

"Yeah. I think I am," she had said.

They were havens of comfort for each other in a place where they had both become instant celebrities. He was overcome with bliss every time he thought about her.

Michael paused on his walk home and sat down on the nearest bench. "Out of every bad thing comes something good," he thought. He had heard that once. Now he realized just how thoroughly it was true. Of course, when he had heard it, the opposing thought that out of every good thing comes something bad had also been included. But he was in too joyous of a mood to give that part any credence right now.

And now the late sunlight had returned for the better part of the year. He closed his eyes. He loved those moments when he could shut his eye lids but the light of the sun would still shine through. He had a girlfriend. And to him that was more of a miracle than anything he had been able to do in the labs.

"Praise the lord!" he heard someone scream in his ear.

He opened his eyes. A homeless man was kneeling before him.

"I am your servant. Tell me what you ask of me and I will do it."

"Um. I think you have the wrong guy."

"You're Michael Bailey aren't you?"

"Yeah."

"Then you are the one God has chosen."

"Right. Well I really ought to be going."

Michael got up and walked off at about one and a half times his normal speed.

"Don't run from the gift God has given you!" the man screamed as Michael departed in his awkward half jog. "You are the chosen one!"

• • •

Zooey rested her head on Michael's chest. Her eyes were closed. Michael just looked at her. He couldn't stop thinking about how beautiful she was.

But something was bothering him. He had started feeling off after the interaction with the homeless man, but as sometimes happens, the discomfort over this particular issue led him right into a far more pressing one he had been doing his best to ignore.

"Zooey?"

"Mmm."

"I need to talk to you about something."

"Yeah?"

She opened her eyes and smiled. She pushed back her hair in a way that made him fill with desire. He wouldn't let his lust distract him.

"I've been afraid of bringing this up because I'm afraid of ruining everything. I'm just so unbelievably happy."

"I'm happy too."

"But I have to know. It's been killing me."

"Yeah?" she said apprehensively. She knew what was coming.

"I have to know why you were trying to kill yourself."

"You do?"

"Yeah. I do. I just care about you too much not to know."

She sat up.

"I haven't felt like that since that morning, you know?"

"Okay."

"I'm so glad you saved me."

"I know."

"It's just, really tough for me sometimes... Have you ever just felt sad for no particular reason? Like not because of anything at all. But just the feeling?"

"Uh. I'm not sure."

"Well I did. All the time. It started when I was about fifteen. I was okay most of the time but I would have these spells of just the deepest sadness. And I just couldn't do anything. I couldn't get up out of bed. I couldn't eat. Just everything seemed so pointless. And I'd feel like there was no meaning to any of it. Any thing I did would just vanish and there was no point in wanting anything because nothing could bring me any happiness. Most of the time the spells would pass after a few days and I'd feel fine. Like it was a completely different person who couldn't find the will to move just a couple days earlier. Or maybe I didn't feel fine but I felt better. I still felt like there wasn't too much to be happy about but I could live my life. I could function. And that's how it was mostly. A spell once every couple of months. Maybe more in the winter. But ever since I got to school a few months ago the spells became the normal me instead of the opposite. And I finally got to the point where the suffering of life didn't seem worth the brief pleasures that came now and again. That morning I just felt like I was suffocating. Leaping off that building was the most immediate way I could think of to end it all. I ran up to that roof feeling like dying was the only thing that could stop the pain."

"Did you ever think of talking to someone? Trying to get some medication or something?"

"I mean it crossed my mind. But only when I felt okay. And when I felt okay there didn't seem to be a reason for it. And when I didn't feel okay I couldn't bring myself to do anything."

"What about your parents? Or your friends? Did you ever talk to them about this?"

"Not really. I was embarrassed. And it made me angry. Everyone else always seems fine and I'm just so sad. Just so deeply sad and it just feels so inescapable."

"But you don't feel that way now?"

"No. I don't. It doesn't even feel like that other person was me now."

"I guess, honestly, it's just hard for me to identify with because I've never felt anything like that. I've always been pretty happy."

"You're lucky."

"But I want to understand what you feel."

"Thanks Michael. But I want you to keep on being happy. That's what I like about you."

"You promise you'll tell me if you ever feel that way again?"

"I promise."

She kissed him and rested her head back on his chest, closing her eyes.

He tried to imagine the wonderful person who made his stomach flutter every time he thought about her as the person she had just described. It made him angry. Angry that such a person had to endure so much pain.

And suddenly he felt incredibly guilty. He had been given a gift. Whether it was from God like the homeless man said was irrelevant. He was able to do things that no one else could and he was using them in absolutely no way that could help other people. He had been selfish. It was time for him to think about people other than himself.

"Don't you think it's time we use some of what we've found more practically?" he said the next day to Dr. Hauser.

"Practically, how?"

"You know, use my abilities to help some people in the world."

"I don't know if we've even scratched the surface of what your abilities are."

"But we know a bunch. I'm sure we know enough that I could do some good."

"What exactly did you have in mind?"

"I don't know. I just feel like I should help humanity somehow."

"Michael, I think you're helping humanity right here in this lab. What you can do completely redefines our definition of what is possible. Not to be too overdramatic but this may just be the most important scientific breakthrough in the history of mankind. You may be the next stage of evolution. A stage where we can manipulate the reality around us. And I honestly think the best thing we can do is keep this as quiet as possible. Right now all the world knows is you might have levitated someone once. And in a giant stroke of luck we've managed to get them to forget for the time being about even that. If people found out what we've discovered here there's no telling the amount of ways they might exploit you. And I bet the government would no longer be requesting your service, they'd be demanding it. I think we should find out completely what we're dealing with here before we take any other steps."

"But we could be finding out what we're dealing with for the rest of my life. I've loved this time in the labs but don't you think it doesn't matter as much why I can do what I can do as the fact that I can do it? And that there are people out there suffering who I might be able to help?"

"Do you want to be a super hero?" Dr. Hauser said with a smirk. "Is that it? Show everyone just how great you are?"

"What? No."

"I've gotten the impression that you were serious about this. This is important Michael. You can't just let your fantasies of being some savior to humanity let us get off track."

"I don't think that's what I said."

"Well you let me know when you're ready to get back to serious work."

• • •

Aaron had been waiting for Michael's call. Through insufferably boring meals, through intolerably tedious class lectures, through afternoon barely entertaining sitcom marathons on a series of ever worse cable networks. He kept his phone next to his ear as he slept, set on the maximum volume, to ensure that even if Michael decided to call at three in the morning he would be there, ready to respond.

He was supposed to be Michael's main ally. His second hand man. The sidekick that provided the essential voice of reason and heart to the more powerful hero. He had tasted the bliss of fantasy dripping slowly into reality and then just as quickly the realization of hope had gone dry. Michael started spending all of his time at the lab or with Zooey. When Aaron called Michael he was too busy to talk, or apparently to call back.

It was frustrating. He wanted to scream at students who he passed, "I'm the only one that knows anything about what's really going on with Michael Bailey!" Then, at one point, he did. The arbitrarily screamed at student responded with the logical, "What's going on with him?" At which point, Aaron realized he no longer even knew that, which frustrated him even more. He only got the briefest snippets of what Michael had learned in the labs. He imagined Michael had been sharing everything with Zooey and didn't feel the need for a second source of daily review.

He didn't want to feel jealous of Zooey. He wanted to be happy for Michael. But he wasn't. He was bitter and exhausted. And yet he continued to wait for Michael's call. Ready to respond at full service when and if he received it.

It finally arrived one afternoon as he was finishing up in the bathroom. He hurriedly flushed and rushed out, answering just before the call was stolen away into the irritating grips of voice-mail.

Michael asked him to meet as soon as possible. He said he had something very important to discuss.

They met at the meal hall. They sat at the table where they had first met.

"Ketchup?" Michael offered with a laugh.

"I'm fine," said Aaron who was eating an ice cream sundae.

"It's time for me to do some good."

"Okay."

"I need your help."

That sentence was much sweeter than the rather extravagant amount of hot fudge and sprinkles Aaron had just put on his sundae.

From there Michael finally recounted exactly what had been going on in the labs to Aaron's ever more amazed gasps. He told of his mostly friendly reactions with the scientists he had been working with and of his most recent disagreement with Dr. Hauser. He told Aaron of the sudden surge of feeling he had to do some good in the world but that he was at a loss for where to start.

"So," Michael said, "Do you have any ideas?"

Aaron felt like he could cry of happiness.

• • •

"Bullet Man?"

"That's what the media have been calling him."

Michael and Aaron were pouring over a giant binder of research on categories of world problems that Aaron had thrown together in about three days. He'd skipped all of his classes and felt doing so was fully worth it.

"I'm amazed you haven't heard about this," Aaron said.

"I've been slightly busy with things going on in my own life."

"But they've been talking about this guy since before any of this even happened. He's been around for months. First he was just killing criminals and everyone was basically fine with it. They treated him like a real life superhero. But then he just started killing anybody and now they're calling him a serial killer. Funny how no one realized before hand how subtle the distinction between those two things is. I guess they might call him a supervillan now if there was a hero to battle him. In any case, they still haven't even figured out who he is."

"And what are you suggesting?"

"You be that hero."

"I don't just want to be a superhero you know," said Michael rather resentfully.

"I know that."

"I want to help people."

"Of course. And this guy's been killing innocent people for months!"

"But if they don't know who he is, there's no good way for me to find him. I'm not going to be able to do a better job than the cops at that."

"Well, not if you stay in the dark."

"What are you suggesting?"

"You go public. Show people what you can do. Challenge bullet man."

"You do just want me to be a superhero!"

"I want you to show the world what you can do! I think once you've proven yourself you'll have the opportunity to do all kinds of good. It's like this episode of Happy Days I once saw."

"Happy Days! You're comparing my life to Happy Days!"

"Just bear with me. So the Fonz is basically a superhero right? He can start a broken jukebox with the lightest of taps. He can summon a beautiful woman with the snap of his fingers. And he can win a potential physical confrontation by the mere fact of his being present. But in this one episode he tells Richie, it wasn't always an automatic. He had to hit someone once in order to establish his reputation. This is what it's like with you. Sure, you could go out there and just start trying to help out like anyone else could. Bring food to the poor. Fight crime alongside police officers one criminal at a time. But as far as I'm concerned the way for you to really do some good is to get into people's heads. Become something more than just some college student who happens to be able to levitate things. Get some serious press. Then do the amazing things you can do. If you're serious about doing good, you have a better opportunity than maybe anyone else ever has."

"And what if I do challenge this Bullet Man? And he takes my challenge? I don't know how to fight someone. And this guy sounds like he's a fucking maniac!"

"I'm not saying you wouldn't have to practice first."

"I don't know. Let me talk to Zooey about it."

• • •

Michael had planned on struggling to bring up Aaron's suggestion for several hours into his time with Zooey but she sensed something was wrong within the first thirty seconds.

"You don't have that trademark spirit about you. There's clearly something wrong," she said.

His answer was not so much a response as an essay. Sentence after sentence of nervous tension released through words, some necessary, some superfluous, all without pause.

"There's just so much suffering ... These scientists are great but don't you think a more practical solution would be better ... This bullet man sounds terrifying ... I can grow plants? I mean really? ... What would my mother think ... I just care about you so much ... ... Sometimes I think Aaron is just trying to live through me ... Am I even human anymore? ... Maybe he's right ... Maybe they're all right ... They can't ALL be right! Can they? ... I don't even know if there is a right or a wrong but I can't just sit back can I? ... I don't want to do anything that would make me lose you ... I cut my finger nails with my mind the other day. The ends just fell right off as if they'd been perfectly cut ... It makes me so sad that you had to suffer like that ... I thought I'd finally gotten back to my old self and now I'm all jumbled up again ... I'm scared ... I mean someone should do something to stop this guy ... I mean do they want me to be a lab rat forever? ... What if I could change my own genetic code to make myself stronger? ... Aaron does read way too many comic books ... If I could some-how make food out of nothing for the poor ... It bothers me that I'm better at destroying things than creating them ... He sounds like a frickin' maniac, right! ... I'm smarter than Aaron. I feel bad saying it but its true ... What he's saying makes sense, I know that ... I can make hair grow faster than usual too. Do you want to see? ...There's so much suffering out there ... I'll just have to get a new phone if I do this because I am entirely tired of having to listen to the entire voice mail before I can delete it ... I like you so much ... Maybe I could try to talk to him first? Maybe there's a chance he's not completely insane? … I never realized I was so lonely before I met you. I always thought I was happy but it's clear now I wasn't. I don't know what that was but it wasn't true happiness … So what do you think?"

Zooey sat still and didn't say anything for several moments. Silence was a necessary aide to digesting the feast of words that had just been thrust upon her.

"I think you need to decide whatever seems right to you."

"But I don't want to do anything you wouldn't want me to do."

"Michael, I'm the worst person to ask advice from! It's a miracle if I even manage to stay in control of myself, let alone make decisions that help anybody else."

"I just don't want to lose you. I need to know that whatever I do your feelings aren't going to change."

"Oh, Michael. I can't promise that. Nobody could."

"I see."

"I'm here with you now though."

She kissed him. For now, that would have to do.

• • •

Dr. Hauser and the rest of the crew were pacing around, waiting for Michael to arrive or at least respond to one of the three voice mails they had left him when someone mindlessly turned on the television.

"Hey guys. Michael's on the TV."

They found out along with everyone else.

"So you're willing to show the world right now what you can do?" said the morning show host.

"That's right."

The host's chair raised into the air. And him along with it.

"It's like I'm back at my bar mitzvah," he said.

"I don't know if I get that joke," said Michael.

"Just put me down," said the host.

Over the next day or so most of the world saw the video of Michael going public with his powers. Changing the color of the morning show logo. Juggling morning show mugs without touching them. Ending a truism by cooking an omelet *without* breaking any eggs.

And challenging the Bullet Man to a one on one duel.

"If you're out there listening Bullet Man," said Michael, "We've had enough. You've killed too many innocent people and I say its time for you to stop. I'm challenging you to meet me face to face. I won't bring any help. We can talk this out if you want. But I'm prepared to do whatever is necessary to stop this killing."

Aaron watched on the side of the studio experiencing a seizure of joy. Michael had brought him with. "Badass," he said over and over again to himself. "Goddamn badass."

• • •

Michael tried to think of a good metaphor for what his life immediately became following his national appearance. A firework constantly going off, having a life-altering conversation while yelling over a blender, and walking up an escalator traveling at the speed of light were all options he threw around that ultimately unsatisfied him. Although having literary sounding answers for reporters' questions wasn't exactly his primary concern.

He had naively figured that his first brush with fame would prepare him for whatever would follow his official demonstration. It was the power of visuals that he later realized he had underestimated. The testimony of hundreds of witnesses spurred only a passing interest in the general public if there was no continual evidence they could watch for themselves. It hadn't occurred to him earlier but it was amazing that in the age of digital photo video cameras and cell phone video cameras and mp3 player video cameras that not one person had been quick enough on the draw to capture the original levitation incident with Zooey. Apparently they were all too fixated to reach for their technological limbs. And though it had generated its own thunderstorm of press and a definitive packet of believers anxious to know more, in the age of unending twenty-four hour stimuli, the average citizen lost faith in a piece of supposed news for which there was no evidence that could be watched over and over again on the internet. His appearance on the morning show changed all that. The world now believed. And the response was unprecedented.

"The president just mentioned you," Aaron said. "The fucking president."

Everyone mentioned Michael. He was on every station. On the cover of every magazine. The primary source of discussion of every blog.

"First sign of the next stage in evolution?" some asked.

"First sign of the apocalypse?" others responded.

Among religious circles there was serious dialogue about whether Michael might fit the description of the messiah.

There were immediate gatherings of mass groups of people making the journey to see him, desperate to know if he might hold the answers they had been seeking all of their lives. The small sprinkling of rambling homeless men wanting salvation that he had come across before was nothing compared to the waterfall of common folk now trying endlessly to see him.

"Embrace God Michael," said Dan in not so much a request

as a demand, while Michael had cleared out of the dorm he could no longer conceivably stay in.

The news networks covered every conceivable angle of the story, generating fantastic rumors about the reasons for Michael's powers, and commentaries from every imaginable standpoint, both praising and ripping Michael for theoretical actions he had yet to actually take.

Most of what he heard directly was praise, even worship, though he did receive quite the tongue lashing from Dr. Hauser as he cleared out of the campus. The professor screamed that he was recklessly irresponsible and nothing better than a lousy fame addict who had abandoned some of the most important scientific work the world had ever known for the sake of free gift baskets and a cult of moronic groupies. He was rather hurt by the rant, particularly because he did not wish to completely desert the labs and stop methodically studying himself, he just felt that he had a responsibility to help the world in some way. He saw no way to continue his scientific pursuit now. Not without the support of the crew he had been working with and not without any sign of a moment of quiet, either sound-wise or otherwise to be found seemingly anytime for the rest of his life.

In the wake of all the madness, while flash bulbs replaced the sun as his primary source of light, Michael tried to spend some time with Zooey.

"You seem so quiet," he said to her as they snuck away a moment at Aaron's parents house that he had generously arranged for them.

"I think everybody else is making enough noise that I don't have to," she said, somewhat despondently.

He held her.

"Hey," he said. "Everything is going to turn out great. You've got nothing to be worried about. I'm always here if there's anything wrong. You're my first priority."

"Thanks Michael."

"You're wonderful, you know that?"

She cuddled close to him, radiating a desire for comfort he could feel through his skin.

• • •

Four days after Michael went public he was invited to a high class Manhattan charity event and he accepted the invitation. They sent down a private limo to bring him. He asked Zooey to accompany him but she declined. Too much schoolwork she said. He brought Aaron instead, who had gotten his own fair share of coverage as Michael's most trusted ally. He had done a few interviews throwing together some standard words he repeated again and again about Michael's amazing character and sincerity in wanting to improve things the best he could. He was on cloud nine.

Michael's arrival brought silence to the room. Followed by the most tremendous round of applause. He walked from person to person, all gazing at him with such esteem he couldn't help but feed off of it. The praise, the admiration, there was an undeniable appeal to it.

They asked him to speak. He said a few bland words about making the world a better place and then did what everyone actually wanted to see and levitated the master of ceremonies.

At some point someone asked him about whether he had heard from the Bullet Man and he realized that he had completely forgotten about him.

"No," he said. "But neither it seems has the public. So maybe

I've scared him off."

At some point during the soiree Michael sensed the briefest moment of escape from attention and made a break for side door that lead to a back alley. He had been wanting to call Zooey for several hours.

"Hey there."

"Hi," she said.

"How's the work going?"

"Fine, I guess."

"I wish you were here with me."

"Yeah."

"I miss you."

"I miss you too."

Michael felt it before he heard it. The most immense pain he had ever experienced. First in the back of his right leg, accompanied by a muffled crack. Then the left leg and the same crack. It wasn't until he turned his head and saw his attacker holding a gun with a silencer that he even realized that it was gunshot wounds which afflicted him.

He looked for his phone to see if Zooey was still listening. It was about a foot away. He had dropped it and it had smashed into pieces.

The man with the gun leaned down in front of him.

"Hi Michael," he said. "I'm the Bullet Man."

He covered Michael's head with a pillow case, dragged him down the alleyway to a van parked on the street and threw him inside.

◆ ◆ ◆

Michael was given the power of sight again after he had been thrown out of the van, dragged across a sidewalk and up a flight of stairs. The pillowcase came off and he saw that he was in a dark dank apartment in a building that was either vacant or should be.

The Bullet Man stood over him.

"Well," he said. "Here I am. I accept your challenge. Do your worst."

He sat down on a rotting recliner in the corner of the room.

Michael focused on the pain. He tried to recall the moment when he healed the scientist who had fallen off of her bicycle. This was far more extreme but he knew it was possible. He needed to somehow push out the bullets and close up the wounds but the relentlessness of the pain severely disrupted his focus. He tried to concentrate with all that he had.

"The name's Jake by the way."

He watched Michael writhe.

"Not in the mood to talk?"

"You're insane."

"All I did was shoot you in the legs. You went on national TV and called me out. I responded. There's nothing crazy about that."

Concentrate, Michael thought.

"Well are you going to vanquish me or what? Isn't that what you wanted to meet me for?"

Concentrate.

"You know they could have stopped me any time if they wanted to, don't you? I'm just one guy. I don't even really make any effort to disguise myself. If they really put their resources into it they shouldn't have had a hard time tracking me down. They just don't care."

Concentrate.

"Actually it's worse than that. The media loves me. They don't want me to be caught. People love their apocalyptic fantasies.

They flock to their television sets every time there's some natural disaster that wipes out some impoverished nation. It's a big fetish for people. The idea of the world ending. People want destruction. They feed off of it."

He couldn't concentrate.

"That's not true," Michael said.

"It's not?"

"No. Most people want good. They want peace."

"People say they want peace. They don't actually want it. Sure, most people don't live their lives going around killing everybody but they don't do anything to stop all the horror. And what's worse, they flock to watch it happen, completely gripped, disappointed almost when the violence stops. It's less interesting. You see, I started out just killing the bad guys. And people loved it. But eventually I realized, it wasn't the justice they loved, it was the killing. And it didn't make any difference who I was killing. It was all the same. Fucking teens would still wear some ridiculous image that looks nothing like me on their t-shirts."

"That's not true. People want good."

"People are so fucking bogged down by their own personal pain they will do or think anything possible to get them through it. They'll watch with delight as other people suffer just to feel better about their own lives, even though they won't admit their real motivations. I know you want to be some Messiah or something, and I hate to be the one to tell you but it's too late. Humanity can't be saved. There is no solution. The world's just going to keep getting worse until eventually we do something to all kill each other."

"So you think we should just do nothing? Not make any effort because no good can be done."

"You know what our best bet is? Just let it all burn. Stop trying to prevent people from destroying one another and just let it happen. And maybe, just maybe, whatever scraps of humanity survive might start over in a better way. But even that's unlikely. They'd probably just kill each other off too."

"You're wrong. People want good."

"Who are you trying to convince by repeating that? Me or yourself? Let me ask you this. Do you really think that you challenged me to a battle because you wanted to make the world a better place by getting rid of me? Or do you think that you just thrive on all the attention you're getting? People telling you how fucking great you are?"

"I want to make the world better."

"Okay then. Well here I am. Human virus known by the ridiculous name of the bullet man. I've accepted your challenge. Make the world better. Get rid of me."

Michael closed his eyes. He was shaking. He needed the bullets out of his legs now. His life depended on it. He pushed. They wouldn't come. Goddammit! he screamed to himself.

He opened his eyes. Jake stood over him. He smirked.

"This is pathetic," he said.

Out of the corner of his eye Michael spotted a gun sitting the window sill. He snapped his wrist and it flew across the room.

The gun was less than two feet from him when Jake caught it in the air.

"Nice try," he said. Then shot Michael in the stomach.

Michael screamed and clutched himself as the blood started to pour out. Jake dropped the gun.

"I think I'll do this the old fashioned way."

Jake rested on his knees. He punched Michael across the face with the force of a falling brick. He punched him again and again.

Michael tried to fight back. He was in a panic. Every time he lifted an arm Jake knocked it away. Every time he lifted his head Jake's knuckles slammed it back to the ground. His body was slowly and painfully being pummeled to the point of breaking. He knew if the beating went on much longer he would just expire.

In his chest he felt the seed of a guttural eruption.

And then. The big bang.

Michael's arms snapped back like he was a human crucifixion mousetrap. In slow motion he might have been able to see his hands pass directly through Jake's body. Watch the pieces of the whole separate gruesomely from one another. The fingers fly from the hands. The arms from the torso. Veins torn through the muscles, popping, splattering blood on every surface. The bones separating in the midst of an explosion of organs.

But in real time he only saw a detonation. Jake was a person and then he wasn't. Whatever forces that held the matter that made up Jake together were destroyed in less than an instant.

Michael surveyed the sickening wreckage. Then set about the work of healing his wounds.

III.

Aaron met her in the most surprising of places. At a burrito stand hidden on a sidestreet in a residential beach town of Massachusetts. It was a gray September day. He was there waiting for Michael who was on the beach, trying to squander some private time to think in a place no one would bother him. She was working at the stand selling the burritos and he couldn't resist buying one after he caught the delicious whiff of Mexican food.

"Betty" read her name tag, pinned to the blindingly bright tie die shirt she was wearing.

"I like your uniform," he said.

"I actually don't have a uniform," she said, "It's my choice to wear this."

"Well I like your choice."

She was an unapologetic hippie. A girl from another era who spent most of her time outside, got most of her furniture for when she was inside from piles on the sidewalk that people had left for the garbage man, and believed in love above all things.

She was so friendly that Aaron didn't even realize he was having a conversation with her until well into it. Speaking with strangers was not something he easily fell into. Usually it took an awkward amount of effort but he was asking Betty about her vinyl collection before he even thought to introduce himself.

"I'm Aaron," he said somewhat abruptly, mid-thought.

"It's delightful to meet you Aaron."

He asked her out. She readily accepted. He left Michael on the beach. He was prone lately to spending hours in thoughtful solitude and Aaron knew he would find him when he was ready to move on.

As soon as she got off work they went to some sort of outdoor waffle shack she said she had been meaning to try for quite some time. Aaron wasn't sure whether it was an actual establishment or just a bunch of drifters who loved making waffles. He couldn't recall later whether they ever asked for any money.

He fell for Betty almost immediately. She had so much enthusiasm. She was so unburdened. She lived in a cheap apartment just outside of the beach town and made all the money she needed working at the burrito stand. She was the first person he had ever met who talked about living in the moment and actually seemed to follow her own advice. She hadn't bothered with college. She seemed to think an education of novels she found in the local used bookstore was more than adequate and the life experience of talking with any person she came across provided far more useful knowledge than she could ever find in a textbook.

"What do your parents think?" he asked.

"They disapprove. But I love them anyway."

She was a terrific conversationalist. She brought out the best in Aaron. Within just a few hours she got him to talk about his passions in a way that no one else ever had in the first nineteen years of his life. He talked about his love of myths and classic storytelling. Of the way in which people developed legends and lived by them, organizing their morals through images of commonly shared heroes. It had been so long since anyone had asked him about himself and really wanted to hear the answers.

He had been so satisfied the past few months being Michael's right hand man, being integral to one of the most important stories that had ever unfolded, that he had not previously noticed the small bit of bitterness he felt. The resentment at being important mainly as a side character in another's life. He was so wrapped up in everything that he had forgotten his own identity was even a consideration. He was afraid that when he told her the reason he was in town, she would stop being interested in him and just want to hear about Michael. But she didn't. She was human, certainly. She asked a few questions about the person all the world was talking about. But then she returned to just asking about Aaron. About his relationship with Michael, his feelings about his famous friend.

"Come with me," he said, completely out of character, as their evening together was nearing its end.

"To where?"

"Just on the road. We'd travel a lot. See the world. I bet you'd love it."

"I might actually."

"Then come. I don't want to stop knowing you after just one night."

It was not himself speaking. He knew that. It was a combination of hundreds of far more confident film and literary characters he'd come across over the years, from whom he borrowed without proper citation.

But it worked.

She came. And although joining him at first involved far less travel than he had originally anticipated, she would later look back at that decision as one of the best she ever made.

• • •

For quite some time Michael knew there was something off with Zooey.

What he wasn't sure of was whether she had returned to her feelings of depression or just lost all her feelings for him. And what disturbed him more was that he was strongly hoping it was the former.

She had become extremely brief on their phone calls. He asked her on several occasions if anything was wrong but she always said no, and seemed to want to talk to him a little less each time he asked.

It was an incredible source of frustration. He tried to see her as much as possible but it just wasn't feasible more than once every couple of weeks with his increasingly hectic schedule. Everyone expected so much of him. There was so much pressure. The least she could do was comfort him by sounding like she meant it when she said "I miss you too."

He didn't want to wish that Zooey was chronically and uncontrollably sad, that the happiness he'd seen was the exception not the rule, and that her increasing distance from him was only a side-effect of her genetic disposition. But he did. Anything was preferable to the ache that came with the thought that there was some flaw he possessed which would not allow her to maintain her affection for him.

Zooey wasn't the only one acting differently towards him. Actually, the whole world was.

Everything had changed when Michael had walked back into that high society Manhattan event covered in the splattered remains of a human being. When he heard the disgusted gasps of the socialites. He saw someone vomit in the corner.

"I killed the bullet man," he said. He waited for a round of applause. He got silence.

Michael related his story to the police who, picking through the debris of the Bullet Man left in the apartment, corroborated the facts with little investigation, likely more out of fear than anything else.

Fear. It was a reaction he got used to very quickly. He scheduled more television appearances to assure the world of his good intentions but that did nothing to quiet the intense intimidation he spotted in the eyes of everyone he looked upon, just before they looked somewhere else as a result of that same intimidation.

Apparently it wasn't possible to explode a man with your mind and not have people become afraid of you.

Most still believed he was the proverbial good guy. Though there was the occasional newspaper columnist or twenty-four hour news network pundit who ranted about stopping him before he realized how much power he might possess. He had imagined that the love affair the religious had been having with him might end after the display of violence but apparently there were enough fans of the Old Testament out there that the worship only increased. It was hard for him to make any public appearance without a crowd of the awed following him around, declaring that he was here to bring the wrath of God to the world of sinners. Asking him anxiously to preach what he knew.

His parents, his extended family, everyone he had known in his previous life arranged times to see him only to mutter incoherent half sentences, failing to convey any thoughts but perfectly explaining their emotions anyway. He let them ramble but was always relieved when they departed. The truth was he really just felt no connection to these people anymore. The change had been too dramatic. He wasn't the same person they remembered and they weren't the same people that used to provide him with comfort. Very little did that at this juncture. He'd given up the expectation that he would ever feel comfortable again. There were too many people watching him for that. It used to be a great deal of his directed purpose in life to feel comfortable. With all the tumult and the recognition and the fear that had engulfed him so quickly, with all the tension he felt now whenever he walked out the door to the pestering crowds wanting to catch a glimpse of him or persuade him to be their savior, and with the increasing frustration of waiting for the girl he had thought he had fallen in love with to sound like she actually wanted to talk to him, he motivated himself every morning with one louder and louder thought.

"I will make the world a better place."

He was extremely thankful for Aaron who kept a clear head and rationally suggested that he follow up the graphic Bullet Man incident with a series of positive public clean up and rebuilding appearances. What better way to contrast destruction than with construction? He cleared disgusting garbage ridden parks with a snap of his fingers, watching the insane amount of litter fly into his open bags. He removed graffiti with a wave of his hands. He repaired unpleasant cracks in buildings and dangerous holes in bridges. He helped communities grow just planted flowers in a matter of seconds. He really liked this work. It was a delight to see smiling faces watch their decrepit neighborhoods improve. It was a great boost to hear genuine thanks from people who for the first time in their lives might have something nice to look at.

But even with the great satisfaction he was getting out of this neighborhood repair he was very quickly worn thin. Communities everywhere heard of his efforts and requested his services. He did his best to serve as many as possible. The airlines were all offering him complementary flights in return for the press they got from having him fly on their airplane. He had discovered a great many amazing powers, but he had not yet figured out a way to be in two places at once. And he couldn't help but get a bit pissed at the nasty attitudes he heard from people who he simply couldn't yet manage to schedule the time to help.

These community activists weren't the only ones pissing him off. There was also the military and the government, who were no longer exactly requesting his services, but instead publicly attacking his character. They called him reckless and irresponsible for sitting by when there were forces of terror in the world that needed to be destroyed. He counterattacked by saying it was irresponsible of them to let thousands of people die merely so the United States could have a continual supply of oil. He had no idea whether he was fully informed as to the specifics of government hypocrisy or not, but he was fairly confident that there was enough hypocrisy that he could fairly tell them they were hypocrites. Which he did. It wasn't that he didn't eventually hope to eradicate certain larger forces of destruction in the world. It was that he wished to do it on his own, using his own methods, instead of taking orders that trickled down from bureaucrats.

Beyond all that, he wished to do everything possible to avoid killing again. It wasn't a moral issue so much as a control one. He had felt completely out of control of himself when he had killed the Bullet Man. It hadn't been some action of his own that blew his opponent into pieces. It was a reflex. His deepest concern was that someone else might be able to harness his power better than even he himself could and he would become nothing more than an immobilized weapon used by others. And besides, murder had not been pleasant. It had been gut wrenching. No one would ever know how hard it had been to concentrate on reconstituting his skin afterwards. How hard it had been to leave that wreckage and walk back to that event, unstoppably crying the whole way from what he had done, forcing composure only because he thought he would receive a round of applause that he never did.

Anger, sadness, turmoil, transitioned through him with equal frequency.

He focused on the smiling faces of the children playing on the swing sets he had just repaired.

"I will make the world a better place," he said to himself.

His community work lead directly into his next major effort in the goal of achieving his stated purpose. Those paying close attention to the situation noticed that when Michael was in town, even in the most dangerous areas of particular cities, crime would decrease significantly. It was a remarkable statistical trend. Apparently criminals wanted to take no chance of having a pool of their own flesh fill the street and suspended all action for the day when Michael was near, resuming only when they were sure he was somewhere else.

Aaron read the reports and made Michael aware of the positive effect he was having. Michael was encouraged but he wanted to take it a step further. He wished to ensure that when he was around crime would dwindle down almost to nothing. The system he came up with involved changing the colors of city skyscrapers to solid blocks of red when he was in town. It was like his own bat signal except that it was he who was calling his own services. For good measure he would throw in some embellished displays of his own presence, sending obnoxious gusts of wind down alleys known to be used by drug dealers, shaping the clouds overhead to resemble hand cuffs and electric chairs, and occasionally walking down the street engulfed by a human shield of flame if he felt so inclined. His goal was to scare the criminals into silence through spectacle alone, avoiding all forms of violence. And the theatrics did seem to work. People were terrified of him. He had to give Aaron credit for his apparently not so ridiculous Fonz metaphor. Hitting (or blasting someone into oblivion) once did appear to be enough.

Cities throughout the country, the continent, and soon the world were requesting his services. So as to not have to hire some sleazy untrustworthy business man with shiny sunglasses and shinier skin, Aaron personally volunteered himself for the task of acting as Michael's agent, embassy, and press secretary. Michael made sure to thank his friend often for all that he was doing. The world didn't realize it, but the transition Aaron had undergone in the past several months was even more extreme than the one Michael had, even with his ability to convert his skin into fire. The spike in Aaron's confidence, the assured way he spoke to people, his organizational skills, all made it hard for Michael to believe that he was even communicating with the same person he had met in the meal hall some time before. He supposed that Aaron was living his dream of glory, and achieving what you always wanted was capable of doing wonders for your character. But the truth was, he was jealous. When they had met Michael had been the contented one, satisfied with life as it was. Aaron had been the one with vague personality jitters, searching out some purpose to make life more satisfying. Now the roles were reversed as Aaron seemed to take on the burden that came his way with a composed poise and Michael struggled to maintain a single state of mind. Or at least that was how Michael saw the situation. He didn't actually talk to Aaron about it, apprehensive that a discussion might reveal more complexity than he actually wanted the situation to have. Instead Michael just frequently thanked him for his services and tried to focus on his own ambitious goals.

"I will make the world a better place."

And for a brief period of time following each visit to one of the world's most crime plagued cities he seemed to be doing just that.

But it didn't last.

The problem was that as soon as everyone was sure he was gone, witnessing his exploits in some other metropolis on the international news, the crime would just resume as if there had never been someone there controlling the lightning and amplifying his voice to frightening volumes, screaming in every applicable language of the consequences to come from continued wrongdoings. It was only the immediate danger of telekinesis castration (which he also threatened) that kept the peace. But as Michael was caught up scampering around the globe, offering up his performance in each of the world's largest markets, those he had already visited started to doubt his convictions or follow through. They figured he was too caught up and as soon as he departed, they resumed their regularly scheduled programming.

"You have to show them you mean it," Aaron told him.

"Shut up Aaron," he said in his mind.

"Yeah, I know," he said in reality.

So he went back to cities he had already been to and froze hundreds of those who had committed crimes in giant blocks of ice.

Somehow the cryogenic display of felons only made crime increase.

"Maybe you froze higher class criminals who were somehow keeping the low class ones in check?" suggested Aaron.

Shut up Aaron, he said in his mind.

"That's a theory," he said in reality.

He had spent over a month exhaustively running around the globe, threatening the scum of the world with supernatural punishment completely free of charge and increasingly the only sentiment he heard from the public was "What have you done for me lately?" What the hell was he supposed to do to make the world a better place? No effort seemed to have any long term effect. Should he just wipe out anyone who committed a crime? Wouldn't that make him just as bad as the criminals? And he had the feeling that even destruction wouldn't really do any long term good. Others would soon come about just as happy to steal and rape and murder with no fear of consequences. No threat that he could provide would ever be enough to change the basic nature of certain people. No spectacular manipulation of matter would change the fact that many thrived on destruction. They were just waiting around for the world to end and would be sure to play their part in the process. The whole thing was pointless. There was nothing he could do. His powers didn't make a damn bit of difference. He was just as powerless to make the world better as everybody else was.

"But we've just gotten started," Aaron said when Michael told him of his concerns. "You can't give up so soon. You've hardly tried anything yet."

"I want to see Zooey," Michael said.

So they took a trip back home.

• • •

"Michael. What are you doing here?" Zooey said when she found Michael at her door.

"It's nice to see you too," he said.

"I didn't mean— it's just a surprise."

"Can I come in?"

"Of course."

Zooey was back home at her parent's house for the summer. He walked in and sat down on the right side of the couch. She sat a mile away on the left side.

"I haven't heard from you in a week," he said.

"Yeah. I know. I'm sorry about that."

"Is everything okay? Have you been feeling alright?"

"I'm feeling fine."

"You're not feeling depressed?"

"No, I'm okay."

"Then how come you won't talk to me?"

"Michael, I— I'm sorry."

"Sorry for what?"

"For a while I just haven't been feeling right about us."

"What do you mean?"

"I mean, just that. I just haven't been feeling right about us. About us being together. It just doesn't feel right anymore."

"I haven't even seen you lately!"

"I know. But it's been since before that. It's been a while. I know I really should have told you sooner. But you've been doing such important stuff all around the world. I didn't want distract you."

"You didn't want to distract me! Well you did! I've spent more than a month worrying about you! Wondering if you were okay! Wondering what the hell was going on! And now you tell me that you've wanted nothing to do with me, for, how long exactly?"

"I don't want nothing to do with you. I just don't feel right about us being in a relationship anymore."

"How long?"

"I don't know. A couple of months I guess."

"A couple of months!"

She started to tear up.

"Michael, please don't scream."

"So what's wrong with me?"

"Nothing."

"Something must be. What is it? You can tell me. I'm not afraid."

"You're a great guy. What you're doing for the world is amazing. You're just not right for me."

"Is it my powers? Is it too weird for you to be with someone who has powers?"

"I mean, yeah it's strange that you have powers, but it's not the powers."

"Well what is it then?"

"It's not anything specific about you."

"Have I meant absolutely nothing to you?"

"No. You meant a lot to me. The way you are, the way you're just so happy and enthusiastic about life, it's really had an influence on me. You've made me want to be like that."

"But you want to be happy without me?"

"Michael."

"What am I supposed to do now?"

"What do you mean?"

"What am I supposed to do with my life?"

"Michael, there's so much for you to do. More than anyone. The world's counting on you. You're going to do such great things."

"There's nothing to do."

"But you've been helping out in all of those cities—"

"I've been accomplishing *nothing.*"

She noticed that he was now on the verge of tears as well.

"Oh Michael. I'm so sorry."

He stood still. He tried to hold in his tears and pretend that neither of them had detected their appearance.

"I'm so sorry if I hurt you," she said.

He stood quietly. His lips quivered. He walked out the door.

• • •

"What should I tell them?" asked Aaron.

"I don't know," responded Michael, face down in his pillow, "Tell them I'm sick. Tell them I'm dying. Tell them I've lost my powers. Tell them anything you goddamn want."

Michael had holed himself up in his current hotel room in Boston for three straight days. He refused to get out of bed. He barely ate. And he would say nothing to the city officials, the reporters, or the crowd of eagerly anticipating public who didn't seem to care if his actions actually did do anything to prevent crime as long as they boosted tourism, made a good headline, and provided some solid entertainment, respectively. For all his effort he was now seen as nothing more than a popular touring act. Even his current situation with Aaron, refusing to go "on stage," stunk of bad musician biopic. He'd done nothing to make the world any better and he didn't even care. He'd lost Zooey. That was the only thing he cared about. It disgusted him that his own suffering over a breakup he'd long known was coming made him distraught when all he could feel for the far greater suffering of humanity at large was an impersonal objective vague moral obligation. But that was the way it was. He could think about other people's problems but he could only feel his own. And that's how it was with everyone. And that's why the world would never get any better.

"What's the point?" he said.

"The point is that there are people who want to see you do what you can do," said Aaron. "The point is to make the world a little better. Remember? You'll get over Zooey, Michael. I'm sorry to say it but it's true. There are bigger issues at hand."

Michael was in no mood for Aaron being in no mood for his sulking. It was bad enough trying to ignore the irritating cacophony of those outside the hotel calling his name as if he was a useless teen pop star, loving him because he was a fad while they ignored brutal deaths in third world countries and all the other ceaseless horror surrounding them. It was worse having to ignore Aaron who over the course of the three days of hotel room cabin fever went from being a kind compassionate friend to a self righteous motivator who thought he had the entitlement to tersely tell Michael what his priorities should be, laying out a time line for his grief.

"I need to get out of here," Michael said.

"Good. That's more like it," said Aaron.

"No. Not just out of the room. Out of town. To somewhere quiet. Somewhere I can think without anybody bothering me."

"Where?"

"I don't know. I just have to go."

"Ok fine. I'm coming with you."

"I just want to be alone for a little."

"There's no reason I can't come with you for the journey and let you have alone time."

"Afraid that I'll leave you and you'll be left a nobody?"

"What? No."

Michael smirked, pleased at having struck an uncomfortable chord.

"Fine. Come with. But no talking in the car."

Michael managed to locate a quiet beach on the Massachusetts coast which served his purpose of obtaining some solitude.

It was there that Aaron met Betty.

While Aaron ate his burrito Michael thought about genetics. He wondered where in the brain emotions formed and if that was the same place that they solidified. He fantasized about manipulating the gray matter in Zooey's brain so that she would fall in love with him. But rationality kept creeping in, ruining the satisfaction of the daydream with the realization that if he tried to play with the matter in her brain he would likely just kill her, having far too little knowledge of what goes on beneath someone's skull. He was furious with himself for having left the labs when he did. If he had stayed perhaps he could have found out more about human chemical makeup. He could have changed not just Zooey but also the scum of the earth, forcing them, on the level of their DNA, to be good upstanding citizens. That the whole thing reeked of moral and ethical quandaries didn't bother him at the moment.

While Aaron ate his waffles Michael thought about desire. What if Zooey could be influenced to love him? Would he even want her to anymore? If he knew that she only loved him because she had been surgically forced to, her love would no longer mean anything. She would be a machine that had been programmed to show him affection. That would hardly be satisfactory to his ego. But why did people feel certain ways for some people and not others? Why was it that every time he saw a pretty girl he automatically wanted her without any time for thinking whatsoever? Did he really have that little control over his own mind? Was he just a series of cogs designed to respond in different ways to different situations? In what would surely be labeled ironic from any other of the world's residents, Michael felt increasingly powerless. He had already felt powerless to help the world and powerless to maintain the affections of a female. Now he felt powerless to even control his own actions. He could change the physical reality that surrounded him. Alter the tide, transform the sand into grass. But he had no influence over the one thing that really mattered. The mind. Neither the minds of others nor his own. And that made free will seem like a pretty foreign concept.

While Aaron asked Betty to join him on the road Michael wondered if he would be now be ruminating over gargantuan ideas like free will if he had just managed to have sex with Zooey before she broke up with him, ending the nuisance of virginity. For a moment he believed his restlessness was this simple before he quickly recognized that any time he had achieved what he wanted he had just ended up either wanting more or later wishing that things had stayed the same when they inevitably changed. He had once felt that he was chronically happy. All so soon his mindset had changed so dramatically that even the past seemed less worthwhile than it once had. Sex would have been just a momentary satisfaction that spurred on more wanting. He knew that. But he also still wanted it.

There is perhaps nothing that Aaron could have done to rupture his relationship with Michael except what he did following the events of that day at the beach. He got a girlfriend. And became insufferably happy.

As Michael wallowed over his lost love and tried to figure out whether he was any longer capable of committing any action at all, Aaron, giddy over the new member of their entourage, dealt without complaint with the public's pressing demands that Michael come out from his hermitage. Betty attempted on several occasions to speak with Michael and comfort him, assuring him, entirely reasonably, that a person with his level of fame could win over any female he wanted. But the sting of his specific rejection and his general growing lack of confidence in the point of existence did not allow him to feel anything but jealousy towards Betty and her out of nowhere relationship with Aaron. He felt a quake of anger every time he saw them embrace. It was he who deserved happiness, not them.

If Michael had turned on the TV at any point during this period of barricading himself in hotel rooms, he would have seen newscasters debating the mystery of his sudden disappearance from the public eye. They ran through any number of ridiculous rumors. He had taken work with the mafia and was now only venturing out secretly to whack those who needed to be whacked. He was actually an extraterrestrial and the disguise he had created to make himself look human was wearing off. He had been using his powers on his own body in lurid fetishistic ways and had somehow managed to get himself pregnant. The fictional suggestions of why Michael was behind closed doors got more coverage than the actual extraordinary actions he had executed. The public's thirst for controversy was more essential to their social survival than their hunger for attempts at humanitarianism, regardless of the reality that either might be built upon. The only ones who did not cast Michael's reclusion in a negative light were the ever growing group of followers, some formerly religious and some not, who believed Michael was to be the savior of humanity. They spoke on Michael's behalf, saying that the untrusting, bitter, sinful masses had driven him away through lack of appreciation for his attempts to rid the world of evil. They said that Michael needed to be respected and esteemed. That every act he undertook might be just a test of those he was here to save. If Michael had watched TV he might have noticed that someone he knew had risen quickly through the ranks of these followers, given credence because he had spent significant time with the savior before the rest of the world had come to know him. That he was now a major spokesperson of this group. And that he promised he would communicate with Michael, and apologize on the rest of human kind's behalf, asking him kindly to reveal himself once more.

Michael didn't know any of this. And therefore thought very little when Betty, taking over Aaron's usual job while he was out getting them lunch, asked Michael if he was willing to see his former college roommate Dan who was waiting at the front desk.

"Why not?" said Michael, who figured Dan still had delusions of grandeur about him, but could never have predicted quite the devotion Dan had given his views.

Dan entered the room wearing his best Sunday suit, in considerable contrast to the uniform of imitation Polo shirts and football jerseys he had dressed himself with at school.

"Michael," he said, dropping to his knees and bowing his head.

Michael looked around to see if there was someone else by his name in the room for whom this bow was performed.

"Yes?" he responded, somewhat confused.

"I have come to apologize on behalf of the world."

"What did the world do?"

"We have let you down. You have been trying to teach us something and we have not been listening. We know that you have been isolating yourself to tell us that we have not been listening. Many of us are ready to listen Michael."

The room became silent. Michael supposed that Dan had already begun listening.

"Dan...what are you talking about?"

Dan stood up.

"I will show you."

He walked over to the window and gestured for Michael to follow. He opened the blinds.

Outside was a crowd of hundreds, all kneeling, in a massive formation of prayer. They were spectacularly silent. Dan pushed up the glass and stuck his head out.

"I am speaking with *him*!" he screamed.

Completely in unison the heads of everyone in the crowd were raised.

"Tell him!" said Dan.

"FORGIVE US MICHAEL," they all said at once. "FORGIVE US MICHAEL... FORGIVE US MICHAEL... FORGIVE US MICHAEL... FORGIVE US MICHAEL..."

Satisfaction swelled in his Michael's chest. For a full minute or more he just listened to the chant. Telling Dan the real reason for his isolation could wait for another time. For the moment, all he wanted to do was give the people who so benevolently asked for his forgiveness precisely what they were seeking.

"I FORGIVE YOU!" he exclaimed.

The crowd roared. They jumped up and down. They hugged on another. It was a sight of complete joy. Of people coming together. Of enormous harmony.

A tear formed in Michael's eye. He felt deeply moved.

• • •

"But this is all a bunch of nonsense!" said Aaron as Michael packed his bags.

"I'm glad you have so little faith in me," said Michael.

"You know that's not true. I think you can do great things. But these people expect you to be Jesus Christ. You can't live up to that expectation!"

"Maybe not. But I'm going to act like I can. For the good of those who believe in me. I've got to reward their faith."

"You're being an idiot. I'm sorry but it's true."

Michael paused in the middle of folding his underwear. He walked up to Aaron and looked him directly in the eye. Their noses were uncomfortably close.

"Where do you get off? Huh? Less than a year ago you were just an anti-social nerd with no friends who begged me to let him run some experiments and see what I could do. Now all of the sudden you think you're some kind of big shot who thinks he can pick up girls on beaches—" They both looked at Betty who was awkwardly doing her best to pretend she wasn't listening. "—and can tell me what the hell to do. Well let me tell you something. I made you. You're nothing without me! Nothing!"

"You sound like a bad mafia movie."

"Well you sound like an asshole."

"Michael, what are you going to do when these people realize that you're not directly communicating with God? When they expect you to save them from every problem that ails them and have all the answers? You can do a lot of good. But you're just not capable of what these people want."

"That's your opinion and you're entitled to it."

"If you tell them that you are who they seek you're a liar. Plain and simple."

Michael resumed packing.

"These people have hope. I used to think that was something that was easy to come by but after what I've been through and after seeing people around the world I've realized that it's a pretty rare thing. I won't kill anyone's hope. I just won't."

"There's a big difference between not killing hope and pretending to be something you're not because you get satisfaction out of being praised."

Michael stuffed in his final item of clothing and zipped up his suit case. He lifted it off the bed and carried it towards the door.

"And what if I am who they seek? I still have no idea why I can control things the way I can."

"Do you really believe that that's who you are?"

Michael paused for a moment. He opened the door.

"Goodbye Aaron."

He walked out.

◆ ◆ ◆

Dan rented out the largest high school auditorium he could find. Originally, he thought it proper to arrange for Michael's speech in a place of worship, but the church's official position on Michael was still undeclared, even with many of its members flocking in his direction, and no priest wished to make a decision that would officially endorse him. Any indoor facility would be limited, but there would be news cameras and a live feed so that every person who wished to hear his words would be pleased. Though the chances of actually getting in were slim, thousands made the journey in the hope they might get to see him in person, and be present for what was rumored to be an event of complete revelation, in which all of the mystery surrounding Michael would be uncovered. It was to be one of the most important moments in history, they said, in which God might finally again speak through one of their own, and show how he would heal the dreadful pangs of those he had created.

Michael waited in a classroom and listened to the ever growing noise of the crowds pushing their way into every available crevice of the auditorium, flagrantly violating fire code, stuffing into the just outside hallways in the hopes of seeing through the doors, pressing up against the windows of the high school for a possible glimpse of he they had come to see, before rushing to the front steps to catch the speech on one of several jumbotrons that had been installed. Michael was playing with a pencil he had found on the teacher's desk. Doing the old rubber pencil trick he had been so fond of in elementary school. He could likely actually turn the pencil into rubber now if he wished, but he still found the optical illusion entertaining. And more importantly distracting. So he didn't have to think about what it was exactly he was going to say.

Dan knocked on the door.

"They're ready for you," he said.

Michael took a last long look at the pencil, as if pleading with it to find him a way out of his current circumstances, then put it down and took the long walk to the auditorium stage. He heart beat fast. He tried to slow it but apparently that was out of his control. His body was covered with goosebumps. He was hot and cold at the same time.

"You ready?" asked Dan.

"Sure," he said.

"I can't wait to hear what you have to say."

Michael pushed the edges of his lips up in what was supposed to be a smile.

He walked in. The crowd erupted.

Michael looked from one hopeful pair of eyes to another, saw the bliss which he was providing people, and he immediately forgot that he was not the person they were cheering for. For a reaction like this, he must be that person. All he had to do was say what that person would say. He quickly ran through his mind to times in his past when he came across celebrity style preachers on the television. He never watched these programs for more than two seconds at a time but that was knowledge enough to know how to behave.

"Hallelelujah!" he screamed into the Microphone, delighting the crowd. "Thank you, all of you, so much for coming here today," he continued, quieting the people, eager to carefully listen to what he had to say. "I know you all have a lot of questions. I understand that. There are questions I have too. You have not been given all the answers. I have not been given all of the answers." (They look disappointed by that, he thought) "But there are some answers we all have. And that you don't even need me to know. Love!" (That's good) "We are all united by love. God! God is love! Love is God! Love and God are one and the same!" (Now I'm preaching) "All we have to do is look inside of each of us and we can find the source of God that's always been there."

"Why has God been hiding from us?!" someone yelled out. The crowd murmured.

He thought for a minute how to respond. He looked at the members of the crowd. In the front row he spotted a little girl in a wheel chair. Could he do it? If he was going to attempt what he was thinking he would have to be sure he could succeed. He could. He knew could. The confidence that the crowd had in him gave him a level of confidence he had never before felt.

He walked down the steps and up to the little girl. Eager eyes followed him.

"Hello there," he said to her.

"Hi," she said, smiling sweetly.

He looked over to her mother who was sitting with her.

"Do you mind if I try something on her?" he asked.

The mother started to cry. She must have had a sense of what he was implying. "Ask her," she said.

"Can I try something on you?" he asked.

"Okay," the little girl said.

Michael placed his hands on the girl's legs. He closed his eyes and concentrated. He didn't know enough about biology to specifically repair whatever it was that was broken, or even to know what it was that broken, but he tried to reach for something deeper. Some more fundamental connection with the matter that was the little girl. Then suddenly, he felt something. Some transference. He opened his eyes. The little girl was looking directly into them. She conveyed a look of the most improbable understanding.

She stood up.

The crowd gasped. The girl's mother broke down in a storm of tears. She hugged the little girl so tightly she could hardly breathe. The little girl smiled awkwardly.

"Mom, you're embarrassing me," she said quietly.

Michael walked back onto the stage. He took in the ultra fulfilling awe.

He forgot all of the thoughts he had while working with the scientists about how the deeper you investigated reality the more complicated and impossible to understand it became. These people needed an answer they could grasp. And so did he.

"God is not hiding," he said. "He is here with us right now."

• • •

Michael resumed his tour of the globe. But in an entirely different capacity than he had last seen it. Before his primary destinations were civilization's biggest cities. This time they were small towns, villages, farms, following historical tradition by gathering in any place with a field large enough to contain the massive amount of people who wished to see him, and a population small enough to not overwhelm him with the more difficult questions or criticisms which had no easy answer. Last time his list of companions consisted of one, Aaron. This time, it consisted of a constantly growing assemblage of over a thousand people who had vowed to follow their new savior wherever he might go. In this go-round, his focus was not on lowering the crime rate amongst the cities' poorest inhabitants, who unfortunately tended to be the ones who created the crime rate. He now realized his former attempts were purposeless in the shadow of the impossibly imposing societal changes that would have to be done to change the system and the ideas that produced the criminals. In the end these were worse than the criminals themselves, but they were also harder to know what to do about. So this time he focused on helping specific individuals. He healed those who were sick, mended those who were broken. It was good work. It made him feel positive. It kept a steady stream of adoration coming his way and let people believe in something. Somewhere in him was the thought that these small efforts still lacked something. Still didn't go far enough. However, he was surrounded by enough optimistic energy that he was able to banish those thoughts to the farthest reaches of his mind.

Fairly often he would be asked about the specifics of his relationship with God. Was he God in another form?

"I am human just like you," he would answer, trying to avoid the dangerous line of questions that the first one might lead to.

"So you're a prophet?"

"Yes, I think that's the best way to describe me," he would say.

"Does God speak to you often?"

He had deliberated for a long time on how to answer this question. He really did not wish to lie. But sometimes, he thought, bending the truth is necessary for the common good. If he told them that he spoke with God they would be far more likely to listen to what he said. To follow his directions of acting in the name of good. To work together to gain peace. To promote loving thy fellow man instead of hating. (He had started inserting ancient words like "thy" into his speech to see how it sounded). This one little lie was his major hope for doing something real and permanent. For not just performing isolated charitable acts, but for truly making the world a better place.

"He does speak to me," he said. "But in some ways, he speaks to all of us," he added in, feeling this extra detail somehow took a little of the harm off of his fib.

After struggling through saying it the first few times, talk of his conversations with God became quite natural. Whenever he said something he really wished for people to remember, all he had to do was add one little detail.

"It is the word of God."

• • •

And for a glorious time being that was how it went. Michael performed miracles and spoke of peace.

And his followers loved him and that sustained him.

And his words spread.

And much of the world came to believe that he was the true vessel of God.

And people came from far and wide to catch sight of him.

And many did everything they could to live their lives the way he preached.

But time passed as it always does.

And the miracles started to seem less miraculous, being now commonplace.

And most people noticed that their lives remained rather the same. They asked him if the end of the world was coming if they did not change their actions. He denied it. They seemed strangely disappointed with his answer. They asked what the threat was if they did not change their actions. He said that the threat was the world as it already was, full of pain, and misery, and suffering. He said that good should be done for its own sake. They seemed to want to be threatened.

And they continued to believe in him but their adoration lessened.

And Michael noticed himself becoming bored with the proceedings. He preached ideas of peace and love that he knew in his mind were right to preach but which he could no longer feel connected to. He started wanting. He wanted Zooey back. He wanted to be loved. He wanted to curse off the crowds of followers who were increasingly less grateful, tired of the same old answers and desiring a new set of even more enlightening ones. He wanted to lose his virginity with one of any number of gorgeous religious girls who came to see him, but who would likely never go for it because of their annoying devotion to chastity. He wanted the people who kept asking if he would die for humanity's sins to shut up. You go die! he wanted to retort. He wanted to know why he *could* do what he could do. Was it actually God? Was it something else? Was there even a why? He wanted a break from the ceaseless traveling, the constant attention. He wanted a moment alone.

And the questions about what God had to say came more and more endlessly. And Michael became more and more tired of answering them and made less and less effort to pretend that he knew what he was talking about.

And many seemed to notice his increasing reluctance to speak about God. And they started to doubt him.

And then the unthinkable happened. At a shopping mall in Kansas a man went on a shooting spree, killing thirty-five people and injuring forty-two more before killing himself. He left a note that said the Devil told him to do it to wage war against Michael. The incident was a tragedy that was mourned for weeks in the United States, but other than a few maniacs who did not accept the public's diagnosis of the killer as a psychopath, no one really put the blame on Michael. Except of course, for Michael himself. He knew the man's actions weren't technically his fault but he still felt inseparable from them. If he had never made himself out to be a prophet of God then maybe the man would never have had the proper trigger to fully snap and live out his fantasies of demonic possession. He had done nothing to encourage anything but love and kindness but these murders could still be directly traced back to him. If he had never existed those people might still be alive. The incident destroyed Michael. He kept ruminating over it. Picturing the dead bodies soaked in blood spread across the mall. Imagining the families in their inconsolable grief.

And the same old haunting thought kept pounding the borders of his brain. That nothing he did would ever make any difference. That every act of consolation would somewhere be balanced by a moment of pain. That the larger the good he tried to enact, the larger the tragedy that would spring up to compensate for it. He finally understood what Zooey had meant when she had been describing her depression. It was an inescapable circularity. It was a continual return to pointlessness. It was an erasure of any drive to do anything, fully knowing that everything would bring you back to the same aching feeling.

And so for the second time Michael gave the world the silent treatment. His followers kept finding him, kept asking questions, but he refused to open his mouth.

And this time they were far less accepting. Doubts rose and spread among Michael's legions. Many started to vocalize their concerns that he was not the prophet they thought he was. That he was sorely lacking in answers. That he could certainly create miracles but seemed at a loss to answer the essential question of what God was really thinking. They were restless and tired of his routine, ready for some new material he was unable or unwilling to produce.

And while the potential apostles complained that Michael's greatest hits no longer did the trick, Michael managed to sneak away a moment to call his mother for the first time in months.

"Michael?"

"Hi Mom."

"Where have you been!? I've been completely unable to get in touch with you! I see you on the television and everyone is talking about you and a man said the Devil is going to get you and I've been worried sick!"

"Yeah, I'm sorry about that."

"It's not right to treat your mother like this! To just run off and become a prophet and not talk to me at all!"

"You're right. You're right. I've been a bad son."

"Are you talking to God? Is it true?"

"No. It's not. I don't even know if God exists."

"Then you're lying to all those people?"

"I guess I am."

"That's not right Michael. You need to tell them."

"You're right. I should. But I probably won't."

"When are you coming home? When am I going to see you? You can't just do this to your mother!"

"I'm sorry mom. I really am."

He hung up. The guilt was too overwhelming.

Michael went quickly from place to place. He stopped checking into hotels because the attention was too immediate. He slept on the street.

But people kept finding him. They kept asking him questions. Some were angry with him. Others were genuine and kind but hurt that he did not seem to be the savior they expected him to be.

"I'm sorry," was all he would say before fleeing for another town whose alleys he could attempt to hide in. "I'm so sorry."

• • •

In the back of a donut shop in a suburban shopping center in-distinguishable from any of the hundreds of others he had passed through, Michael considered a bag of the day's uneaten donuts that had just been thrown outside by an oblivious teenage girl employee too busy texting to notice the supposed prophet trying to hide behind the dumpster. He was hungry. He had been eating less and less. The attention that came with buying food was one he preferred to avoid. And his attempts at morphing inedible objects he found on the street into delectable morsels had thus far failed miserably. He thought he had turned a piece of cardboard into an adequate graham cracker at one point, but it tasted like burnt hair. So he considered the donuts. Which were perfectly good and apparently going to go to waste. They should really be going to those starving and in the grips of poverty around the world, he thought. But in the meantime, while society had not yet realized the selfish waste it produced, there was no reason he shouldn't have a cruller.

As he ripped into the bag he heard a voice behind him.

"You're Michael Bailey, aren't you?"

"You know you're really wasting perfectly good donuts," he responded, preparing to be accosted by the pastry shop's manag-er, but instead finding a man only a few years older than himself who had a look in his eyes that was just as dejected as his own.

"I've been trying to find you," the man said. "I've been follow-ing you all around the country but you keep disappearing just before I get to wherever I've heard that you are."

"I'm sorry about that."

"It's okay. I've been searching for you for several months now and I kind of realized that I didn't even know what I would do once I found you. I know that the chances of you living up to my expectations are pretty slim."

"Oh."

"You're my only hope left."

"For what?"

"I don't know. Something good I guess."

Michael looked at the donut bag he had just torn open.

"Cruller?"

"Why not?" said the man. He walked over and Michael handed him a donut.

"What's you're name?" asked Michael.

"Justin," he said.

• • •

For some reason, most likely the cynical acknowledgment that he had accepted Michael as a savior because he simply needed something to believe in, fully expecting to be let down, and vaguely disappointed that he even found him at all, Michael felt comfortable telling Justin Giacarozzi the full truth of everything that had happened to him in a way that he had never had with anyone else.

He told him of his initial baffling discovery of moving ketchup bottles and switching on lights. Of his fear and confusion over his new unexplainable condition. Of the incident with Zooey and how he fell for her. Of the constant pressure he felt once he went public. Of his lies about communication with God. Of the growing pestering feeling of hopelessness that appeared that first moment he realized what he could do, which he had repeatedly tried to bury to no avail, desperately missing his old content self.

Though he had spent the past three months imagining Michael as an all powerful being who could suck the desolation from him like a vacuum cleaner sucking up dirt from a carpet, Justin betrayed only an expression of resignation as Michael relayed the specifics of his story. This was how any positive expectation always ended. In disappointment.

"I know I've handled things badly," said Michael.

"I don't think that's true. I can't see any point at which you should have done something differently."

"I shouldn't have lied. And I probably shouldn't have ever thought that I could have made a difference."

"You were given a burden of ability you never asked for. You did the best you could."

"Then my best was pretty bad."

"Your best is a lot better than mine. You've at least helped some people. Look at all those people you healed. They're going to be grateful to you forever, even if they figure out that there is no God."

"You don't believe in God?"

"Do you see any evidence of him?"

"I don't know. I would've said maybe the things I can do but I know that probably boils down more to some complicated physics or chemistry or something that no one understands yet. That's what I really thought before. I just convinced myself differently so that I could be the person people wanted."

"So what are we supposed to do Michael?" asked Justin, still lingering on his image of Michael as the one with the answers even though he had just explicitly been told he was not. "We're here. What are we going to do with ourselves? Is there anything worth sticking around for at all?"

In one of the oddest reactions he had experienced for some time, Michael felt a small stirring of encouragement. He later hypothesized that interacting with someone just as defeated as he was had provided the proper opportunity for contrast. But that was just a theory. In truth, he had no idea where the spark of optimism had come from.

"Life does have its pleasures," he found himself saying. "If there's no real point to anything, maybe we should just be trying to enjoy ourselves."

• • •

Before he had become a universally recognizable performer of miracles Michael had never thought the gasp was a sound people actually made. By now he was so used to that particular shocked intake of air as a reaction to his appearance that he would have been more surprised had he not heard a gasping chorus when he and Justin entered the bar. The only ones not gasping were a few girls vigorously dancing, already too drunk to be distracted, and a few threatened males preserving their image as tough guys by staring him down as if they wanted to stab him in the eye with a pool cue.

"C'mon," said Justin, directing Michael over to the bartender.

Justin ordered the beers for the both of them, since Michael was not yet twenty-one, although no one seemed to care. While Justin started consuming, Michael stared at the alcoholic beverage sitting in front of him. He tried to recall why it was he used to feel so strongly about not drinking. He ran through all the excuses he used to give to people. None of them seemed to fit. Then he remembered. He had just never wanted to. It wasn't any active reason. It was quite a passive one. The complete lack of desire. But desire was there now. Desire to rebel against some unknown force he considered responsible for ambiguous cruelty. Desire to show life itself that it had driven him past a point of no return. Desire to engage in a complete abandonment of his former self because life had not given him the chance to remain in the happiness he had once known. He didn't know what specifically he thought he was fighting by having his first drink, but as he tasted the beer a faint but sharp "fuck you" filled his thoughts.

Michael looked to his left. A very attractive young female was investigating him closely.

"I'm sorry," she said, upon being spotted.

"Nothing to be sorry for," he said.

"You're Michael Bailey aren't you?"

"That's me."

"What are you doing here?"

He glanced back at Justin who was watching the interaction closely. He nodded his head up slightly, encouraging Michael, and with this small gesture putting pressure on him by reminding him that this was why they had come here in the first place.

"I'm here to try to meet girls I guess," he said to her.

She giggled. "You're cute," she said.

Though it took Michael twenty years to lose his virginity, the delay between the first girl he slept with and the second (as well as third and fourth for that matter) was what could be casually described as slim.

Justin had been right. All that was required to get them both laid was Michael showing his face at an establishment filled with drunk, young females, who were informed enough to know who he was but oblivious enough to not see any implications in his powers, other than the fact that they were the reason for his fame.

It only took about a week of his new lifestyle for Michael to end up in the tabloids, next to an article about the wife of a football player who had supposedly obtained the largest breast implants ever devised and directly under a twelve year old singer suing her father for backing out on some contractual one pony a week clause. The public attention given to his very sudden party lifestyle only increased his success at the bars, which increasingly tried to obtain pre-notice of his arrival to boost business. The establishments gave him free drinks and the girls flocked to him, hoping to be the next ones on his list, and wondering what his matter manipulation skills might imply for pleasure in the bedroom.

Many of his former followers gave up on him completely, feeling betrayed. Their hope evaporated at seeing their potential savior disappear into the reprehensible world of those famous only for their fame. Others still tried to make contact, yelling that he had become weak and let the devil in, some meaning it metaphorically, others literally. Perhaps they hoped that if they were the ones to bring him back from the dark side, they would be rewarded in some special spiritual way. But Michael just ignored them. He knew he had let everyone down and his goal was just to think about responsibility as little as possible.

As he fell quickly into this routine of indulgences, he tried repeatedly to convince himself that the frequent momentary bursts of physical pleasure added up to a satisfying existence. But after the initial thrill of mutiny against his own mental establishment, all the lifestyle really made him feel was empty.

He closely watched his new companion to sense if he was at all affected the same way and realized that he knew almost nothing about him.

Justin seemed at once completely devoted to their mission of pleasure and completely indifferent to it. He took every action necessary to ensure their maximum success under the guidelines they had set but never relayed the smallest indication of enjoyment.

"Tell me about yourself," Michael said at one point. "I've selfishly talked on and on about me but I never asked about you."

"There's nothing to tell," said Justin. "My life consists of one failure after another."

"There must be more to you than that. Everybody's got a story."

"Michael, my whole existence has been nothing but waste and frustration and I'm so deeply sad I can't possibly even describe it. I've wanted all the wrong things and gotten none of the few actual good things I've wanted. I've had nothing to live for for years and I can't ever seem to find the courage to just end it all. I keep finding something to hope for. It's fucking debilitating. Thinking that something good can come out of any of this. But I just can't manage to give it up. And that's my biggest failure of all."

"Do you think we should keep living this way?"

"I decided several months back that I was going to search for you. And if I found you I was going to do exactly what you said. You told me to live this way, so I'm living this way. That's all there is to it."

"But I'm not the person that you thought I was."

"You're someone. That's enough."

Later, at the apartment of the girls they were spending the night with, Michael stumbled across Justin in the bathroom doing cocaine. He looked far from euphoric. He seemed to be doing it just because it was there.

"You want some?" he asked.

Michael walked away. He was afraid. Afraid of the person he was becoming, who in no way resembled the person he thought of himself as. And afraid that that he had almost said yes to the new drug. Why not, he had thought for a moment. Because he didn't want to become a junkie, he reprimanded himself. Because he didn't want to be controlled by a fucking drug. He didn't want to be controlled by anything. Not by his own desires. Not by masses of people expecting him to perform acts of salvation he was incapable of. Not by instincts that told him it was his responsibility to help people just because he could do some crazy things he never asked to be able to do. And not by the crazy powers themselves.

Since that first moment of unexpected levitation he had not felt in control. And he was sick of it. Trying to live life just for its pleasures did not return the feeling of control at all. It had actually made him feel far less in control than ever.

Michael ran out of the building. He desperately needed some fresh air.

He went through the doorway and a flashbulb went off. There were two groups of people waiting for him outside. A sect of paparazzi, hoping to capture some juicy image of the most sought after icon of trash mags today and a group of former followers, sitting around a lit candle, praying for Michael's salvation.

Michael wanted to explode. He wanted to scream at the leeches who wouldn't give him a moment's peace to leave him alone forever.

But before he did, he was struck again with the memory of that first levitation. Feeling his own body float above the ground. The one feat he had never been able to duplicate.

He looked his observers in the eyes and smiled.

Then he rose from the ground and flew away.

IV.

Michael watched a lizard scamper by in the sand and felt the pangs of hunger in his stomach. He wanted to capture it, to kill it, to eat the little bit of meat that could be located on its scrawny frame. But he held himself back as he had for the last fifteen days. He already had his day's meal. A pair of leaves off a resilient tree growing in the middle of the arid desert. That was all he was allowing himself. Any more would be an indulgence.

Michael's flight had descended in what he imagined was an unpopulated area of Arizona or New Mexico. He landed in a gorgeous open region of cactus and canyons and for the first time in months felt the peace of solitude. He watched the stars. He listened to the wind. He looked into the distance for long periods of time, taking in the beauty and heavenly quiet that surrounded him. And he set about the task of taking control of himself.

There was a tremendous relief that came with being completely alone. From knowing there was no chance the satiating silence would be interrupted. It had never occurred to him before but every time he was in the presence of others he would become something, quite automatically. As soon as he interacted he was a particular person, whether that person was an enthusiastic optimist, a love-sick fool, a naïve superhero, a prophet of God, a lying delusional con man of religious folk, or a party hopping man slut. When he was alone, however, he was free to be nothing. To just exist as he was without having to define himself.

He thought about all sorts of things at night in the desert as he stared at the sky and lay down next to a fire of his creation. He let his mind go like he used to be able to do before any chance for a contemplative moment had been completely wiped away. Let his thoughts flow as they would. No direction. No pressure. It was sometimes painful. He kept thinking of Zooey. He kept long-ing for her and for those first days with her when there seemed to be no end to the feeling of ecstatic possibility. He thought about his parents. He felt horrible for ignoring them the way he had. He thought about Aaron, who had been such a supportive friend and who he had abandoned so callously because he was too over-whelmed with envy. He thought about the dreams he used to have for his life that were now nothing more than past specula-tions never to be. But whenever his mind wandered down dark alleys he was able to rein it in by focusing on the notion that he could seize control. That he could dictate his emotions. That he could be unaffected by negative thoughts. And that he could pre-vent his desires from getting the best of him.

He started with eating. Food consumption would have been a problem in the desert anyway. There was a serious lack of any kind of nutrition and Michael had still never figured out how to make something edible that wasn't. However, the more fun-damental issue was that eating disrupted his intended practice of taking charge over every instinct he had, whether mental or physical. Every time his stomach sounded the alarm, loudly de-claring it wanted to be fed, he was acting in the service of some desire he had not chosen to have. So from the end of his first day in his new isolated life he made the conscious decision to eat and drink only enough to keep him alive, deciding with his own men-tal awareness when he would perform this intake, and ignoring his body's warning calls that he was running low on fuel.

Other desires were easier to reel in. Sexual yearning was at a minimum with no female within what could be as many as a hundred miles. Thoughts of ego and praise and unnecessary cravings of pride were silenced in the absence of any companion-ship. Desire for love and happiness was still the most determined to have itself heard, but Michael battled it with his own unwavering attention to the peaceful environment that surrounded him. Nature, which existed quite contentedly without any wants at all.

The lizard made its way back to Michael and paused in front of him. It was taunting him, he decided. Challenging him to reach out and end his physical strife by tearing its skin off with his teeth and inhaling its muscle. It looked at him curiously, like a scientist coming across a heretofore unknown puzzle. Michael's stomach turned up its volume in an honorable attempt to drown out his focused refraining. The lizard waited for a minute, then apparently got bored and turned in the opposite direction. Michael stood up and followed it.

On the end of his second day of isolation Michael had located a cave towards the bottom of an imposing canyon that he slept in and retreated to whenever the sun got too hot during the day or the wind got too cold at night. The cave became his home. He decorated it with cave drawings, scratching small rocks against the walls to create images of buffalo and coyotes and cell phones. (He found it humorous to incorporate modern technology into classic cave imagery. He liked to imagine an archaeologist discovering the lair, seeing the images and coming to the only conclusion he could – time travel.) In the corner of the cave was a formation of stone perfectly suited as a seat. It was here he often sat still and tried to settle his mind when it started screaming for a return to civilization.

These mental fits didn't become full fledged until midway through the second week when they teamed up with his vociferous hunger. The first few days had been a tremendous relief in which he basked in the calm of his surroundings and appreciated the abandonment of the unyielding pace of society for a lifestyle in which he didn't have to do anything at all. The next few days after that the transition settled slightly into routine and the contrast with his former lifestyle didn't present as much active satisfaction. But he still took in the open atmosphere with a tremendous amount of appreciation. By the start of the second week, however, his identity began a minor rebellion. His thoughts started pestering him with the possibility of upcoming boredom. Not that he was currently bored, but there was the threat that he would inevitably become so. Same with loneliness. Sure, he was relieved to be away from others right now, but just how long could he live in complete seclusion before his social needs overwhelmed him. Like a good dictator of his self he repeatedly squashed these rebellions but he wasn't sure just how long he could keep the serfs down. By the time the thoughts united with his hunger, he realized he might be facing a full out revolution.

The lizard steadily marched forward, apparently determined to progress although Michael doubted its ability to have a destination in mind. As he followed it for the better part of an hour, feeling the crunch of sand on his bare feet as a part of his newly chosen lack of footwear method of travel, he glanced down at his chest and took note of his increasing skinniness. It was amazing how quickly he had lost most of his body mass. His ribs were sticking out as if they were reaching for something and his skin became not much more than a thin coat for his bones. He imagined that he might be able to use his powers to bulk himself up the way he had been able to heal abrasions but the hunger made utilizing his abilities more difficult. In fact, the hunger made everything difficult. Walking, sitting, sleeping, thinking. The hunger was all consuming. Tearing him open from the inside, demanding satisfaction he refused to give it.

The lizard paused. Michael collapsed next to it gratefully. He and the creature looked at each other. He swore he caught a glance of understanding from the tiny reptile. Of empathy for his starving desert companion. And then it hit him, powerfully and painfully. He had not been hypnotized into following the lizard because the little guy was a potential source of food, although that had been his immediate reaction. No. He had been following the lizard because he had appreciated the company.

"Hi. I'm Michael," he said to the lizard, speaking for the first time in over two weeks. "I'll call you Lorenzo," he said playfully.

The lizard stuck his tongue out.

"I'll take that as an acknowledgment," he said. "So what brings you to the desert?"

The lizard ate an insect that was passing by.

"Not much of a conversationalist, are you?"

Then the dam broke. The boredom and the loneliness and the misery that came with the thought of spending the rest of his life alone, out here, was finally too much for him to bear. He had been holding it back but it all came flooding out along with miraculous tears, somehow produced despite the fact that he couldn't imagine much liquid left in his body, having only been drinking a slight amount of moisture he sucked each day out of the air.

And he was starving. And he wanted something to eat. And he suddenly felt that the whole venture of trying to renounce any and all desire had been utterly pointless. Eventually he would lose. At some point the desires always won. At some point he always lost control. The anguish of hopelessness which he had been able to lock away for a small period of time broke out of its cell and pummeled him with a newly strengthened poise.

The lizard watched him cry. He wanted someone to comfort him but there was no one around.

He didn't know what to do. He felt trapped. If it had been purely up to him he might have locked forever into that moment of desperation, frozen until he withered away. But his hunger saved him.

He needed something to eat. And he needed it as quickly as possible. Scrounging the desert would not be enough. He needed to go somewhere where people were. Somewhere he could buy a full course meal. Somewhere he could end his god forsaken hunger for good.

But how could he ever show his face to the world again? He never wanted to be recognized anymore. Never wanted to deal with the pressure of expectation, of being constantly watched. If he was going to return to civilization he needed to know that somehow, someway he could avoid the suffocation of the being the person he had become.

Michael put his hands on his head. He realized what he had to do. He did his best to quiet his mind and concentrate completely.

Then he slowly deformed his face, morphing his bone structure until he was unrecognizable.

• • •

Michael located a small town on the edge of the vastness. He had flown until he spotted buildings, then circled overhead and doubled back so that he would enter the town by foot. He figured arriving via flight might have been counterintuitive to his goal of not drawing attention to himself. Walking in, he caught a sight of his reflection in a window. He was not the prettiest of sights but he didn't look like a monster either. Just an uncommonly ugly individual. He considered his work on his face, done without a mirror or any reflective surface, to be a success.

He stopped at an ATM, luckily having kept his wallet, and

even more luckily finding that his old bank account had not been closed. Then, he made his way to the first restaurant he could find.

Despite his craving for a filling entrée of meats and pastas when he sat down at a local diner, Michael felt his bones, saw the waiters' stares that had nothing to do with who he was and everything to do with his emaciated frame, and intelligently decided that he should start slow so as not to combust whatever was left of his internal organs with a single meal. He ordered chicken noodle soup and sipped it slowly, each spoonful a painful but necessary coating of his digestion system.

While he ploddingly pushed through his meal, determined to consume the entire bowl of soup despite the hurt that it caused him, Michael stared out the window.

On the bench across the street sat a man, late twenties, who stared straight forth and did not move for more than a half hour.

Michael watched him. It was hard to see the man's face from the distance he was observing, but Michael had the strangest hunch that if he could see his expression he would see contentment in its purest form. There was some aura about the man that radiated all the way across the street and through the glass to Michael's booth. Something remarkably peaceful.

Michael returned to the restaurant the next day. He requested the same booth. And once again outside sat the man, staring forward, unmoving, completely content. Michael ate as slowly as possible so he could just continue to study the man. Wait for him to do something. Anything. But he just sat there.

Michael returned again. And again. For five days in a row. Steadily working his way up the menu to more and more substantial food. Steadily regaining his strength. And all the while watching the same man, sit on the same bench, and do the same amount of nothing. Apparently happy to just sit on a bench for days on end. Needing nothing more.

On the sixth day, as Michael approached the restaurant, finally starting to feel physically like his old self again, he stopped. He walked around the side of the restaurant and sure enough, there across the street, sitting still on the same bench, was the man. He realized he could not take any action until he spoke to the man. Until the mystery of the his stillness and the strange impression of peace he gave off was solved, everything else needed to be put on pause.

As Michael took small steps to make it across the street, he felt himself shaking. The man seemed to pay him no mind. Michael's approach did nothing to distract him from the important task of nothing.

Then finally, Michael stood there. Right in front of him.

"Hi," he said.

"Hello," said the man.

"I couldn't help but notice that you spend a lot of time on this bench."

"Time is relative."

"I suppose it is."

The man looked up at him. Michael immediately averted his eyes. There was something in the way he was looked at. Something knowing. It was disconcerting.

But it was too late to leave. He needed to understand this man. There was no other thought in his head but doing so.

"Do you mind if I sit down?" he said.

"Not at all," said the man.

Michael sat down.

"I'm Michael."

"Nice to meet you Michael. I'm Colin."

Michael waited to see if Colin would initiate any conversation. But his bench companion seemed to have none in mind. The town was exceptionally quiet. The skies were cloudless. The birds chirped in the background. And for a moment Michael forgot about his curiosity all together. He became caught up in the surrounding atmosphere the way Colin apparently was. He lost track of time. But then he looked over, and remembered his determination.

"Listen, I have to ask. Don't you get bored just sitting on this bench day after day, not doing anything?"

"Not particularly. I used to get bored. That was before I realized there wasn't anything to be done."

"I'm not sure I understand."

"No. I didn't used to either."

Colin seemed awfully ambiguous, thought Michael.

"It's just that, I don't know why, but I've seen you sitting out here, and you just seem so...happy."

"I haven't thought about that word in a long time. Yeah, I guess you could call me happy."

"But how can you be so happy doing nothing?"

"I take it you're not very happy?"

"I used to think I was."

"Then what happened?"

What happened? thought Michael. I discovered that I had superpowers. I got a girlfriend and fell in love with her only to watch her drift away from me. I realized that there's no good that can be done in the world not balanced out by some bad. I stopped thinking that there was a point to existence. I failed to find satisfaction in every single method I tried.

"Life," he finally answered.

"Ah yes, life. It can be a painful thing," said Colin.

"You bet."

"Can I tell you something Michael?"

"Sure."

"I used to be sitting where you are. Not literally on the bench. I was there too. But I mean, I was in the same emotional place. Probably worse."

"I don't know about that."

"You're right. I don't pretend to know your history and you don't pretend to know mine. The point is I was in a very bad place. And I spent several years traveling, doing anything and everything I could to bring myself that feeling of satisfaction. Of some lasting fulfillment. I wanted to feel something. Because feeling was meaningful. And if I didn't feel something, then what was the point of anything? Even pain was preferable to nothing. Or so I thought for a while. Until the pain became too much itself. And I really thought my best bet was probably just to kill myself."

Michael listened, gripped. He had no intention of interrupting the gap of silence.

Colin continued. "But then something hit me. As I went all around and watched other people, trying to see if anyone else felt as much despair as I did and figure out why the people who didn't, did not feel that that way, I experienced the most powerful realization I ever had in my life. People continue to love. Despite all the horrors throughout history and every bit of pain everyone feels throughout their own lives, including that poisonous need to feel itself, people continue to love. Despite the way that we hurt each other and every pleasure eventually passes people continue to love. And that's a pretty astonishing thing. Despite all the suffering in the world and our own lives, me and everybody else continues to want to not suffer, as a basic aspect of ourselves. We continue to want love even when there's no love to be found. And

I thought about this a lot. I just sat around and thought about it. For hours and days. And it helped. But it still wasn't enough. It still didn't quite give life meaning. The fact that there might be a need for peace in ourselves didn't actually make the world less violent. And the fact that there was a need for peace in myself didn't make me feel calm. But then I realized the truth. As suddenly and clearly as if it had been there all along. Which maybe it has. I realized the truth while I was sitting on this bench. And that's why I've stayed here. The truth is Michael that there is no meaning to life. That's where the peace is. That's what a baby feels. That's what an animal feels. And that's what we somehow lose and try to regain through love throughout the rest of our life. It's only this belief that there is meaning which causes us to hurt so badly. This idea that we'll find some ultimate fulfillment, that there is some answer to all of this, that there's somewhere to go. Because there's nowhere to go. We're here right now and we always will be. And when I realized that there was nothing I needed, because nothing would bring that ultimate satisfaction, I stopped wanting anything because I was already fine. So I just stayed here on this bench. I just came back here day after day and stopped caring about doing anything or going anywhere. I used to be so bored with existing. That was because I thought there was something to do. But there's nothing to do. And that's okay. You asked me if I was happy. I am happy. But I'm happy right now. Not before. Not later. Because now is all there is. Let go of your need for meaning and all that remains is peace."

Colin looked at Michael and smiled. Then he returned to his stillness.

Michael sat still himself for quite some time, trying to take in everything that he had just heard. Trying to comprehend all the aspects of the speech, which was surely a condensed version of countless thoughts from Colin's head over a long period. He wasn't sure he grasped it all. He wasn't even sure if everything Colin had said was consistent. But he did feel good. He felt inspired by Colin's words even in spite of a sense of apprehension. He had actually felt pretty good all week. Ever since he had come to this town. But how long would that last? He had felt good when he first went to the desert. But that feeling passed. He had felt good when he first jumped into the world of pleasure with Justin. But that feeling passed. He had felt good when he had first declared himself a prophet. But that feeling passed. He had felt good when he had first started trying to lessen the crime in the world. But that feeling passed. He had felt good when he had first been with Zooey. But that passed too, along with her affection. Every feeling of contentment always passed.

But it also returned. Every time he felt down he eventually felt up again. And maybe that was the key to understanding it all.

Michael suddenly missed his parents. And his old friends who he had felt so disconnected from after he had discovered his powers. And his new friend who had discovered his powers along with him.

I should give Aaron a call, he thought.

But for the moment he remained on the bench and let his thoughts fade away until he was thinking nothing at all.

ABOUT THE AUTHOR

Jeremy Dorfman is a graduate of New York University's Tisch School of the Arts. He lives in Philadelphia with his seven parakeets and is at work on his second novel. He can be contacted by email at jid204@gmail.com

www.ingramcontent.com/pod-product-compliance
Lightning Source LLC
Chambersburg PA
CBHW030242030726
47493CB00023B/426